Lifestyle

Lifestyle

PETER WARNER

VIKING

VIKING
Viking Penguin Inc., 40 West 23rd Street,
New York, New York 10010, U.S.A.
Penguin Books Ltd, Harmondsworth, Middlesex, England
Penguin Books Australia Ltd, Ringwood, Victoria, Australia
Penguin Books Canada Limited, 2801 John Street,
Markham, Ontario, Canada L3R 1B4
Penguin Books (N. Z.) Ltd, 182–190 Wairau Road,
Auckland 10, New Zealand

First published in 1986 by Viking Penguin Inc.
Published simultaneously in Canada

LIBRARY OF CONGRESS CATALOGING IN PUBLICATION DATA
Warner, Peter.
Lifestyle.
I. Title.
PS3573.A766L54 1986 813′.54 85-31514
ISBN 0-670-80072-4

Printed in the United States of America

Set in Caledonia
Design by David Connolly

For Jill

PART 1

ONE

I am not the kind of snob that I was raised to be.

I was raised in the smug confines of the Best Families of Morrisburg, a tired industrial city of 225,000 in central Ohio. The Best Families were, by virtue of the city's modest size, obliged to include a number of families such as mine who had history on their side (four generations in Morrisburg!) but whose fortunes were somewhat more equivocal: I was the embarrassed heir to the second largest insurance agency in Morrisburg. To the dismay of my parents' friends—but with the secret encouragement of my father—I fled my patrimony.

The Best Families were unhappy to see me leave since those without *real* fortunes (most of us) sustained their businesses, law practices, political careers, by circulating money among themselves. Which is to say that much of their incomes required little more initiative than the clapping of each other on the back at the Willow Green Country Club. What would they do without the Werble Insurance Agency: Quality and Service Since 1923? For many of my parents' friends the prospect was bleak, as in their hearts they knew that Anthony Morelli (quality and service since 1969), to whom my father intended to sell out, would not dream of sharing a drink with them, much less an assumption.

Virtually every small city in America has a group like us. We go to second-rate prep schools or local "country day" schools (and a day in the country is about all you get) and then go on to fairly good universities in the East and South where ivy attitudes, if not scholarship, run deep. At college we recognize each other almost instinctively: Hello there Roger of the Best Families of Duluth; Hi Lindsay from Tacoma. It's a frightening thought, but the truth is that this hierarchy is itself organized into hierarchies. I mean, Roger and Lindsay begrudged their acknowledgment of Pamela, the best of Plattsburgh, New York, and they in turn received short shrift from Cincinnati's finest.

Sometime in my sophomore year of college I realized that I shared few values with my social set. In fact, since I shared few values with almost any set, I was lucky to develop the unoriginal but marvelously organizing goal of earning a lot of money. So five years later, when my goal-directed class of MBAs graduated, I headed for New York and began the corporate clamber. I went to work for a group of magazines whose editorial concerns were of little interest (*Hot Cars; Auto Test; Quarterly Review of Drag Racing*) but whose marketing and financial departments were wonders of efficiency and aggression. I rose steadily, moving every 1.8 years to a new and larger group of magazines until my current employer, Schaefer Communications, Inc., owned five of the most successful trade magazines in their industries; one medium-sized and mediumly successful astrological entertainment magazine called *Stars 'n Stars* (this month's feature: "What's ahead for the stars of *General Hospital?* Mona Robbins' astrological charts tell you what to look for"); two lucrative cable TV outfits; three radio stations; and a small, hopelessly unsuccessful book publisher (*Selected Essays of James Branch Cabell; Tombstones of the British Isles*).

I should also add that my scamper up the corporate ladder had been marked by good luck, very good luck. A case in point was the morning that my secretary, Frances Toomey, a.k.a. Frankie, entered my upper-middle-management cache of chrome and glass with the sort of saunter that implied she knew something and I didn't—not the most uncommon state of affairs.

"Big news!" she said, dramatically indicating the position of *Big* and *news* on the front page of an imaginary tabloid. "Your lunch has been canceled."

"But that's with my best friend Milton."

"Him? That pigfart's your friend?"

"Well, it *is* nearly April and he *is* my accountant."

"Gotcha. But I have other plans for you. You're having lunch with Helmut at his club."

I'm sure Helmut would have been appalled to know that Frankie did not refer to him as Mr. Gernschaft. He no doubt believed that it was a major concession to American informality to permit "Mr." instead of "Herr."

"Speaking of nearly April," I said, "are you pulling one of those disgusting jokes that tend to occur in very early April?"

"Hey!" Frankie said. "When Helmut Gernschaft says cancel, I don't just cancel, I eliminate. Milton's been zapped. Right?"

"Right."

"Maybe Gernschaft's going to fire you," she suggested maliciously—though I suspected she was a bit nervous at that prospect. After all, who else would put up with her? Though Frankie was the most skilled secretary I have ever encountered, as well as the shortest, the stories of her personal life that ricocheted about the office had always managed to offend her previous bosses. In addition to flaunting a life of breathtaking sexual complexity, she was a walking pharmacology of controlled substances.

"He'd never fire me in public, at his club."

"Well, then it's a promotion. Hey! All right!" She punched the air several times in joy.

"Twenty dollars says it's neither a promotion nor a pink slip."

"Listen to *him:* Mr. Big Bettor! I'll tell you this. That air-head Rosalie—you know, the one with the teeth who used to be Schaefer's secretary—well, she says that Helmut has never had lunch at his club with a single one of us Americans. Only his Panzer pals get to eat there with him."

The Panzers were, inevitably, the way us Americans had come to refer to the little blitz of Germans who were sent over to supervise the operations of Schaefer Communications, Inc., which the huge Gruppmann Group of Frankfurt had purchased fourteen months ago.

I shrugged nonchalantly. "Don't bet. I wouldn't if I were you."

"My five dollars against your twenty?" At her insistence, the size of our bets was directly proportional to our respective salaries, which ensured that over the long run she cleaned up on me. I could tell that Frankie believed I was in for a promotion, but I figured it was an easy five dollars for two simple reasons: happily, there was no reason to fire me; sadly, there was no place to promote me to.

During the first six months of the Gruppmann reign at Schaefer, the previous owners and management team had been eased out. Old Man Schaefer, who had negotiated a long-term consulting contract when he sold the company, discovered that he was consulted three times, each time to be asked which smaller office he wanted to move to next. Once he left, so in short did his nephews, cousins, and cronies. The devastation was so complete that Mrs. Schaefer's radio program, *New Perspectives in Modern Dance,* which had run for twenty years on our network (Jacksonville, Battle Creek, and Bakersfield), was finally put out of its misery. Without receiving a promotion, I was left as the top-ranking American at Schaefer Communications. It was one of those peculiar situations in which a great deal of power tacitly came my way. The other Americans on the staff looked to me to negotiate their little objections to the new regime, and the new regime expected me to negotiate their large objections to the staff. I did this very well, and the Germans appreciated me with two nice raises and four fervent handshakes. But I had no illusions: without a dueling scar, I had nowhere to go but sideways.

At about eleven that morning a media consultant (i.e., a gossip with connections) named Albert called me.

"I hear you guys are getting into the big leagues." He spoke in the teasing, insinuating tone that men of our corporate ilk use as a substitute for friendly conversation.

Rather than ilk right back at him, I asked, "What do you know or want to know?"

"The magazine you guys bought. A very hot one. Or at least that's what everybody says. How much did you guys *really* have to pay?"

The Panzers were hardly my idea of a bunch of guys. And Albert knew that a big move by Gruppmann would probably have been kept a secret from me. So Albert wanted to tell *me* something. Given my unexpected lunch with Papa Panzer, I had a real need to know.

"Okay, Albert. I know nothing. They've left me in the dark. I'm an insignificant schmuck and you have fabulous sources. Tell me what you know."

"You remember my brother-in-law . . ."

"The investment banker."

". . . who handles . . ."

"Mergers and acquisitions."

". . . for Morgan Stanley . . ."

"Who told you what? Please, please!"

". . . that Gruppmann has just . . ."

"What? Bought? Traded? Stolen? Hurry, please hurry."

"Well, it seems that Gruppmann has just bought LIFESTYLE Magazine. You're not going to pretend that you didn't know."

"Good-bye, Albert. I owe you."

I was very angry, but not at the Germans for hiding the news from me. After all, the deal was probably handled at a corporate level that began with Helmut and went up. But I have always prided myself on my good instincts, on my ability to sense that something is in the air and then to ferret it out (a flying ferret). I was angry at myself. I closed my eyes, leaned back in my chair, and put *zwei* and *zwei* together.

I called Frankie into my office. "Here's two dollars. Go downstairs to the newsstand and get me a copy of LIFESTYLE. And put the magazine into your bag so no one sees you bring it into the office."

Frankie gave me a Look, which involved raising one dramatically sculpted eyebrow.

"By the way," I added, "here's twenty bucks. You win."

"A promotion?"

"I'm reasonably confident it is."

"He's 'reasonably confident,' is he?" she mocked. "Well, you better take me with you, buddy-boy."

"And you better keep your mouth shut. And hurry. Get that magazine. I've only got an hour before lunch."

I was no longer angry. Perhaps I had lost twenty dollars, but my luck was running.

The telephone rang at twelve thirty. "Here comes Helmut," Frankie whispered.

Like a furtive schoolboy, I hid the copy of LIFESTYLE in my desk as Helmut entered. He was a short man with a high voice and a contrived expansiveness.

"Ah, Mr. Werble, how lucky I am you are able to join me. But it is you who is not so lucky, no? You have to put up with the food at my club." He cackled in short staticlike bursts—a Blaupunkt on the fritz.

Helmut had evidently learned that New Yorkers coyly brag about their clubs by complaining about the food. Helmut's club, however, was not one of the traditional cathedrals of self-congratulation but a businessmen's eating club of only modest prestige to which, according to Frankie, Mr. Schaefer had introduced Gernschaft so he wouldn't have to run into Helmut at the clubs he really enjoyed. Helmut's complaint about the food was all the more hollow since eating clubs generally provide pretty good food to make up for the lack of squash courts, libraries, and overly risible middle-aged men whose marriages have just broken up.

"So, we will go downstairs and get a taxi," Helmut said.

When we arrived he said, "So, we will go upstairs and have a drink in the bar before lunch." Helmut liked to be sure everyone understood exactly what the plan was.

The club occupied the fortieth floor of a large Park Avenue office building. It was a triumph of decorator colors and contemporary paintings, though one could have carpeted the floors with the paintings and framed the rugs with no noticeable difference. After we ordered our drinks, Helmut brought up the only subject of informal, personal conversation between us, the Werble family dog.

"I'm afraid that Gretel got into a terrific fight," I said. "She came home with a cut under the eye and an injured paw. But she's very proud. She won't let us clean the wound, which I think means that she lost the fight."

The subject of the dog was rather problematical for me. At a get-acquainted party for the Gruppmann people and Schaefer Communications last year, I mentioned to Helmut that I used to have a dog. After two martinis it seemed to me perfectly clear that Helmut would be fascinated since Gretel was a German dog, a Giant Schnauzer. Although Gretel had died thirty years ago, when I was seven, Helmut misunderstood me to say that Gretel was now seven years old. After several futile attempts to correct him, I gave up and allowed his misapprehension to become my lie. Hardly a week passed that Helmut didn't ask after Gretel and I didn't invent some new doggie adventure. When my imagination faltered, I hit upon the clever scheme of borrowing the adventures of Sara, the ten-year-old daughter of our neighbor, and applying them to Gretel. Today's story had been inspired by a recent schoolyard fight that left the feisty Sara with a black eye. Sara adored the idea that I translated her life into a dog's life to please my boss. I suppose I could and should have dispatched poor Gretel beneath the wheels of a speeding semi-trailer, but then I would have lost my free and easy rapport with Helmut.

When our drinks were finished, Helmut stood up. "Now we will go get ourselves some of that food I warned you about."

One of the things that I genuinely liked about the Panzers was that they didn't beat around the bush. As soon as we were seated, Helmut looked directly at me. "I am pleased to tell you that Schaefer Communications is the new owner of LIFESTYLE Magazine."

I was visibly astonished.

"I'm very impressed," I said. "By all accounts LIFESTYLE is the most successful new magazine since *People*. And it's still growing. Until you bought it—"

"*We* bought it, Mr. Werble," Helmut corrected me gently. "You must feel that you are one of us."

I nodded with humble gratitude and thought that Frankie's twenty dollars were pretty safe. "Until *we* bought it, it was one of the very few successful independent magazines."

The waiter appeared.

"We will order now and talk about the magazine later. Yes?"

Helmut was delighted with himself. He ordered another round of drinks, taught me how to say *"Prosit!"* and kidded the waitress about the way the sauerbraten was prepared. During pauses in the conversation he hummed. We seemed to be celebrating an alliance only slightly less important than Brest-Litovsk.

Helmut finally brought the conversation around to the magazine. "So, I am very interested in your thinking about LIFESTYLE. I want you to tell me why it is such a big success. In Germany we don't have such an interest in ourselves or in what you call 'lifestyles.' "

"I guess we Americans tend to search within ourselves for *Lebensraum,*" I said blithely. I winked so Helmut would know it was okay to laugh, and he laughed heartily.

"You Americans, you are such big kidders," he said.

So I laughed just as heartily and hollowly.

"LIFESTYLE's basic premise," I said, "is that having a good time is a kind of pilgrimage during which you perform a series of semi-ecstatic rituals with your body, your mind, and your loved ones." I then launched myself upon an extended pontification about LIFESTYLE's editorial profile, marketing, promotion, and potential, as if I were summing up a lifetime of study.

After a while Helmut said, "You are a regular reader, no?"

"Not really. But I take a look now and again just to keep up." I was pushing my luck so I signaled for a turn. I asked about Larry Roth, the whiz kid who created LIFESTYLE and sold it to Schaefer. Helmut inferred a hidden question here—as he was meant to—and quickly assured me that the only reason Roth happened to sell was because he was a mercurial genius and they made him an offer when the mercury was low. Helmut repeated at least four times that LIFESTYLE was a very successful magazine.

"If it's so successful," I finally said, "why isn't it making any money?"

"Ah-ha," Helmut said. "This is a very clever man. And I think you are pretty much right. It does make money, but nothing like it should be making. They run it crazy. Put money into big projects that have nothing to do with the magazine business, sell discount subscriptions when they do not need to. . . ." Helmut shook his head. "So I think you are going to be very happy."

I took a deep breath. "Why am I going to be happy?"

"Because when you have a basically sound business that has been a little mismanaged, it is an easy challenge for a publisher to be very successful. And you are the new publisher of LIFESTYLE." He stood up and bowed stiffly. "Congratulations."

The rest of the lunch was warm and pleasant, devoted as it was to mutual reassurance: I, by my murmurs of delight in the job and my eagerness to take charge, assuring Helmut that he had made a brilliant choice of publishers; Helmut, with his praise of my intelligence and tact, assuring me that Gruppmann stood solidly behind me. Only one of us was telling the truth.

Helmut said one surprising thing to me. When I asked if he saw the need for any changes in the magazine's style, he urged me not to tamper with LIFESTYLE's editorial quality. I was surprised because so far Gruppmann had pursued a rather different policy at Schaefer.

For instance, one would hardly point to the Top 40 hits as an example of all that's right about American culture, but one sensed a decline in values when the Panzers threw out the Top 40 format and made all of Schaefer's radio stations follow a pasteurized, pretested format ("the mellow, contempo sound") that was computer-designed to provide maximum demographic impact. Likewise, while *Stars 'n Stars* was a rather dim beacon of civilization, its decreasing coverage of movie stars and increasing coverage of third-rate television stars could also be considered a lowering of standards (we're talking *relative* values here). The only instance in which the policy failed was when Briggs & Schaefer, the book publishing division, blew most of their editorial budget on a surefire best-seller, a multigenerational Jewish saga called *Lotsa Matzoh* ("From the steppes of Russia to the stoops of Brooklyn . . ."). But surefire does not always spread like wildfire; the book seemed but to pause in the bookstores at its original price before it expired on the remainder tables for 98 cents.

Overall, however, the Gruppmann programming and editorial policy was a smashing success. The radio stations increased their ratings, *Stars 'n Stars* increased its circulation, and Schaefer increased its revenues. I remember reading an early essay by Freud in which he discusses the association, in dreams and folklore, of money and excrement. There is a Middle European wisdom here that Gruppmann had adapted to create a modern alchemy of marketing: take a product, turn it into shit, and it will then be magically transformed into gold.

TWO

FOR RELEASE: *March 15, 1985*

ALL MEDIA

Schafer Communications Inc. today announces that it has acquired LIFESTYLE magazine from Lawrence Roth, the magazine's founder and publisher.

"We are pleased indeed to add one of America's most original and popular magazines to our Magazine Group," said Helmut Gernschaft, President of Schaefer Communications. "We wish to stress that we bought LIFESTYLE magazine because of our admiration of its unique voice and place in American culture. Consequently, no changes are contemplated. We have assured Mr. Roth and the editors of the magazine that its editorial independence will be respected.

LIFESTYLE magazine was founded in 1970. . . .

Because we wished to stress that LIFESTYLE would enjoy total editorial independence under the benevolent Gruppmann thumb, we announced that the magazine would retain its old offices. The fact that Schaefer Communications had no extra office space was just a happy coincidence.

I was given two weeks to set my affairs at Schaefer in order before moving to LIFESTYLE. I spent some of the time reviewing all of LIFESTYLE's issues for the fifteen years of its existence in an effort to grasp the magazine's "philosophy." One reason for LIFESTYLE's success was that in some ways it was a very traditional magazine: it covered many of the usual categories—food, sex, entertainment, health, psychology—but gave each a special LIFESTYLE slant. The magazine itself was a minor triumph of splashy design, and this imparted a certain aggressive authority to such typical articles as "Running and Authenticity"; "When Your Self Grows and Your Spouse Doesn't: A Guide to Constructive Divorce"; "The Whole Truth About Whole Grain Cereals"; and "Twelve Ways to Get More Out of Masturbation."

The key word, which popped up irrepressibly during LIFESTYLE's first fifteen years, was "energy." Each issue was bursting with physical and psychological exercises that promised to increase your energy—for sex or work or, most importantly, for reinventing yourself. By nurturing this energy, the devoted LIFESTYLE reader would have no trouble creating a new profile to adorn his or her divested identity. One thing was clear: the idea of the slow, difficult forging of an identity had gone by the boards. LIFESTYLE had discovered a sort of psychological version of quantum mechanics: instead of gradual development, one's energy simply leaped gazelle-like from lifestyle to lifestyle.

During my last fortnight at Schaefer, Frankie Toomey successfully conducted her campaign to accompany me to LIFESTYLE. She tried a number of ploys, including relaying gossipy accounts of internecine strife at LIFESTYLE: "Hey, listen to this story! You're going to need protection." But her best argument went as follows: "Here's how I see it, buddy-boy. There you are over at LIFESTYLE. But do you know what the Panzers are up to back at Schaefer? No way José. You know squat. And you can be sure that somebody's going to be after your ass around here." The point was that only Frankie's great contacts with the other secretaries at Schaefer could keep me abreast of office politics. She got the job.

I somehow managed to interrupt my rapturous sense of self-importance during the final week at Schaefer to wonder how my arrival would be greeted by LIFESTYLE's staff. No doubt they were expecting a slobbering Visigoth who had swept across the Atlantic in a U-boat. I thought I might ease their fears by meeting with the mysterious Larry Roth, the departing publisher and owner, who so far had dealt with us entirely through emissaries. I had in mind a pleasant, expensive lunch during which I would glow with such charm, sincerity, and concern that Roth would run back to LIFESTYLE's offices and tell everybody, "It's all right; you're in good hands. That George Werble, he's a sweetheart."

It was a perfectly lovely scenario, but unfortunately Larry Roth did not return any of the five phone calls I placed to him. So on Wednesday I called Parker Burns, the magazine's editor in chief, and made a date for a drink after work on Thursday.

We met at one of those bars in the fifties off Sixth Avenue which, because of the proximity of several huge communications empires, fill up at five o'clock for two frantic hours of media talk. When I arrived the room was stocked with hectic men and women who leaned conspiratorially toward each other and spoke excitedly of deals gone awry, deals about to collapse, deals full of double and triple crosses. Escaping the hubbub were gleeful cries of triumph such as ". . . and picked her brain when I already had someone else under contract . . ."; ". . . charged off all the profits . . ."; ". . . and put up a hundred thousand worthless shares as security." I was in a din of iniquity.

I arrived before Parker Burns. I had fatuously described myself to him as looking like a man who appears to be ten years younger than he really is. He wasn't amused. "I'm the opposite," he said flatly—but accurately, since I recognized him as soon as he walked in. Although I knew he had had a pretty long career on a number of magazines and newspapers, I had the illusion that he would somehow personify his magazine by wafting into my presence in the grip of a flamboyant lifestyle. Instead, his pallor suggested that the existence of the sun was a rumor in which he didn't put much stock, and I couldn't decide whether it was indigestion or the prospect of meeting me that gave him such a dyspeptic expression.

To show what a convivial fellow I am I ordered a martini.

Parker ordered a glass of gin. After a few minor pleasantries, we began that feeling-out process of locating a common acquaintance. Parker seemed to know just where to look.

"You remember Jimmy Peterson?" he asked.

"Of course. He worked for me at *Weekend.* How is he these days?"

"All right, I guess. He stopped drinking."

"That's great. But I don't remember that he really drank so much."

"You're right. He didn't start drinking until *after* you fired him."

"But I was sure he'd get another job right away."

"He should have, but even a couple of months out of work were too much for his wife. She split after six weeks. That's when he *really* started drinking."

"I see. I'm glad he stopped."

"Had to. The doctor told him either to stop or his bleeding ulcer would kill him."

"Would you like some hors d'oeuvres?" I said, changing the subject before we were on our way over to Jimmy's wake. "Have you been at LIFESTYLE since it started?"

"Nope," he said.

"I'll bet LIFESTYLE was quite a change for you."

"I guess you're right."

"If I remember correctly, you used to be the editor of a Sunday supplement in Boston."

"Right," he said and then added, as a concession to loquacity, "Boston."

Parker must have decided that communication was his profession and should not be practiced in off hours. Even if I managed to make a wonderful impression on him, I doubted if anyone at the magazine would ever find out.

I ordered another glass of gin for Parker and cast about for a good conversation to overhear. At the next table, two men were discussing the formation of a TV production company called Come Again Productions. They were debating their first project, trying to decide whether it would be more original to remake

The Women and cast it entirely with men or remake *The Dirty Dozen* and cast it entirely with women. "But how could we have women fighting in World War Two?" asked one of them.

"I got it. We'll make them Israeli women. They fight in the army."

"That's it, we'll set it during the Six-Day War. But who'll play the Telly Savalas part?"

"I know. Shelley Winters' agent is a friend of my first wife. Maybe—"

"Forget it. She's too Jewish."

Parker Burns seemed content to sip his gin and stare desultorily at his hands. I ordered another glass of gin for him and tried again to stoke the conversation. "Tell me a little about the magazine."

The question seemed to dumbfound him. He shrugged, held up his hands to demonstrate total innocence, and scratched his head doubtfully.

"Well, how about Enid and Leon Malt?" I suggested. They were the husband-and-wife team of psychologists who had established a national reputation by busily honing the cutting edges of personal fulfillment, interpersonal relations, and impersonal ecstasy.

"Jesus, those two old goats," Parker said in a sudden garrulous burst. "You know, I didn't ever think I'd be editing articles on how meditation can increase your sexual energy. I said to Enid, 'If you meditate about sex a lot, you get horny. What's so original about that?' And judging from Enid and Leon, they must think about it all the time. You wait and see, she'll be crawling all over you. But their articles bring in more reader response than anything else we publish. 'Dear Dr. Malt: I've been working hard at finding my center, but my wife Valerie says that if I quit being a real estate agent and travel around the country in a Winnebago selling my wood mosaics at craft shows she'll leave me. Where do my obligations lie?' "

At least he had begun to talk. I ordered another gin for him. "How about the other editors, like the cooking column?"

"Ahhh, him," Parker said in disgust and launched upon an account of a complicated dispute between Gregory the food editor and Annette of natural nutrition. It seemed their territories overlapped.

On the other hand, maybe that last glass of gin was not what Parker needed. I had hoped to get an editor in chief's perspective on his staff and instead was being treated to petty tales of office lowjinks. And unless my hearing was out of focus, Parker's voice was beginning to accomplish the oxymoronic feat of growing simultaneously thicker and runnier. "That Judy what's-her-face . . . Gruber . . . I call her grubby. Fitness editor and a bitch on wheels and I don't mean her exercise bike. Office smells like a fucking gymnasium . . . socks and bras sweating all over the place . . . thinks she's paid to go running at ten in the morning."

Although I am a tolerant person, Parker's behavior seemed quite curious to me. It wasn't the behavior itself, but the fact that he chose to display it in this particular situation. After all, this was his first meeting with his new boss, and although his new boss had ordered a lot of gin for him, he had not been forced to drink it. Parker did not seem upon first meeting to be such an utterly indispensable member of LIFESTYLE's staff that he could afford such a display. As he lurched into a description of the warfare between the production and art departments, my attention turned again to the neighboring table, where the creative intelligence of Come Again Productions was challenging itself to come up with a cast of blacks for a six-hour mini-series remake of *How Green Was My Valley* with Gary Coleman in the Roddy McDowall part.

The bar was nearly empty, but the war between art and production was like an artichoke from which Parker kept pulling issue after issue. It was time to extricate myself. I started inserting deft little summing-up remarks every time Parker paused. I tried "Well, that's great," and "What a good story!" and finally "What time is it?" But my remarks were just commas; Parker had been sentenced to run on.

I made a scribbling motion to the waitress for the check.

When she arrived Parker ordered another glass of gin. I left twenty dollars on the table.

"Monday at your place," I said.

The Gruppmann purchase of LIFESTYLE had been certified by the full exfoliation of purchase agreements, stock transfers, loans, bonds, and escrow payments. Despite this civilizing veneer of financial documentation, the essential act of acquisition would not occur until I walked into LIFESTYLE's office and took over. There was something primitive here: I had to announce myself as leader of this peculiar pack of editorial hunter-gatherers and convince them that I could guide them successfully in search of the elusive lifestyle.

LIFESTYLE occupied the third floor of a small undistinguished loft building on the fringe of the garment center. In fact, Alpak Fringes: Decorative Costume Products occupied the fourth floor. Other tenants included Kantrowitz Hat Forms on the fifth floor and Robbins Ribbons on the sixth. The second floor was for rent. In the coffee shop on the first floor I met Frankie on the morning of our debut at LIFESTYLE. To my surprise, Frankie had insisted that I escort her in the first time.

"Are you still nervous?" I asked.

"Nah." She winked.

"How much?"

"Ten milligrams, that's all."

"That's a pretty good down for so early in the morning."

"I know. I needed half a red to get back up."

I stared at her angrily.

"Well, you're not going to give me any dictation on the first day, are you?"

"How do all those happy little milligrams get along with this coffee?"

"Espresso would be better," Frankie said. "You look kind of nervous yourself. Maybe you could use—"

"That's all I need. Look, it's ten o'clock. Let's get going."

As we stepped into the elevator, the operator greeted me with a cheery "Hello, captain!" It occurred to me that Parker Burns had alerted the elevator man to my arrival, but when we were followed into the elevator by a grizzled messenger mumbling to himself about Bosnia and Herzegovina, whom the operator greeted with "Hello major," I realized that the operator favored the military form of address and not me.

Depending upon one's point of view, the building either was rundown but serviceable (the other tenants' point of view) or had a kind of *declassé* elegance (my optimistic point of view). The reception area on the third floor was decorated with a number of enlarged covers from LIFESTYLE. One cover showed a beautiful man and woman exchanging gifts; the headline read: "Sharing—What's in It for You?" Another cover, an infamous one, illustrated the burning question "How Much Change Can You Take?"; it showed Drs. Enid and Leon Malt wearing each other's clothes.

The receptionist, a real specialist in the art of greeting, said to us, "Just a minute," and returned to a complicated telephone conversation concerning her mother, her mother's boyfriend, her stepfather, and her natural father. Frankie finally hissed to get her attention. The receptionist held up a cautioning hand but Frankie hissed again, throwing wind to the caution. The receptionist looked up as if to say, This better be good.

"I'd like to introduce you to someone," Frankie said.

"Just a sec," the receptionist said to the telephone.

"I'd like you to meet George Werble, otherwise known as the boss."

The receptionist rolled her eyes heavenward. "Shit!" she said and clapped her palm to her forehead.

Frankie cupped her ear. "Is that an echo I hear?"

"Will you tell Parker Burns that I'm here?" I asked and firmly steered Frankie out of earshot. "I want you to take it easy. They're going to think I arrived with a private bodyguard."

"So I guess you're here," Parker said when he appeared. "Maybe you'd like me to show you around." I wondered if he thought any reference to our drink(s) together would be unfortunate or whether he simply couldn't remember the occasion. I introduced Frankie, and we were ushered into a gymnasium-sized space with glass-fronted offices lining the long sides. Between the two rows of offices was the secretarial pool and a honeycomb of clerical cubicles.

My first impression was one of busy disorder. People were moving quickly and talking rapidly. At least three of the people who passed us stopped Parker to say, "Oh, by the way, I meant to ask you about . . ." Parker handled each question efficiently, but I wondered what would have happened if he hadn't had the conversation. Would the article "Eight Meditative Techniques for Your Pre-Schoolers" really have appeared with a libelous passage? I cautioned myself not to judge LIFESTYLE too easily. Maybe they had planned an "Oh, by the way" management style in which everybody circulated themselves instead of memos.

My second impression was of clutter. At Schaefer, clutter had been eliminated by a management consultant who convinced us that we should have no more paper, only documents, and only meaningful documents at that. There couldn't be as much meaning in the universe as there was paper at LIFESTYLE; it was piled on desks and filing cabinets, pinned to bulletin boards, and taped to doors and walls. One would have thought the fishbowl effect of glass-fronted offices would have restrained their occupants, but instead it seemed to have goaded them to decorate the other walls with posters, aggressive epigrams, and the printing detritus of proofs and mechanicals.

"Maybe we should go to your office," Parker suggested.

"Whatever you want." I tried to smile in a relaxed, confident manner as I felt fifty pairs of eyes bearing down on me. At the far end of the floor we came to a group of offices that surrounded a carpeted reception area. No glass walls here; this was management's arena, where opaqueness reigned.

There were several secretaries at desks in the reception area. We headed for a woman dressed entirely in black. Her dark hair was wound up in a bun, and she held herself stiffly and stoically with her arms folded in her lap.

"George, I'd like you to meet Teresa de la Iglesia, your secretary," Parker said.

I heard Frankie draw in her breath sharply. "Cool it," I murmured as I stepped forward with my arm outstretched. Teresa rose gravely and took my hand.

"And I'm Frankie Toomey, Mr. Werble's administrative assistant. How *are* we both going to fit in this tiny space?"

Teresa's enormous brown eyes filled with tears. "If you'd prefer, I can just go away. It doesn't matter."

"Weren't you Larry Roth's secretary?" I asked.

She nodded.

"But he said such good things about you . . . that you were invaluable. Please don't go away."

I wasn't exactly sure what going away entailed, but when a woman dressed in black threatens to do so, it's worth a lie to stop her. Teresa bowed her head, yielding to my plea, and sat down again at her desk.

"And I guess this is your office," Parker said in his authoritative manner. "If you want it, that is."

Appropriately, it was a corner office, but the only view I had cornered was of a street full of trucks. We all entered cautiously, as if we were violating a graveyard. "By the way," Parker whispered, "Teresa's in mourning."

"Since when?" Frankie said.

"I don't know, maybe two years."

"Would you excuse us, Parker?" Frankie asked and closed the door behind him. She whirled on me. "If you think I'm going to let Teresa de la Dismal push me out of my job here, you better think again. No way Frankie's going to crawl back to Schaefer just because Teresa turns her big wet eyes on you."

"Well, there's no danger of your crawling back to Schaefer because no one there will take you back. You get what I'm driving at, don't you?"

She nodded.

"So you go off and fume for a while and try to make some more enemies around here and then we'll figure things out."

Frankie stalked off and I surveyed my new office. Although I had expected it to be cleaned for me, it gave the appearance of having never been occupied. There were no bookcases, pictures on the wall, or casual furniture. In the precise center of the room sat a gray metal desk of the sort that governmental agencies use to eliminate any sense of pride among their employees. Tucked beneath the desk was a matching chair which had been designed to eliminate any sense of comfort. On one wall there was a large bulletin board from which hung a calendar whose month had not been changed since December.

"Oh, Teresa," I called gently. "Could you come in for a minute?"

She entered tremulously.

"Tell me: when Larry Roth left, did you pack up a lot of papers and files?"

"Oh no. There was almost nothing to take. He hardly used this office."

"Did he have another office?"

"No. He just kind of hung around the whole place. He was always in someone else's office. He just used this office to dictate letters and make phone calls."

I was beginning to fear that I had a title but would have to invent the job to go along with it.

"He's here. He's come at last!" I heard someone say in a hushed, excited voice. A strikingly handsome white-haired man had entered the office. "Enid, come quickly!"

An equally attractive white-haired woman came into the office. "Oh, Leon; our new publisher!"

They stood away from me as they exclaimed upon my arrival: the baby publisher had been found in the bulrushes. Then, in an eruption of joy, they flowed toward me with their arms extended.

"You must be . . ." I said, backing away.

"We are, we are," she keened as they trapped me against the window. "I'm Enid Malt and this is Leon: my husband, my colleague, my lover, and my friend."

Leon clutched my arm while Enid rested her hands gently on my other arm as if they wanted to assure themselves of my corporeal existence.

"You must allow us to make you feel welcome. What can we do to make this difficult transitional period as easy as possible for you?" Leon asked.

"We know—don't we, Leon?—how stressful such major life changes are. We want to help."

"Often, when I am lecturing," Leon said, "people come up to me with anguish on their faces. And I say to them, 'Something is terribly wrong. Tell me.' And they say, 'I don't know what's wrong. Everything is right. There's a wonderful new person in my life. My new job is terrific. We love our new house. Yet I'm choked up, nervous, fearful.' And I say, 'What is that word I hear? *New?* Did you say *new?*' And of course, George, so much stress seems to go along with each new life experience. Many people who come to me tell me that that is why they won't move forward in life—there's too much pain. They say, 'Dr. Malt, what shall I do?' And I say, 'Call me Leon.' And then I say, 'Dumbbell! You're nervous about being nervous. Might as well be nervous about something else . . . like *wonderful changes in your life!*' "

"Leon, Leon," Enid said, tugging his sleeve. "we must let George get settled in his office. We'll have lots of time to talk later on."

"Yes, you're right. But I just want to tell George about my Danish grandmother, who never had any stress at all. Do you know why?"

"Maybe she just didn't give a shit about anything." Frankie had reappeared.

"This is Frankie Toomey, who has come here with me and who is soon going to have lots of stress to deal with. Listen carefully, Frankie."

"Well, Frankie, I once asked Grandmother Helga why she was able to take everything in stride. And she leaned back in her chair and gazed out of the farmhouse at the neatly planted rows of fennel, and she said, 'I don't worry about changes because . . . because I'm very very old.' "

We all gazed at each other for a few moments.

"Think about it," Leon said.

"I am, I am."

I thought about it for what I guessed was an appropriate length of time and then thanked the Malts for their advice. They floated out of the office and I spent the rest of the morning reading correspondence and deciphering some strange scribbled figures on a crumpled sheet of paper, which Teresa told me represented LIFESTYLE's budget. After meeting the Malts, I decided to take my time with the rest of the editorial staff, so in the afternoon Frankie went off to hunt up a new desk for me and I introduced myself to the advertising and circulation departments, which were more familiar territories to me. I told these departments that I wanted to have a meeting, and we did.

When Helmut called at the end of the day and asked how my first day had gone, I told him I had organized a meeting. He seemed very satisfied.

THREE

In nice weather, I rode a bicycle to and from the Finchmont Village train station. Finchmont is a tasteful suburb which used to be thirty-eight minutes from Manhattan by train but seems to be creeping farther away. I took up the bicycle when, trembling with rage after a particularly horrendous ninety-minute trip to Finchmont, I got into my car, stomped on the gas, and bulldozed an original exit through the parking lot fence. My rule as I pedaled was to refuse to think about any problem that could not be solved in five miles. What did I not think about? Mostly, I didn't think about my marriage.

Because I had concentrated rather single-mindedly on my career, it was a relief to have the attitudes and tastes of my origins—believe in them though I did not—to fall back upon when making those potentially messy choices such as wife, home, and children's upbringing. So my wife, Helen, came from one of the Best Families of Topeka—she was a known quantity, in other words—and we lived in a good suburb in a good house with plenty of room for the future appearance of two small known quantities. Sometimes I wondered if Helen didn't share my casual contempt for our background, if I weren't simply a known quantity to her, chosen so she could concentrate on some mysterious inner life or secret goal. It is a mark of my fairness that I am perfectly capable of entertaining this idea with equanimity, or even approving of it. But I never asked Helen; there are certain issues every good marriage must skirt.

After seven years of graceful issue-skirting, we tripped. For Helen, the problem turned out to be not an inner life or a secret goal but the very absence of such a goal. So she decided to embark on a voyage of self-discovery and I became one of several anchors that needed to be cast off. Such events are rarely unilateral; I too had recently embarked on a voyage, mine one of sexual discovery. On my voyage I had already explored the Archipelago of Ethnically Exotic Women and I was making full steam for the Atoll of Arrogant Models and Dancers.

Helen and I confessed all to each other on the most honest night of our marriage. Hindsight suggests that honesty was the worst policy. The very next morning we realized that the guilt each of us felt over our separate needs could now be assuaged by blaming the other's failure. And when guilt and blame arrive, can lawyers be far behind? Since the "roomy handyman's special with a nice piece of land" that we had purchased for $68,000 was now worth $350,000, the lawyers advised us to stay put until we could reach an agreement.

So began the "phony divorce." We continued to live in the same house—with just a bit of territorial rearrangement—and, true to our origins, behaved toward each other with great politeness and even a kind of exaggerated solicitousness. I discovered, to my surprise, that my voyaging urge disappeared. Was it the consequence of confession? Or was it my discovery that on the Atoll of Arrogant Models and Dancers no one spoke my language? (As far as I could tell, no one there spoke any recognizable language at all.) Sometimes I wondered if Helen's voyage had come to a similar end. But I never asked; there are certain issues every good divorce must skirt.

I parked my bicycle in the garage and with perverse pleasure surveyed the signs of incipient neglect which stippled the house and grounds. A few stout daffodils had managed to push their way through the mass of wet dead leaves and twigs that had accumulated in the flower beds. Although Helen and I had not widely announced our long-impending separation, untended flower beds seem to be the suburban equivalent of posting divorce banns. With the elation of a convicted murderer when the governor calls, I realized that this was the first year I would not have to massage our grass with manure.

"Down with lawn ordure!" I announced to the neighborhood.

I entered my half of the house and hung my coat in my half of the closet. Certain domestic conventions had been abandoned during the phony divorce: I no longer entered the house and said, "Hi, I'm home!" in a loud cheery voice (which I used to do at least once a year), nor did I announce myself in any other way that might imply that my presence mattered to someone who was already home. On the other hand, it was now necessary to slam the door and then cough or hum so that the someone in the house would know that I was not the burglar come to take his tithe.

"Is that you?" she called as I rasped my fifth cough.

I went into the kitchen, where several other conventions had been jettisoned. We no longer consulted each other on shopping lists, though both of us shopped for food and shared whatever we bought. This created strange eating patterns. We would each fill the refrigerator with extremely ordinary food (once we ate nothing but permutations of ground beef for two weeks) and then find ourselves simultaneously stocking up on lobster tails, tripe, rabbit, quail, and venison. What we didn't share were meals. I often had to wait until ten o'clock to get into the kitchen.

Our situation had its amusing and annoying aspects, but we neither complained about them—too hostile—nor joked—too friendly. Instead we improvised a kind of tacit decorum to advise us on the appropriateness of our behavior. The news of my new job, for instance, prompted measured but sincere congratulations from Helen. Then she said, "I suppose you're going to be so wrapped up in the job that you won't be able to think about a divorce for a while."

I shrugged my shoulders.

There was a pause, during which, I am convinced, she debated whether she should ask me how much more money I was making. But decorum suggested she feign uninterest since she couldn't feign disinterest.

Tonight, as I busied myself with chicken breasts—we were on a bland streak—Helen came in and watched me.

"I need to talk to you," she said, and ran her hand dramatically and messily through her hair. The even-featured, fair-haired, clear-eyed, self-composed, well-groomed woman I married because her hyphens matched mine had, in recent months, acquired an air of distracted intensity. Her new interest, Finchmont Village politics, appeared to be so absorbing that the fine points of neatness and restraint paled before her responsibilities. And there must have been a lot on Helen's mind. Finchmont is one of those suburbs with an overdeveloped sense of national importance. The town council not only wrestled with school budgets and zoning variances but also felt compelled to take authoritative positions on the destruction of the ozone layer (against it), the Falkland Islands (maybe, but), and sexual freedom (an unqualified right; however . . .).

I feared a Serious Discussion was about to take place. At least once every three weeks, one of us felt obliged to remind the other that he/she was indeed searching for a way out of the current impasse and that the other was not to assume that the lack of ostensible progress meant that he/she was changing his/her mind. We had felt the need of Serious Discussions most acutely following the two occasions when we blundered into that rarest of sexual events, an "illicit" interlude with one's own spouse. "Totally meaningless," we assured each other before the sheets were cold.

"What's the problem?" I asked Helen.

"It's Irene. She's coming for a visit." Helen threw up her hands in exasperation. "I don't know what I'm going to do with her. There's a council election coming up, and I've agreed to be Bud Horner's campaign manager."

Helen's sister Irene was married to a semi-alcoholic minister named Emerson Miller.

"Has Pastor Miller got himself into another professional scrape or is this a marital eruption?"

In our seven years of marriage, Irene had visited us four times: twice during scrapes and twice due to eruptions. This may not sound like a particularly troubled marriage by modern standards, but there was a third sister whom Irene also visited.

"If you're asking if I mind, I don't," I said. Decorum, as usual, restrained me from raising the possibility that Irene's arrival was some sort of tactic, a way of driving me out of the house.

"Thank you," Helen said in a cool formal manner which indicated that she didn't need my approval. "That's not the problem. The problem is—God, I can't believe this!—I don't remember if I ever told Irene that we were breaking up."

"I see. I see."

We finally grinned at each other; the ludicrousness of our situation was sometimes too obvious to be concealed by decorum. When we originally decided to split up, we began to tell selected friends, family, and professional acquaintances, but then we shut up when it became apparent we couldn't deliver a nice juicy divorce right away. Helen was especially cautious about telling her own family. They did not communicate very much on a casual basis, but come a crisis and they would cramp up into an urgent nexus of misunderstandings, accusations, and recriminations, as if they had collapsed into a black hole of such great emotional gravity that not a single ray of good sense could escape.

Helen and I discussed the problem for a while. We finally decided that the sister whom she had confessed to and sworn to secrecy was Katherine, the spoiled rich sister who was married to a man who lived in Tulsa and manufactured drill bits for oil rigs.

"*Should* we tell Irene?" Helen asked.

"Why bother? She'll never notice, if I know her. She's usually pretty wrapped up in her own problems."

"But we're in separate bedrooms."

"Lots of couples—"

"On separate floors? In separate wings?"

Helen's pretentious streak insisted on defining my bedroom over the garage as a wing (even though I had to use the bathroom in the cellar). "But don't you see, Helen? People with topsy-turvy lives like Irene will regard the seventy-one feet between our beds as a slight spat. She won't notice a thing."

I suspect the real reason I didn't want to tell Irene was so she didn't feel she had to take Helen's side and thus outnumber me in my house. And I actually liked Irene; she might even dine with me on lonely evenings. She was a large, gregarious woman with a quick temper but also great generosity—the sort of person who would give you the shirt off her back as long as you didn't cross her. These qualities stood her in good stead as a minister's wife, but since the Reverend Miller went from failure to scrape to failure he was rarely in one post long enough for her skills to be brought into play.

It should be said that Reverend Miller's peccadilloes were not the only cause of their separations. One of Irene's visits was launched by the Reverend's discovery that on several occasions, as she counseled unfortunate parishioners, the shirt off her back was followed by her skirt, bra, panties, and shoes. "I mean I felt so hopeless," she told me. "Those poor men, out of work, deserted, struggling with drinking. Often I was the only woman they could speak to frankly. I just wanted to make some comforting gesture."

I looked at her skeptically.

"I guess I'm just a sucker for a hard-luck story," she said and smiled. "And the harder the luck, the luckier I felt."

Before I went to sleep that night I picked up my phone and called Helen. "George Werble here, calling from the West Wing."

"Yes?"

"I just wanted to make sure I didn't miss something tonight. Did we decide to tell Irene about the separation or not?"

"Not. At least for now."

"Good night."

FOUR

On the professional front, things at LIFESTYLE got off on the right foot. It appeared as if I were going to glide effortlessly into a long, friendly relationship with the staff, even though I had alerted myself to sensitively apply my managerial techniques to those inevitable personnel problems that crop up with changes in management. The best solution to such problems is to make the very worst threat of all: one simply announces that anyone who creates difficulties for a manager will be forced to read a book on management—*any* book on management. But there were no problems; to the contrary, I got to know the staff through their generous willingness to share their troubles and thoughts.

Publishers are often considered to be money-obsessed lummoxes by their creative people; they are expected to market the magazine, sell advertising space, and step back from the day-to-day concerns of editors and writers. Even though I scrupulously stayed out of editorial meetings, the staff seemed to have no reluctance to wander into my office and bounce ideas off me or solicit suggestions.

One morning, for instance, the Malts came in to show me their plans for a collaborative article on sexual jealousy. They usually published separately and had their territories divided so that Leon wrote about feelings and Enid wrote about sex.

"Jealousy is a perfect subject for two perspectives," Enid said.

"We want our readers to understand that jealousy is *natural,*" Leon added. "It's always there, ready to leap out when you don't expect it. But in our sexually permissive society, many people feel guilty about feeling jealous."

"And we know that there should be no guilt," Enid said firmly.

"But hurt is okay?" I asked.

"Hurt is wonderful!" Leon said. "That's our point. First you work through your jealous stage—which we call 'Plateau One: Blind Rage'—until you get to where you hurt. Then you're at 'Plateau Two: Wounded But in Control.' "

The empirical side of this collaboration was an incident from the semiprivate lives of Enid and Leon in which, as in their writing, Enid got the sex and Leon got the feelings.

"Of course Leon was very jealous when I told him I was having an affair with a sixteen-year-old boy—we had only been married for eight months at that point. But I was able to help Leon get to Plateau Two by developing such techniques as Adjective Suppression, which we describe in our article."

"What is it?"

"Well, it didn't help matters for me to refer to the young man as a *delicious* boy or a *lithe* Adonis."

"I can see that it wouldn't."

"It wasn't easy for me to get to Plateau Two," Leon continued. "But by God, my pain was real, my pain said to me, 'Leon, you're bleeding, therefore you're living.' And once I reached Plateau Two I was able to understand that it was because *I* am so sexually masterful that Enid had a profound need to be a teacher herself, to be master to this inexperienced young man."

"And when you get to Plateau Three," I said, "the wounds have started to heal and you just pick at the scab occasionally."

"In a manner of speaking," Enid said with a forced laugh. "We call Plateau Three 'Acceptance.' Finally we were both able to take joy in the fact that what I was doing with the young man was a tribute to Leon, for if I were a good enough teacher, another masterful Leon would go out into the world to make another Enid happy."

"And so we arrived at 'Plateau Four: Reconciliation,' " Leon said.

"That sounds just fine," I said. To encourage more communication with the writers, I tried to confine my remarks to praise and occasional questions. I figured any critical comments I had could be made through Parker.

"You like the article the way it is?" Enid said. She sounded surprised.

"From what you say, it seems just right. But perhaps Parker has some thoughts." I felt I was being exquisitely politic here.

"Oh no, he doesn't," Enid said. "That is, he's satisfied with it the way it is."

"There is one little problem, George," Leon said. "It's Frankie."

"Don't think we're not appreciative," Enid added quickly. "We've never before had a secretary just for ourselves."

"But she has some very peculiar attitudes," Leon said. "She doesn't seem to be—how shall I put it?—*sympathetic* to what we're trying to do."

"I don't think she's really hostile," I said. "I've known her for a while and I suspect that what you stand for challenges many of her beliefs. I'd take it as a personal favor if you'd try to put up with her a little longer. Maybe if you share your world with her. . . ."

They looked at each other doubtfully. "Do you know what she told Leon when he was dictating part of this article to her? She said she liked sex *because* it's dirty." Enid clucked disapprovingly.

"If it's not working after a few more weeks," I said, "I promise to make some other arrangement for her."

They smiled gratefully; we had a deal.

Perhaps I exaggerated when I implied that my early days at LIFESTYLE were without any difficulties; but a few rough edges here and there hardly qualify as Problems.

As I got more into the swing of things, I became aware of the peculiar habits of Judy Gruber, the fitness editor, whose very popular column was called "The Better Body." My office was one of the few without a glass front wall and door, but when my door was open I could just see into one corner of her office. And what I saw in that corner was the regular appearance and disappearance of Judy Gruber, as if she were pacing back and forth like a caged animal.

Judy and I more or less avoided each other for the first week or two. When we passed in the halls she would give me a cool, knowing grin, as if to say, The first move is yours.

So I made the first move and dropped into her office one day. I was encouraged by the sign on her door that said ALL THE NEWS THAT'S FITNESS. Her office had the appearance and faint odor of a locker room. I had to maneuver around her exercise bike, from which dangled sweaty clothes, and step over a set of weights that lay on the floor.

"Where do you shower?" I said hopefully.

"I belong to a gym a block away," Judy said without looking up from her typewriter.

Although I was glad to be finally breaking the ice, I was not sure the feeling was reciprocated.

"You have the guarded reserve of someone who suspects the worst in someone else," I said with my most winning smile.

"This is quite a day," she said with a quick insincere smile. "Le Grand Fromage at last decides to pay *me* a visit. I think I'll put the nicest interpretation on it and assume that he saved the best for last."

I would become accustomed, after a while, to Judy's frequent habit of addressing me in the third person, as if she were speaking to me through an intermediary Higher Authority. She had a short, compact figure and dark curly hair. She was dressed in slob-jock attire: a T-shirt three sizes too big; shorts pulled over sweat pants which had been cut off at the knee; and, of course, elaborately designed running shoes. There was an Ace bandage wrapped around her right knee.

"What happened to your knee?"

"Could it be a work-related injury? No, just a little chondromalacia. I need new orthotics."

I nodded as if I understood. To show my interest in her subject, I asked her if she could help me select an exercise bike.

"What kind of regular exercise do you do now?"

"Nothing," I said. I was unwilling to admit to my daily bike ride to and from the station—probably because I feared she would sneer at it.

"You must have a good tailor, then."

"And you have a good backhand," I said.

We reassessed each other for a few moments.

Judy explained to me the relative merits of eight different brands of exercise bikes. Then, to my surprise, she showed me a column she was working on about the way athletes psych themselves up to perform well under pressure. I was relieved by the subject of her column: perhaps she had been pacing in her office as research in psyching oneself up into an aggressive frenzy.

"I like to write about aspects of fitness and sports which my readers can apply to other areas of their lives. When I took over this column it was full of pieces about the runner's high and your body as a temple. You know, a real 1970s attitude. Today, people want fitness to be useful. They stay fit because they have to compete with each other at the office or they work out to work off tension. Or, frankly, they want to meet each other at the gym. And because they like to show off, they're into gear, into buying the best equipment and outfits.

"Take this column, for instance. There are lots of situations for which you have to psych yourself up, get the adrenaline flowing, be on, be ready—"

"I get the idea."

"The techniques in my article can help you to control difficult meetings or dominate those who are more powerful than you." The look she gave me said, I'm testing you.

"Or even dominate those who are smarter than you," I said. "I think it's a good idea for a column."

She proceeded to ask me a number of very specific questions about the piece, the sort of questions that invite critical comment. My instinct was to treat Judy more gingerly than anyone else. I offered my comments in a charmingly modest manner so she would feel free to reject them—which she did. Her continu[…] suspicious reserve indicated she wasn't charmed either. Before […] inexplicable tension between us went from palpable to palpitating I brought the conversation to an end by suggesting, in my politic way, that Parker Burns might help her with a couple of her questions.

"Parker? Help *me?*" she said incredulously. She snatched up her article and stalked out of the office. A few seconds later she returned. "Hey, this is *my* office. *You* leave."

So I left. My uncomfortable encounter with Judy Gruber couldn't depress me, however. After all, one could scarcely say that I faced Serious Problems.

Why, even the extremely superior Gregory Duplessix, LIFESTYLE's food writer, glided into my office one morning for advice and encouragement. He was a lean, handsome man of such aristocratic bearing and facile charm that I felt clumsy and humiliated in his presence. He was the sort of person who could successfully use the word "amusing," as in: "Ah, George, it's high time we became acquainted. Perhaps you will come with me soon to a wonderful little Chinese restaurant which prepares the most amusing jellyfish." His speech betrayed just enough of an accent to enable one to catch his continental drift.

Gregory's food articles ranged from recipes to reviews of restaurants to appreciations of wine, all of which expressed his belief in food as the most civilized, sensual experience in life. His latest article was a theme piece on the delightful versatility of coffee. The recipes included a Swedish-style roast leg of lamb cooked with coffee, a coffee ice dessert, and precise instructions for brewing perfect coffee from the three acceptable kinds of beans. Also included was a thoughtful discussion and taste-testing of coffee liqueurs. "Though some object that coffee keeps one awake," Gregory's article concluded, "these are pedestrian souls. Those of us who are eager for all the succulent pleasures of life think of insomnia as a benefit of coffee."

I was appropriately interested and impressed. Though I can't say that Gregory found me amusing, he seemed to be satisfied when he left my office. No problems there, I told myself. But that very afternoon Annette Norris, our natural nutritionist, appeared in my office to announce she was working on an article about the dangers of caffeine.

Annette was a tiny, perfectly proportioned woman who spoke in hushed, conspiratorial tones. "Do you know, George, how many unfortunate conditions are linked to excessive consumption of caffeine? Arrhythmic heartbeat for one. Quite scary. And fibrocystic breast disease in women. Very frightening, I'd say. The coffee producers are engaged in a desperate attempt to cover up these facts, I've been told."

I mentally added up my weekly consumption of coffee. Annette must have read my mind, for she regarded me with disapproval and said, "You have every reason to be worried. And ashamed."

I tried to look contrite.

The heart of Annette's article described an experiment she had performed in order to prove the unfortunate psychological effects of caffeine. Annette had a happy, contented husband who never ate or drank substances containing excessive amounts of caffeine. "Except we do permit ourselves a weekly square of chocolate."

Over a period of several months, Annette had secretly increased the amount of caffeine in dear Fred's diet by slipping real coffee into his decaffeinated version and by dissolving caffeine tablets into certain foods. She gradually got him up to the equivalent of eight cups of coffee a day. Lo and behold, amiable Fred became tense, irritable, and moody, given to fits of depression, and of course he became a complete insomniac.

"Wasn't he rather disturbed to discover that he was the guinea pig in an experiment?" I asked.

"To tell the truth," she whispered, "he still doesn't know. I suppose I'll have to tell him before the article is published."

"But hasn't he wondered why he mysteriously went crazy for a while and then, just as mysteriously, got better?"

Annette cleared her throat nervously. I had to lean over and lower my head to hear her. "Between us, George, and I mean strictly *entre nous*, I haven't yet removed the caffeine from Fred's diet. He's such a nice man, so pleasant, so smart, so good. But he's also boring as spit. It's much more exciting around the apartment these days. He may be moody, but that's fine with me. I like surprises. Why, sometimes he'll just seize me at three in the morning."

"You're going to have to tell him sooner or later."

"I know," she said mournfully. "The article is scheduled for July. Only three more months of surprises."

When Annette was gone I called Gregory. "I forgot to ask you something. What month is your article on coffee scheduled to run?"

"July, I believe, George."

I called Parker Burns. "It has come to my attention that Gregory is going to have an article in the July issue on the joys of coffee."

"Yeah," said Parker alertly. "I think I remember."

"But Annette is preparing an article for the July issue about the dangers of caffeine. Don't you think it will look a bit silly to have both of these articles in the same issue?"

"I guess so."

"And don't you think that Annette and Gregory may feel somewhat annoyed when they discover the conflict?"

"You could be right. Well, it will all come out in the wash," he said.

"I'd rather not destroy the washing machine in the process. I want you to take care of this now so we don't have problems later."

"Okay," Parker said.

I suppose that coming out in the wash was Parker's euphemism for the imbroglio that erupted at the end of the day. At five o'clock, Teresa de la Iglesia rushed into my office with one hand over her mouth and the other waving frantically in the direction from which she had come. There was no need for her to speak, since she was followed into my office by the sound of two voices joined in loud disharmony. I made several reassuring faces at Teresa and stepped out of my office.

Annette and Gregory, whose offices were on opposite sides of the secretarial pool, had waded into the pool, where they stood splashing invective upon each other. Although I had missed the opening sallies, I was just in time to hear Annette say, "Do you know how many little children can't sleep or think straight because of the caffeine in their cola drinks? No, your type doesn't care. Your type has governesses and nurses to take care of the trouble."

There was no point to my intercession if they were already reduced to using little children to score points.

"My type! How dare you, you self-mortifying little prig. This is the fourth time that you have tried to make a mockery of me and my many devoted readers with one of your vicious columns."

"So that's how you reward your devoted readers—you poison them. This magazine won't stand for treating the bodies of our readers with such contempt."

"I'll tell you what this magazine won't stand for: it won't stand for some fraud telling people they must live like frightened rabbits who are afraid to nibble a carrot just because you've decided that vitamin C makes your nose itch."

"Vitamin A is in carrots, you food illiterate."

Rabbits and tiny children: they were pulling out all the stops. I looked around. The secretaries had created a small circle about the combatants, and a few of the editors and writers had left their offices to watch from the outer fringe. Judy Gruber had opened her door and was pacing while she watched.

I marched back to my office to the tune of Gregory charging Annette with responsibility for the epidemic of anorexia nervosa because she made people afraid of food. I shut my door and called Parker Burns and asked him why he had not taken care of the caffeine conflict.

"But I did," he said indignantly. "I called each of them and told them what was going on and suggested that they work it out."

I hung up.

In a careful, calm manner I tried to assess the matter. Perhaps I had been naïve to assume I had no problems at all. But I still didn't think one could fairly say that a somewhat clumsy editor in chief and a simple though savage personality conflict amounted to Very Serious Problems.

At that moment, the door to my office flew open and Judy Gruber stormed into my office and started yelling.

"So he thinks that he can sit on his ass and the magazine will run itself. He's got another think coming. I love your type with your MBAs and your nice suits and your assumption that your job is to come up with ingenious ways to count the money and figure out who reports to whom. Well, you're just empty suits to me. Parker Burns hasn't had an original idea in twenty years, and if you haven't realized that you're even stupider than you look. Why do you think all of us have been coming in here and asking you to think about what we're doing? Because we like your handsome, blank face? No, we had the faint hope that you might actually have some creative thoughts in you. This magazine made it because it was novel and unusual and because Larry Roth had lots of good ideas. Parker was just Larry's errand boy; he made *schedules,* for God's sake! I can see it all now: without Larry this magazine is going right down the tubes while you make great plans for circulation promotions."

She stormed out again, slamming the door behind her.

The proper managerial thing to do in such situations is to calm down and tell yourself that an outburst demonstrates that the outburster *cares* about her job despite her unfortunate way of showing it, and her manager must redirect that care in a positive, constructive manner. I took a number of deep, calming breaths.

As I was thinking positively and breathing deeply, Teresa came in looking extremely apologetic, as if she should have tackled Judy before she got into my office.

"I'm so sorry, Mr. Werble. She just—"

"Get the fuck out of my office!" I screamed at Teresa, who burst into tears and got the fuck out.

There was no getting around it: I had Very Serious Problems.

FIVE

Judy Gruber's words rang in my ears for several days like the tolling of a cracked bell. Empty suit? *Clink.* Uncreative? *Clank.* Me? *Clunk.*

I had always fancied myself as rather inventive. For instance, I had yet to work with a copywriter whom I could not outwrite. And my success as a marketer and communications manager was not so much because I was smarter than anyone else but because I was more original. Plenty of my peers could handle a given project better than I (I am so modest . . .), but I was usually the one who created and defined the project (. . . yet so proud).

It is one thing, however, to produce a steady stream of good marketing ideas and quite another to infuse a magazine with a sense of direction and excitement. Especially when your German boss has Germanically suggested that you concentrate on organization, on promotion, on "the numbers."

As I mulled my problems, I came to one conclusion which surprised me: aside from her unfortunately superficial characterization of George Werble, Judy Gruber was right on target: LIFESTYLE needed creative stimulation. Granting this, I was left with two options. The first was a cynical short-term solution. I was pretty sure I could dramatically improve the marketing of the magazine, building newsstand sales, circulation, and advertising before the decline in editorial pizzazz hurt sales, circulation, and advertising. Then I would get out fast, leaving my successor to be blamed for screwing it all up. The thoughtful, long-term option meant convincing Helmut that he was wrong, that the real investment in time and money should be on the editorial side. Parker Burns would have to go, and we would hire a really first-rate editor in chief and spend lots of money upgrading the editorial product.

What was I to do? Although it's nice to luxuriate in moral quandariness for a while, in that state one is also vulnerable to quick fixes and shortcuts. I was finding it hard to resist the personal challenge Judy had flung my way. Why couldn't I provide enough creative input for marketing *and* editorial? With even a smidgeon left over for finance? If Larry Roth could pull it off, why couldn't *I*?

In short, my pride was getting ready to goeth. . . .

I just might have left well enough alone at LIFESTYLE if my perception that it needed editorial improvement had not been quickly followed by an idea of *how* to improve it. Like the sort of joke with which you offend someone not because you intend to but because the joke itself is too irresistible, my idea had such an alluring logic that I surrendered myself to it. The springboard for the idea, I must admit, came from Judy Gruber's remark about updating her column for readers who were now more interested in the material than the spiritual benefits of exercise. But I have to admit that Judy's remark was *only* the springboard; it was I who measured the board and blithely leaped.

While my idea was in the R and D stage (I worked on it mostly while I showered), I began to attend LIFESTYLE's editorial meetings. Once a week the editors and staff writers would gather to review the three issues that were in various states of progress at any one time; they also developed ideas for future issues and divided submissions from free-lancers among themselves. Judy's outburst had led me to believe that the staff was eagerly awaiting my intercession; my presence was actually greeted with a kind of grudging propriety.

As my idea moved out of R and D, I began to make editorial suggestions, such as "Annette, would you mind if we called your column 'Eating Power' instead of 'Natural Nutrition'?" and "Leon, don't you think people are more interested in career growth than in personal growth? How about doing something on stress?" As I made these remarks, sullen glances would be exchanged around the conference table.

If I had known that my new office furniture would symbolize for the LIFESTYLE staff the decline of the West, I might have canceled the order. I imagined that my vast slab-of-glass desk mounted on chrome saw horses, my four Barcelona chairs gathered around a coffee-table version of my desk, my Vasarely prints on the walls, and my magnificent ficus tree would impress them. Sure it was a cliché, but I thought it was the sort of cliché of taste and authority that would send a message to the staff. Instead, those who didn't shudder and sigh when they entered my office teased me: "Ouch! Turn down the lights. Your furniture is too bright."

I also initiated several changes that spoke for themselves. Bob Bickford, the marketing director, began to attend editorial meetings. Both the editor whose responsibility was the mythic oneness of the cosmos and the art director for whom earth tones and a tabloid format were articles of faith disappeared from our meetings (and offices). The rock music critic left of his own accord shortly after I announced that the kind of rock musician I wished to see in the pages of LIFESTYLE collected art nouveau book bindings and maintained a *pied-à-terre* in Paris designed by Mongiardino. And then there was the appearance of Toni Marmoset and Oswald Propper, respectively LIFESTYLE's first-ever fashion and decorative arts editors, and Cynthia Poly, the new art director. They made a rather dramatic presence at the editorial meetings; none of them was especially attractive by conventional standards, yet, like many people for whom the eye is more important than the mind, they were extremely striking in their manner of dress, composure, and expression.

Not all of the old hands had a difficult time with my new direction. Gregory Duplessix, for instance, had never been permitted to write about a bottle of wine which cost more than $5.95; he was only too glad to extol the glories of Montrachet, sun-dried tomatoes, caviar, and llama cheese ("The best thing to happen to llama milk since the llama udder"). I tried hard to keep Enid Malt happy. Leon Malt's point of view made him an alien in my brave new world but Enid, who stood for a slap-happy gymnastic approach to sex, seemed more able to adjust. They were the best-known members of LIFESTYLE's staff, and their departure would have alerted Helmut to my editorial fiddling.

As I increased the rate of suggestions, I awaited the inevitable challenge: Werble, do you really propose to replace the proud traditions of LIFESTYLE with your sleazo values? There would certainly be no challenge from Parker Burns; he was doing his best to be inconspicuous. And the rest of the staff began to give me the silent treatment. Oh, they would make perfunctory responses to direct questions, but aside from the people I had hired, no one even asked me what I thought about the weather, much less about LIFESTYLE. I was surprised, then, when Judy Gruber took the initiative with me. She began to offer helpful hints about which writer might like which assignment, whose wonderful contribution had been overlooked, and how to unruffle many of the feathers I had disordered. I discovered that her advice was accurate: when I acted on it, the employee in question would usually smile with surprised gratitude before remembering again to treat me as if he were the brine and I the cucumber.

Judy appeared to be the staff's wise person to whom they turned with personal as well as professional problems. I found it difficult to understand how she had earned this role, since she would hardly provide quiet counsel. As might be expected from her style of dress, she had a noisy, sloppy personality, full of yelps, chortles, shouts, sudden invective, and sudden exuberance. In other words, hardly the sort of person who would get along with a well-dressed publisher from the Midwest who approached the world with ironic restraint. But since she was making an effort, so did I.

Early one morning I ran into Judy in the coffee shop downstairs from our office. "Instead of getting coffee to go, let's have it together," I suggested. I led her to a booth in an isolated corner of the shop. After a bit of awkward chitchat I broached the subject of the staff's cold shoulder.

"Wait a minute, folks," she said, "I've just been handed a bulletin: 'Our Leader has today announced that he is lonely.' "

"I didn't say I was lonely."

"Of course not. You said, after meaningfully clearing your throat, 'Do you have any suggestions about how I might overcome the staff's very understandable shyness with me?' Do you always talk that way?"

"No. Only when I feel ill at ease."

"Oh people, people, he *is* lonely!"

"Okay, okay, you're right." She sure didn't let one off the hook. "But my loneliness isn't the point. I have to run a business, and I don't think the atmosphere around here will help us to move forward in a cooperative, efficient manner."

"So that's what we're supposed to do. My preference is for something that's more like a large disorderly family, full of feuds and bad behavior but also lots of fun."

"Right now, I'd even settle for that. Instead, nothing's happening. They're so busy freezing me out, they've frozen themselves as well."

"Okay, I'll make one suggestion—though I can't believe you haven't figured it out for yourself. It might help matters if they knew that nobody else is going to be fired."

"Don't you mean '*if* anybody else is going to be fired'?"

She clenched her teeth. "I said it was a suggestion, not a question."

"Sorry. And yes, I can honestly say that I don't intend to fire anybody else. Except for the fact that they won't speak to me, I think I have a good team in place now."

" 'Team'! What a stupid term for a group of professionals. Well, I'm glad at least that no one else is going to be fired."

"It occurs to me," I said, "they might not believe it if I told them no one else is going to be fired. Maybe you could—"

"Oh no. What do you take me for? Just because I try to be helpful, you think I'm some sort of *tool?* Look, I've been making these suggestions because I care about the people who work here, not because I'm your friend."

"I can see that."

"I didn't mean it that way. I mean I'm not your friend but I'm not your enemy either. I mean you seem like a decent sort, but friendship isn't the point." She rolled her eyes. "I can't believe I'm sitting here talking about our *relationship*. Okay, I've changed my mind. I will spread the word that you're not going to fire anyone else. But *you* have to act on another suggestion."

"What's that?"

"Nobody really understands why you're making all these editorial changes. I think it would help if you explained what you're up to. And don't give me that innocent look. You've got a lot more in mind than fine-tuning LIFESTYLE."

"I was afraid you'd say something like that. But okay, we have a deal. In fact, I'll explain at the meeting this afternoon."

I brooded all morning about what I was going to say. There was a reason I had not described my new LIFESTYLE philosophy to the staff: once defined, I feared it would get back to Helmut, who wanted me to change nothing. I had the hope that Helmut's sense of cultural ambience was so clumsy that he wouldn't catch on to what I was doing until it was a successful *fait accompli*. Of course if he did figure it out too soon, the party would be over (*fête accompli*). Though I was tempted to offer the staff a glowing vision of LIFESTYLE's future when the opportunity presented itself that afternoon, I opted for a more offhanded description of my intentions.

Actually, the opportunity didn't present itself. I just waited until I was tired of all the unpleasant looks cast my way; until, as usual, high-minded repudiation from the old hands at the editorial table had exhausted the rest of us. My style at meetings is to remain totally impassive while I twirl a pencil between the thumb and index finger of each hand. Even if you have nothing to say at a meeting, it makes you appear to be a silent, judgmental presence. And when you're ready to say something . . . I waited for a pause in the whining drone and broke the pencil angrily. It always gets everyone's attention.

"I think it is time for all of you to understand what I think LIFESTYLE should be about. In Morrisburg, Ohio, where I was raised, one of the worst things you could be was ostentatious. Among my parents and their friends, yawning dullness was preferable to ostentation—which they defined as the flaunting of bad taste. It seems to me that values have changed. There is something afoot now which I call the New Ostentation, and I would like us to pay more attention to it."

I paused and looked around. I had everybody's rapt attention but no one would play straight person. I looked at Judy, who clamped her mouth shut and shook her head. I helped myself. "No doubt you are all thinking, 'What is the New Ostentation?' It is the flaunting of good taste."

Finally I got some feedback. Harvey Grunwald, our travel writer, whose basic premise was that his readers' interest in any of the four corners of the earth was only to find a place to pitch the same tents and prepare the same freeze-dried foods that are pitched and prepared on a weekend in Yosemite, said, "What does that have to do with having a lifestyle?"

"People want to acquire a lifestyle now and display it. And those who can't afford one like to read and talk about those who can. Besides, credit cards give everybody access to the New Ostentation in small doses. People want to know not just a *good* resort in the Caribbean but the best resort. And usually what makes it best is that the best people go there."

Leon Malt drew himself up indignantly. "And what does that have to do with man's search for his feelings, for his true center?"

"Nothing, I'm afraid. I want LIFESTYLE to be for people who design their lives, people whose furniture, clothes, relationships, food, careers, and interests seem to cohere into a glossy harmony of effects."

Our book reviewer spoke up. "I suppose this means that books and ideas are out."

"Not at all. But the books we will find of interest are the books that stylish people find interesting. And yes, ideas are out. But opinions are in."

In the event, I became more specific than I had intended. I pointed to Oswald Propper's new essay, "A Neo-Georgian Ranch House in Fort Worth—A Designer's Ineffable Approach," as the cutting edge of the new LIFESTYLE. And then there was Gregory Duplessix's two-part epic on the food served by New York's most important hostesses to their intimate collections of powerful people.

The editorial meeting received my words mainly in silence, but in a thoughtful silence. I restrained my curiosity. It was ten thirty the next morning before I barged into Judy's office. "How did I do?"

"I haven't taken a poll." She was hunched on her exercise bike, pedaling away.

"Come on. What's your feeling, your intuition?"

"You weren't exactly inspiring," she said, "but I think everybody got the message."

"Oh."

"Oh? He wants more! He wants to be adored." She stopped pedaling. "Tell me something: Have you always been the fair-haired boy wherever you worked?"

"Well, I don't want to seem . . . I mean—"

"And he's modest too! You know, you're on your own here. There's nobody to tell you how brilliant you are all the time. You're the boss. Now don't look so sad." She patted me patronizingly on the head. "There, there, you did real good."

But after a few days I could see that I hadn't cleared the air. Much as I hated to, I went back to Judy. "It didn't work. Now what do they want?"

"Am I some management spy?"

"No. You care about the people who work here."

"I guess the problem is that even though many of us concede that your scheme—"

"It's not a *scheme*. It's a good idea."

"That's the problem. Who are you to have a good editorial idea?"

"You mean if the same idea came from someone else they would accept it?"

"Maybe from someone they respected editorially. But you're not a creative type. You don't *believe* in your idea. For you the numbers come first, then the idea. You're going to have to earn our respect."

If she knew what my R and D Department looked like, she wouldn't have said that. I saw there was nothing to be done quickly. But I still felt that my idea was perfectly respectable editorially. After all, a society which says that one is nothing on the great lithograph of life without a vividly contrived image surely *needs* the new LIFESTYLE.

The time for my official hello from the ad agency arrived in the midst of my lonely exile. I had had several meetings with our account executive, an overly assured young clothes horse named Kirk. Now was the occasion for his boss, the famous Gloria Pastore, to take me to lunch and re-cement the relationship between LIFESTYLE and Pastore, Horowitz, and Nickerson. Gloria Pastore was known as an advertising genius, though "genius" is an appellation assigned in advertising about as frequently and accurately as "statesman" is used in politics.

Pastore, Horowitz, and Nickerson, known as PHN to their close friends, was a medium-sized agency ($125 million in billings) with a reputation for classy creativity. We were hardly PHN's most lucrative account; we required only a modest identity campaign to remind prospective advertisers that we existed and our readers were special. The disingenuous line that ended each of our ads read: "LIFESTYLE? Never heard of it." We had been with PHN from our first issue and had grown large and putatively successful—a condition for which the agency was glad to assume as much credit as possible.

Kirk greeted me in PHN's reception area. He wasn't dressed to kill exactly, but I was maimed by his successful combination of three different patterns, any two of which I had always believed could not occupy the same body at the same time. "Here you are, George!" he said. "Eager to meet all the members of our team. And they're all eager to meet you." He gleefully rubbed his hands together. "I'm going to take you on our extra-special forty-five-minute tour. And then you're going to meet Gloria Pastore! Let's get going."

As Kirk took me from department to department, I realized that he was one of those formless young men busy creating themselves in the images of their employers. His assurance came from his confident assumption of the best fashions (art department), jokes (copywriting), and ethics (media) of his colleagues. With a few years' practice, Kirk's patchwork personality would probably become seamless and the other Kirks of this world would nod approvingly and say, all too accurately, "Hey, that Kirk has really got his act together."

I had tried to be realistic about having Kirk on our account. Our little campaign had been developed by Gloria and the other important people at the agency, but it could not continue to command such high-priced talent. Kirk's job was simply to supervise a holding action. But I had decided to nudge Gloria for more high-level involvement to keep our ads from getting stale. It would give us something to natter about over lunch; I didn't want her to start off taking me for granted.

I could tell we were at last approaching Gloria's lair because Kirk became nervous and uncoordinated. "Wait here," he said breathlessly and fell over a chair as he scrambled off. After a few moments he returned to escort me into a post-modern sanctum of tutti-frutti colors, aggressively klunky furniture, and kitschy details such as Dutch doors between Gloria's office and her secretary's and a green plastic television set on top of a marble pedestal.

Elaborately designed offices usually overwhelm the resident executive but Gloria was an easy winner. She was a vivid, sharp-featured woman with an enormous mane of black hair, a trademark which gave her a slightly freaky quality. She shook my hand. "Delightful to meet you, George Werble. First encounters are always a special pleasure. There's a kind of eagerness and anticipation. A sense of promise. Expectations are *great!*"

There was a suppressed chortle in her voice, as if she were

languidly amused by anything she had to say. For a moment I was sure I had heard her speak somewhere before, but then I realized that Kirk had been assimilating her inflections.

"Let's go to lunch," she said. "I'll see you later, Kirk."

We had a short walk to the restaurant, and while we walked Gloria held up both ends of the conversation. "Did you get a feeling for the way we operate? A walking tour is really not enough. Even going through several ad campaigns with PHN may not reveal our essence. But I think we have a certain style. A certain way of speaking. Seriously yet insouciantly. That's our signature. When you sign on with us you get a signature."

Gloria also explained why advertising was the warp and woof of marketing's rich tapestry and why New York was a wonderful city (because there's no distinction between work and play). I didn't interrupt her once because I was greedily consuming her rich, thrilling voice.

The restaurant Gloria had chosen, the Seven Seas, was a good subject for a scholarly monograph I'm going to write entitled "Demography and Hierarchy in New York City Restaurants." The Seven Seas was a television restaurant in the way that there are also movie, book publishing, sports, and fashion restaurants. And it was a very senior executive television restaurant; it wouldn't do for the boss to see middle management paying such extraordinary prices for monstrous lobsters, huge drinks, great mounds of fried potatoes, and immense desserts. At the Seven Seas, television was still a vast waistland.

Advertising people seem to fit in almost everywhere. Gloria's entrance was the occasion for a salvo of fond hellos from the First Maître and his jolly tars who navigated the aisles. After we were seated and Gloria had nodded, smiled, and waved at an impressive number of impressive people, she said to me, "You know, George, just because your account isn't our biggest doesn't mean it's forgotten at PHN. I think about it. Tom Nickerson thinks about it. It's one of our favorite accounts. Even if it were not, you'd always get our most professional effort. And I've been thinking that your account is due for a little refresher course. Kirk is one of our very best young account executives, but he's too close to LIFESTYLE. We have a special high-level team that reevaluates accounts periodically. I think we should have a look at yours. Don't be surprised; you should expect this kind of service."

She had anticipated my complaint and disarmed it. I asked her if she had any specific thoughts about sprucing up our ad campaign.

"Let's not put the cart before the horse," she said. "You're new, you're fresh. You probably have some changes in mind. We have to follow your lead."

She was very good; the ball was back in my court again. I would have to beg. "Oh come on. I need your help. You've obviously thought a lot about the magazine. I'm especially interested in what a smart person like you has to say about LIFESTYLE."

She looked at me sharply. "May I speak frankly?"

"That means I'm not going to like what you say, right? Be careful. If I get really upset I'll run screaming from the restaurant. You'll be horribly embarrassed."

"Don't tempt me," she said good-naturedly. "I'd like to see you lose your composure."

"Only last week . . ." I sighed. "But you were speaking frankly."

"Okay. LIFESTYLE is a good idea. A clever idea. But it's also a hothouse flower. It needs a lot of nurturing. It's not one of those sturdy concepts that go chugging along on their own."

"*Reader's Digest* it's not," I conceded.

"LIFESTYLE needs to be constantly primed, always—"

"—creative."

"That's it. Well, it got pretty slack, I think, when Larry Roth made up his mind to sell. Once it became an investment, he stopped investing any—"

"—creativity," I said.

"Yes. Without novel ideas—and even a few lurid ideas from time to time—LIFESTYLE is just an ordinary book."

"You're absolutely right," I said.

Gloria smiled contentedly. She had, like me, the media biz

habit of being less interested in what is thought of our good ideas than in what is thought of us for coming up with good ideas.

"I think I can handle the problem," I said. "After all, I'm not just some administrator, some managerial empty suit who is interested only in promotion and in who reports to whom. My strength, as I see it, is that I'm—"

"—creative."

"There's a good word."

"It seems to be in the air lately."

We were hitting it off pretty well. I'm a sucker for a good voice and hers was great. Once we we had business out of the way we achieved an inspired level of banter. As we were finishing our main courses, Gloria nodded toward a man and a woman who were being led to a table. She knew each of them—along with his and her spouse—separately, she confided. She had seen this couple together once before recently; she was now sure they were having an affair.

"I find him quite unappealing," Gloria said. "But she's rather winsome."

"Well, you win some and you loathe some."

"Oh yeah? I loathe them and I leave them."

"Are you surprised they're seeing each other so publicly?" I asked. "Maybe they're trying the old no-one-will-believe-we-would-be-so-brazen-if-we-were-really-having-an-affair ploy."

"Maybe. But since I've already seen them before, it won't work. It doesn't make any difference what you do to hide your affair; someone always catches you anyway."

I disagreed. I declared that with a little care one could fool around semi-publicly and never get caught. "Those who get caught," I said pompously, "are those who unconsciously want to get caught. You married?"

"Was. You?"

"Am. Sort of."

"Well, I still say you're wrong."

"And I say you don't have to be caught if you don't want to be caught."

Our conversation and relationship were taking a suggestive turn more rapidly than I could have hoped. I knew my next remark would be very important.

"It occurs to me," I said in my smoothest, most I'm-coming-on-to-you tone of voice, "as I reflect upon our conversation, that such exchanges between a man and a woman are rarely as hypothetical as they seem."

She gave me the benefit of a few seconds of thought before she said firmly, "Sorry. They're always hypothetical for me when they're with a client. I'm afraid it's a necessary rule."

"Then you're fired," I ruefully kidded and she laughed. At least I was able to blame it on a rule and not myself.

We finished our meal and managed to restore a friendly but professional relationship between us. Though my point about getting away with an affair was now academic as far as Gloria was concerned, I still wanted to win it. As I walked her back to her office I said, "I'll bet that even here in midtown the odds are remote that either of us would run into an acquaintance."

She grinned. "You mean you would have no fear at all if I were to affectionately take your arm and gaze foolishly into your eyes?"

She took my arm.

"No fear at all," I said.

It was a lovely afternoon in late April. We strolled in our fond manner for a block or two, smiling and chatting. I thought about coming on to her again, but I too have a rule: in the interests of preserving my self-esteem I limit myself to risking one turndown per woman.

"George!" a woman said loudly. "I can't believe it's you."

I stopped and sighed heavily. How, I wondered in a mind's voice full of self-pity, had I twice contrived to have the rug pulled out from under me with the same conversational ploy? The smile of the woman facing me gradually melted into a look of vague unease. The smile of the woman on my arm erupted into a gleeful smirk.

"Gloria," I said, "I'd like you to meet my sister-in-law Irene Miller, who has come all the way from Fergus Falls, Minnesota, to greet me here on Park Avenue. Irene, this is Gloria Pastore and she is smirking because she has won a bet."

As I dutifully pulled my wallet from my pocket, my mood changed. Suddenly I felt lighthearted, joyous. Although poets and scientists have variously described the paroxysm of inspiration, I shall be modest and say simply that in comic-strip terms I had unexpectedly arrived at the frame in which a lightbulb appears over one's head.

With exaggerated formality I presented $20 to Gloria. "I am happy to have lost this bet. Twenty dollars is a small price to pay for a truly creative idea."

This was the second bet I had lost in less than two weeks. As far as I was concerned I had come out ahead both times.

PART 2

SIX

Why, it may be asked, was the usually poised George Werble to be seen dashing from his office at 4:48 P.M. on a hot Tuesday early in May? And why, as his necktie trailed over his shoulder and driblets of sweat ran down his forehead, did he head for the subway instead of his commuter train at Grand Central Station?

Had I not been glancing so anxiously at my watch I might have seen the pudgy man who followed at a discreet distance, snapping at me occasionally with a 35mm camera. At Sixth Avenue and 41st Street I plunged into a nether region where clashing monsters snaked in and out of smoky caves. Those who take the subways more frequently than I tell me that thanks to the graffiti there is no need for directional signs; all it takes is a good eye to distinguish the chiaroscuro of the Sixth Avenue line from the elegant scumbling so characteristic of the E and F trains.

My uptown train lurched along in fits and starts and I didn't get to Central Park West and 72nd Street until 5:20. Rather than trust the train to make it to the next stop, I got off and began to walk at a pace as close to running as the dignity of a bedraggled publisher would permit. I still had not looked back and seen the photographer puffing along behind me. At 75th Street I turned west and walked another block before I located the small nine-story apartment house.

My key was new so it took a bit of wiggling before the lobby door opened. The photographer had caught up to me by now, and because I'm a polite person I held the door for him. A quick look around the lobby sank my heart: the elevator was out of order; I would have to walk up seven floors. I took off with the sound of the photographer scrambling and cursing behind me.

Out of breath, damp, and frantic, I leaned against apartment 7D's door while I fumbled for the other key. My gasps must have been heard because someone opened the door and I spilled inside, barely keeping my balance.

"Ah," said Judy Gruber, "my demon lover has arrived."

"Ah," I said, "and here's my little Sensuella to greet me."

"Don't call me little, and shut my door," she said.

I started to shut the door but Paul, the pudgy photographer, called out for me to wait for him.

"When did you leave?" Judy asked.

"Four forty-eight."

"Thirty-seven minutes door to door; that's not very good."

"How many contenders have tried for the record?" I smiled so she would know it was all in good fun, but it seemed we had different ideas of fun.

"George!" Gregory Duplessix called out from somewhere. "Don't waste time talking. My food is ready to be eaten. My drinks are ready to be poured."

"That man is going to make me insane," Judy said. "I would have to stay up all night to prepare the kind of feast he's made for my hypothetical lover."

"Ah, but if I weren't hypothetical, I'm sure—"

"Look, you're the one who decided that our readers would be amused by a tongue-in-cheek guide to carrying off adultery in great style. 'The Fashionable Affair' is *your* idea. I'm just going along because I'm due for a raise soon. But don't push your luck, pal."

Since I have observed that "pal" is almost always used as its own antonym, I decided to back off.

I glanced about Judy's apartment and was reminded that one of the reasons I hadn't moved from my home in Finchmont and into the city was the fear that I would be reduced to this sort of place. It was so small that three "so small" jokes laid end to end would get a laugh in the elevator. It was basically a single L-shaped room with a six-foot alcove in one of the walls; this gave it the appearance of being constructed entirely of corners.

"It took me twenty-seven minutes to get here," Judy said, "and I left ten minutes before you. Just enough time for me to redecorate. Don't blame me for all this gauze; this is Oswald's idea of how a woman gets her place ready for Mr. Right."

Oswald Propper had draped the apartment in bleached muslin and white organdy. Above the bed, which was nestled in the alcove and doubled as a couch, he had created a canopy of organdy in great romantic folds. Even the lamps and tables appeared to be wearing tutus.

Toni Marmoset, our fashion editor, materialized around the corner at the foot of the L. "Poor Oswald certainly didn't have much to work with. So dark, so drab here. But when we shoot we'll have lots of lights and everything will look wonderfully airy and gossamer." She turned to Judy. "My dear, my heart goes out to you. How you manage to live with all this dreary exposed brick is just a tribute to your spirit. George, come back to the kitchen and meet the models." She hurried back.

Judy encouraged her departure with an obscene gesture. "I've never liked any woman whose first name ends in *i*. It took me six weeks with chisels, acid, and wire brushes to expose all that damn brick."

"Let's check out the models," I suggested.

The idea of the Fashionable Affair was that Judy, the other editors, and I would be photographed as we enacted or investigated various events—running to and fro to show, for instance, how today's *cinq-à-sept* could be pulled off in graceful style. For the fashion close-ups, however, we would use models.

The models were seated at a tiny table that was covered, like everything else, in white material which Toni was busy arranging. Paul was hovering over the models with a light meter, and Cynthia, the art director, was hovering over Paul. At the sink, twenty-eight inches away, was Gregory. It was very hot and crowded.

"Soon as I get that raise," Judy said, "I'm going to buy an air conditioner."

"Meet the models," Cynthia said. "This is Rusty and this is Katrinka."

They were breathtakingly beautiful. Rusty, who had been named after his tan, slumped languorously in his chair, his shirt unbuttoned to his naval. Katrinka wore a little froth of a house dress. Her bargain with the devil for her exquisite cheekbones must have been that she would accept any flaws and blemishes as long as they were restricted to the largest, ugliest, most distorted pair of feet I have ever seen. I would have made the same deal.

"They're playing us?" I said to Judy.

"Don't worry. You've got just as good a back as Rusty."

"And your feet . . . ?"

"Hers are really something, aren't they? It's pretty perverse of her to take off her shoes."

"Is this pre-coital or post-coital bliss they're shooting now?" I asked.

"Definitely pre," Judy said. "Fashionable' means that you don't just jump into the sack and hump away. You admire each other first."

"Here, have some food," Gregory said. "I've made cold pieces of chicken breast tossed in tarragon. We'll call the recipe Chicken Intime. We're serving it with an amusing Chablis. Unfortunately, the Chablis is all gone."

"A bottle of wine makes for cooperative models," said Katrinka.

"Is there some food for me?" Judy said. "I'm part of this incredible project too."

I chose not to ask what 'incredible' meant. "Let's get out of the way," I suggested to Judy.

We took our chicken from the kitchen/dining area to the living/sleeping area and sat on the sofa/bed.

"Don't eat so much," Judy said. "How will you leap into the sack with hypothetical me?"

"Come on, we can't be that literal."

"You want to play journalist, you better follow through on all the details."

"All right, all right." I put down my food. "Why do you have that splint on your finger?"

"Oh, I had a little accident with a weight-lifting machine. Nothing serious." Judy furrowed her brows suspiciously while she thought of something else with which to challenge me. "You're not thinking of shooting those models thrashing about on my bed, are you?"

"Look who doesn't want to be literal now. Don't worry. That would be too tacky. We'll confine ourselves to before-and-after shots and let Enid Malt comment on the events in between. I'm really happy about the way this project is involving so many of us. I think it's really going to work." This last remark was a cheap bid for approval but Judy wouldn't budge. I tried again. "And I must say, I'm enjoying working with you."

"Just stop right there. You're not going to get me to play in all the rest of these little episodes with you."

"Well, how about checking out intimate restaurants?"

"Gregory should do that. Send Annette with him; that'll be a real riot."

"And then we're going to do something on the joy of nooners."

"Oh no. You're not getting me into some sleazo hotel with mirrors on the ceiling and handcuffs from room service."

So I didn't get any approval. We sat silently for several minutes listening to Cynthia and Paul dance around Rusty and Katrinka.

Judy jumped up. "It's six twenty-five and you're not even in bed yet."

"I mean this part *is* hypothetical."

"But you have to keep to a schedule so your readers will have some guidance. But I guess you're the best judge of how little time you take in bed."

"Very funny." I lay back on her couch and embraced a pillow. "Oh my God, the ecstasy, the ecstasy! Where, my sweet wisteria of the West Side, did you ever learn to perform that act? What's that? You will? Thank you. You know how I love to be tied to the bed with dental floss."

"Very clever," Judy said and stalked off.

I tried to relax for a little while. I would soon have to begin my dash to catch the 7:18 train home. At 6:40 Gregory came over to me.

"Ah, George, let a slice of mocha dacquoise melt in your mouth before you leave. I thought our couple should bid *au revoir* with a sweet and some sauterne. Unfortunately, Katrinka drank the sauterne."

"That woman has hollow feet," Judy said as she returned. "What's this? You're munching away and it's getting really late now."

"I intend to eat my mistress and have my cake too."

"Really. Aren't you forgetting something?"

"No. It's six fifty. At this hour a cab will get me to midtown in plenty of time."

"Maybe it has conveniently slipped your mind, but one of the things you told us when you unveiled your grand scheme was that you were not even going to tell your wife. She was going to be the ultimate test of your right to tell our readers how to do it in style."

"So?"

"So one of the tests you have to pass is going home with the bottom two inches of your hair wet."

"Why should—"

"Your shower, you fool. You've forgotten your shower."

"Shit! Where is it?"

She pointed to a small door I had assumed was a broom closet. It probably once was, but the conversion to a bathroom was quite adequate for people under four feet. There was no bathtub but a shower stall so narrow it was like bathing in an envelope.

I whipped on my clothes again, grabbed my briefcase, and ran out of the apartment. As I rattled down the stairs, Judy called after me with ringing insincerity, "Good luck!" Paul trotted along behind me.

I hailed a cab quickly. I had an ace up my sleeve which only another commuter would anticipate: I didn't have to go back to midtown. I told the cabdriver to take me uptown; I would intercept the 7:18 at 125th Street with plenty of time to spare. How infuriated Judy would be when I laid my ace on the editorial table. Come to think of it, I had another ace up my sleeve as well: Helen would neither notice nor care if I came home with my entire head wet and hickeys all over my neck. But I thought I would keep that ace to myself. I sat back and hummed a smug little song to myself.

SEVEN

I suppose that earnest believers in poetic justice would have been satisfied if the ace up my sleeve had turned out to be a joker and I missed my train. But who wants to live in a world where poetic justice sentences every sneaky triumph to pay some ironic penalty? I made my train easily.

I settled into my seat, settling also into a furtive world of drained and anxious passengers. The woman next to me, her eyes glazed, kept running her finger gently across her lips. Ah-ha, I hypothesized, her lover begged her to stay later but she and her husband have a date with the marriage counselor. And what about the pin-striped man who got on with me at 125th Street and opened his newspaper upside down, holding it that way for nearly a minute? He was afraid that his lover had taken a new lover.

Maybe my imagination was working overtime, but the mood of softness and distraction was definitely post-coital; I was on the Cinq-à-Sept Express. I was an imposter here, however. The other passengers were in the midst of difficult marriages and sloppy affairs. I could only describe my connubial status in the world as "not separated."

Lately there had not been much opportunity for Helen and me to do much connubial redefining. The arrival of her sister Irene—in flight from Fergus Falls with a badly packed load of emotional baggage—had used up most of the available emotional energy. Not that Irene was weepy or distraught. On the contrary, the house seemed to reverberate with laughter as the boisterous Irene did her best to cover up. But this was Irene's fifth visit; by now the process of revelation and reconciliation was a family tradition.

At first Irene would announce that the Reverend Emerson Miller was dissatisfied with the small-minded folks of Hoosick Falls or Wichita Falls or Fergus Falls (the Millers seemed to have an affinity for white water). And while Emerson traveled about interviewing for a new ministry, Irene had the perfect excuse to visit her little sister. For a week or two we would be uproariously entertained with tales of small-town scandals and intrigues. Only occasionally would a telling indignity slip out about, say, the hypocritical gossip over Emerson's very occasional bourbon and soda. Soon Irene had proved that the town in question had achieved a level of seamy decadence approached only by such fleshpots as Babylon, Sodom, and San Francisco. And from there it required but the slightest stretch of sympathy for us to see that this evil place would use any pretext to dump its guilt on a scapegoat. Exit Emerson.

So far Irene had not given us a clue to the reason for Emerson's disenchantment with the Collegiate Church of Fergus Falls, but Helen and I were experienced enough to know that the disenchantment was invariably mutual.

Emerson was a man of enthusiasms, and there was always an early period of excitement when, burning with conviction, he inspired his new congregation with the glory of his latest idea. For one reason or another his schemes would fail and then, like a bettor who tries to recoup his losses by doubling the next bet, he would come up with an even more grandiose plan. Sooner or later the congregation caught on.

I remembered the missionary school in Zambia which a congregation in Cedar Rapids adopted at Emerson's impassioned urging. The mission was run by a great man—"a virtual Livingston," Emerson had called him. The outpouring of love and money from Cedar Rapids was acknowledged by grateful letters in charmingly garbled English along with photographs of reformed heathens. But a member of Emerson's church had a son who was an agricultural consultant for the UN and who took time out from an African itinerary to look up this new saint of

Africa. He discovered a seedy English colonial for whose saintliness even Graham Greene could not have made a case. The "mission school" which so desperately needed a coat of paint was actually the man's moldering farmhouse, and the pitiful photos of withered crops were the saint's very own fields, untilled and unirrigated since America's farm belt had responded with a cash crop.

The description of the riotous conditions at the farmhouse—the saint was assisted in the composition of charmingly garbled letters by his mistress and a great deal of gin—was enough for the church. During Emerson's last days in Cedar Rapids, humorous types would lurch up to him in the shopping mall and guffaw: "Have you heard from Dr. Living Stoned lately?"

When the 7:18 train pulled into the Finchmont station at 8:00, my colleagues in commutation sorted themselves into their cars and roared away. I seated myself on my bicycle in an environmentally superior posture and pedaled off. Sara, the ten-year-old who lived next door, met me just outside the parking lot on her bicycle. At least once a week Sara would accompany me home from the station while I regaled her with my newest adaptation of her life into a shaggy dog story. Then we would review her recent exploits and work them into another tale to try on Helmut. I had been a disappointment to Sara lately because my new job afforded little personal contact with my boss.

"Isn't it a little late for you to be hanging out here?" I said.

"Two trains," Sara said. "I waited for two trains. I really need to talk to you."

Sara was a slight, earnest child who asked serious questions and expected serious answers. At first I used to tease her, but her scrupulous consideration of my flippancies shamed me into the straightforwardness she deserved.

"What's the problem?"

"You know what the Finchmont Talent Pageant is?"

"Everybody has heard of the Finchmont Talent Pageant. It's famous."

The Talent Pageant was a peculiar local institution that raised money for charity by staging an annual review of town talent. If you wished to arrive socially in Finchmont, you tried to get on the Pageant organizing committee.

"Well, I volunteered to perform," Sara said.

"You never told me you're talented. I'll bet you're a great singer."

"Guess again."

"You dance."

"Guess again."

"Come on."

"I'm a comedian," she said proudly. "That's why I need you. You work in television. You can help me with my act."

"You have an act already?" I didn't think I could persuade her that my very limited experience with Schaefer's cable network hardly made me an expert. I told her to do her act for me.

"First of all I do some imitations."

"Of whom?"

"I do James Cagney." She did James Cagney.

"Have you ever seen a James Cagney movie?" I asked.

"Nope, but I've seen three different people do impressions of him on television."

I thought it was a dubious form of immortality that Cagney had achieved. "What else do you do?"

"I do stand-up comedy. I'm very good at shticking. You be my straight man and ask me about my husband."

"How's your husband?"

"Large. Very large. I don't want to say he's fat, but last fall he painted 'Goodyear' on his stomach and hung around football stadiums. I mean he's *big.* He's worried that the Grain Belt doesn't come in his size."

I laughed.

"Are you laughing because my jokes are funny or are you laughing at me?"

"I'm afraid it's the latter."

"It must be my delivery."

"Can I give you some advice?" I said. "First of all, professional shtickers like us use the term 'material' instead of 'jokes.' And if you want people to laugh at your material you have to get different material."

Her feelings were hurt. "I thought I had good material."

"It wasn't bad, but when a ten-year-old kid tells jokes—"

"Material."

"God, you kids are so literal. Okay, when a ten-year-old does material about her husband, you don't laugh at it. Instead, you laugh—"

"Yeah, I know, I know. Instead you laugh at the kid. Me."

"You have to come up with some material that's appropriate to *you.* Nobody's going to believe you're married. Your shtick has to be that you're a kid."

"Hmmm," Sara said suspiciously. She contemplated the problem while we pedaled on. Suddenly she brightened. "I've got it!"

"Go ahead."

"Take my brother . . . please!"

A small convoy of cars parked in one's driveway at 8:20 P.M. can mean only one thing in Finchmont Village: committee meeting inside. Sure enough, the Elect Bud Horner Councilperson Committee, chaired by Helen Werble, was thrashing out strategy in the living room.

"Do you know everyone, George?" Helen asked, waving her arm at five cohorts. "We've been having the most intense discussion. We're tearing Bud Horner apart and putting him back together."

I nodded at Bud, who smiled weakly. He was famous for owning the only honest car repair garage in town. He was a generous, sincere man, full of concern and kindness for the boys who pumped his gas as well as for his customers. On the face of it, he was an ideal candidate, but he had lost four previous elections. It's not that honesty carries no weight in Finchmont, only that, in Bud's case, honesty meant charging exactly what his very inadequate mechanical skills were worth. His other political liability was his speeches, which could have been put into capsules and sold as Thorazine.

"I don't believe we've met," said a dapper man. "I'm Al Brubaker."

"Al's in marketing. He's given us lots of ideas," Helen said.

"So, Al, how are you going to market Bud Horner?"

"Well," Al said, "I've only just moved here so I don't want to seem presumptuous. And I've only had the chance to talk to Bud Horner a couple of times. So I wouldn't want you to think that I've come to an inflexible point of view. After all, I'm still on the learning curve. But I've come to a tentative idea of what we might do if my present assumptions are correct."

"What's that?"

Al looked around dramatically. "We've got to reposition Bud Horner."

"And how does Mrs. Horner feel about a new position?" I caught Helen's glare. "Oops! Sorry, Bud. Go on, Al."

"The way I see it—and I wouldn't want to imply that my view is the *only* view possible, but the way I see it, and I think that Bud and Helen and Mark and Sally and Frank agree—is that everybody in town knows that Bud Horner *cares.* Right?"

"Right," we all dutifully replied.

"But who cares? We've got to show that a caring kind of guy like Bud Horner can also be a tough guy, capable of dealing with an era of diminishing resources."

"Wait a minute!" I said, striking my palm against my forehead. "It's coming to me. The perfect slogan for you."

"George . . ." Helen murmured through clenched teeth.

"You'll love it, Helen; listen: 'Never have so many needed so much . . . yet deserved so little.'"

Al looked at me warily.

"My goodness, George," Bud said. "I appreciate the suggestion but it sounds rather harsh. I don't mean to criticize or to offend, but—"

"Don't worry, Bud," Helen said. "George's feelings are not exactly on the line here."

Al's eyes darted back and forth from Helen to me. He *knew.*

I extricated myself with a minimal amount of grace and went into the kitchen. Irene was removing a pie from the oven. In addition to her forced exuberance, another sign of distress was her compulsive creation of pies, cakes, cookies, tarts. The neighborhood had gained fifty pounds since her arrival.

"George! My tired, tired brother-in-law. I'll bet you could use a slice of rhubarb pie. Dig in, boy. Dig in while it's hot."

"Please, not on an empty stomach."

"Oh, is my tired brother-in-law also a hungry brother-in-law? Maybe he'd like some yummy fried chicken."

"Empty as it is, my stomach is really yearning for a martini."

She looked at me slyly. "I've got a surprise for you." She took out a pitcher of martinis from the refrigerator.

Some surprise.

"I thought that Helen's committee would like a drink, but all they wanted was Perrier."

"That's reform politics for you. Have you heard from Emerson lately? What about that job in Idaho?"

"Aw, is George getting tired of his little sister-in-law? I can always go stay with Katherine. They appreciate good rhubarb pie in Tulsa."

Irene was pretty shaky. Another martini and I might get the lowdown on Emerson's last job. I patted her arm. "We *love* having you here and we won't let you leave. I'm just concerned for Emerson."

"Good ol' Emerson is the one who should be concerned."

"What happened?"

"Promise you won't tell Helen?"

I crossed my heart.

"Good ol' Emerson lost out on the job in Moscow, Idaho, because some little snitch from Millstream told them about 1975."

Millstream, Illinois: a quiet little town that, until the arrival of Emerson Miller (yes, the Miller of God streams slowly . . .), had never particularly cared that its children could not pray in the small public elementary school. Emerson had other ideas. He took the town to the barricades, pitting friend against friend, parent against child. Emerson thought the campaign for school prayer would unite the town, but when the state police arrived to supervise a pro-prayer demonstration, half the population urged them to kick the shit out of the other half. The problem was solved when the school janitor, a devout idiot, came to believe that the law prevented *him* from praying in the school. One night he blew up the boiler and much of the rest of the school in protest. To this day, I believe, the children of Millstream are still bused fifteen miles to a larger town. As for Emerson: good-bye Millstream, hello Cascade, Washington. (. . . yet he streams exceeding far).

With rather excessive ceremony I poured Irene another martini and she did the same for me. We sipped silently as we contemplated our favorite man of God, scouring America for an innocent parish.

Irene giggled. " 'Course . . . prob'ly could've been a snitch from Hoosick Falls . . . or Cedar Rapids . . . Emerson has what you'd call . . . I guess a talent."

"And what would a snitch from Fergus Falls have told them?"

She sighed so profoundly that I thought one of her lungs would collapse. "Oh my. . . . Fergus Falls . . . Fergus Falls just went blah-blah-blah."

"Mmm," I agreed encouragingly. Helen chose that moment to appear. The meeting had adjourned. "Helen, Irene was just telling me how Fergus Falls went blah-blah-blah."

"Are you two . . . ?" She nodded accusingly at the half-empty martini pitcher.

"Or was it la-la-blah, la-la-blah?" Irene wondered.

Helen rolled her eyes.

"Maybe we should let Irene tell us about Fergus Falls," I suggested.

"Okay," Irene said. "Irene's going to tell us about Fergus Falls."

"Look here," Helen said in her new, excitingly exasperated manner. "If you think I'm going to just sit here while you two amuse each other—"

"Well, have a martini, dammit," Irene said.

Helen sighed but made no protest when I poured her a

healthy drink. We seated ourselves around a small round table and watched the pie cool.

"So?" I said.

Irene took a quick gulp for support. "I don't know how I'm going to explain this. Let's see . . . you ever noticed how sometimes Emerson . . . well, sometimes he gets these ideas in his head?"

"Ideas . . ." I mused as I poured myself another martini. "You wouldn't by any chance have in mind those totally wacko, off-the-wall schemes that Emerson keeps inflicting on his congregations?"

"George! I'm sure that Emerson has been very disappointed that some of his creative ideas have not been understood," Helen said, patting Irene comfortingly. "And yes, maybe some of his riskier inventions have not been entirely successful. But we should admire Emerson for trying. Surely there's a better way to describe Emerson's—"

"Wacko sounds right to me," Irene chirped.

"Have another drink, Helen," I suggested.

"Ever the attentive husband, eh?" she said.

"You guys don't go to church much, do you?" Irene asked.

"Once a decade, I swear it!" I declared. "Helen goes twice as frequently."

"If you went to church you might know what blah-blah-blah is . . . at least that was what *I* called it. . . . 'Course, when I called it that was when Emerson kicked me out of Fergus Falls."

"Oh Irene. He kicked you out." Helen embraced her sister.

"But by the time I packed my bags, Fergus Falls had kicked Emerson out."

"Irene," I said, "by what other name is blah-blah-blah known?"

"Speaking in tongues."

"Oh, my God!" Helen cried.

"Well, he just got carried away. He thought it was the most . . . exciting . . . thing he could do to build up the congregation. Everybody had fallen away. There was this other church in town . . . minister there, he sobbed while he preached. People loved it. Emerson figured he needed like . . ."

"A new product?"

"Kind of, George, kind of."

"But the congregation didn't like the idea of speaking in tongues?" Helen said.

"No, they loved the idea. Loved it . . . loved it . . . loved it. . . ."

"They did?" Helen didn't understand.

But our eyes all met and the miracle of martini telepathy prompted us to chorus together, "*At first!*" We laughed too much.

"That's right, folks," Irene said. "Once again Emerson Miller started off soaring and then: *kaboom!*" She struck the table, rattling the martini glasses.

"*Kaboom!*" Helen said, following suit.

"*Kaboom!*" I agreed.

"It was great at first. Emerson got them mumbling and chanting . . . they were humming and sweating and waving their arms . . . they never had such a good time."

"So?"

"Yeah," Helen demanded, "how did he screw this one up?"

Helen's bluntness struck our well-lubricated funny bones, and we laughed some more and drank some more martinis.

"I saw it on television once," Helen said.

"What'd you see?"

"Speaking in tongues. I didn't *believe* it. But they were sure having a good time with it."

"Even without martinis," Irene added.

"If you drink at the same time," I said, "then you're speaking in thick tongues."

"Hey, that's good," Irene said. "How'd you ever marry such a wise guy, Helen?"

"That's a question I've stopped asking myself."

"Emerson figured they'd all . . . well, it's long in Fergus Falls."

"What's long?"

"Winter. Emerson figured speaking in tongues would help a long winter to pass."

And it did warm up the church, according to Irene. For a while the Collegiate Church was the hot ticket in town. Pilgrims eager for a new high in spiritual transport deserted the minister of tears in favor of the pastor of ecstatic babbling. Only a few older parishioners grumbled that the new product was too downmarket for their tastes.

" 'Course this time I didn't get too carried away . . . by Emerson's success. I was waiting—you know, sooner or later—"

"Yeah, sooner or later Emerson would . . ."

". . . he would find some way of blowing it."

"What did he do this time?" I asked.

"He didn't exactly *do* anything . . . I guess. He just lost the gift."

"Of speaking in tongues, you mean?"

"Sometimes he could, sometimes he couldn't. Sometimes he spoke stupid stuff."

Over the course of three or four months, the gift of tongues began to desert Emerson at crucial moments.

"He'd be getting them all worked up—chanting blah-blah-blah or whatever—and then he couldn't get anything out. It was like he was struck . . ."

". . . dumb."

Emerson tried to cover up at first, wordlessly working his mouth as if he were whispering holy nonsense. But the silent episodes occurred more and more frequently. In the privacy of his study, he claimed, he had no problems; he keened rhapsodically; he spoke languages he had never heard before such as Finnish. But when he stood before a congregation—which happened a lot more often now that the Collegiate Church was popular—fear clutched at his tongue and he became the Philomela of the North Country.

Irene poured the last drops of martini into her glass. "If that'd been all it wouldn't've been so bad. People felt . . . sorry for him, suffering and everything. . . ."

But then came the stupid stuff. Emerson began bursting into

tongue with the most extraordinary banalities. Instead of melodic syllables, he would suddenly shout out old advertising jingles or the current prices on the Chicago Commodities Exchange or the starting lineups for the 1964 World Series.

"Once he even chanted the names of all the state capitals in America. Another time . . . another time he named all the tributaries of the Mississippi River."

What happened in practice was that Emerson would have no trouble getting the congregation tuned up; but just as their tongues started wagging autonomously, Emerson would shout out something on the order of: "Hey, getcha cold beer! Hey, getcha Ballantine beer!" Naturally, the shock of banality left the congregation in a condition of *chorus interruptus.* Though his silences could be excused, these amazing utterances seemed to mock the very idea of divine inspiration. Emerson claimed he never meant to mock; he felt under such pressure to *speak* that he would simply follow the first word or thought that popped into his desperate mind.

"Awful, just awful," Helen said, but I noticed she was trying to avoid meeting my eyes.

"It got awfuller," Irene said. "Emerson wouldn't stop. . . . Tried to tell me he had stage fright . . . all he needed was more exposure."

The vicious bourbon rumors began cropping up again as Emerson resorted to still more bizarre behavior to overcome his stage fright. As his congregation dwindled he sought other opportunities to practice speaking before an audience. On one occasion, while addressing the Rotary Club of Fergus Falls, he abandoned his prepared lecture ("Did Jesus Need an MBA?") and began hectoring them to speak in tongues. When the Rotarians indicated their reluctance, Emerson ranted that they were crushing his spirit.

"I talked him into seeing a doctor—a psychiatrist in Minneapolis—but there was this conference at our hotel . . . microchip salesmen . . . and Emerson walked in on their meeting—fifteen hundred of them, at least—and told them he was supposed to give the invocation."

Irene managed to persuade the hotel to drop the charges, but Emerson couldn't be persuaded to drop his attempts to speak in tongues. He told Irene he felt he was on the verge of a breakthrough.

"Breakdown, you mean," Helen said.

"That's when I called the whole business blah-blah-blah, and that's when Emerson suggested I visit you guys." She put her head on the table and fell asleep.

EIGHT

When Helmut Gernschaft handed me the keys to LIFESTYLE he said to me, "So, you will go there for six months and see what you see. Do not make me worry and I won't worry you. A promise, no?"

I agreed. It sounded a lot like a promise.

"Then maybe in October we begin to make strategic plans for the magazine." He clapped his hands eagerly.

There is nothing like plans of the one-, three-, and five-year variety to make the executive heart beat faster. Planning is such a happy corporate ritual! Even supposedly tough-minded planners profess conditional faith in the future. Chapter 1 of every company's story is a nice, positive plan no matter how often the planners suspect that the last chapter will be 11.

Thanks to Frankie and her network of informants I knew I hadn't worried Helmut so far; in fact, the consensus at Schaefer was that I was doing a pretty good job. I also pumped Frankie for miscellaneous Schaefer gossip, which revealed, I suppose, how lonely I was at LIFESTYLE. I missed those zesty confidences of folly and bad behavior which add leavening to the workday. The major folly back at Schaefer seemed to be the book publishing division, which had defied all attempt to improve its fortunes by lowering its standards. The Panzers decided to aim even lower. Market research had shown that the truly desperate were the fastest-growing segment of the population, so Briggs & Schaefer was about to launch a paperback romance series called *Last Chance at Love.*

Frankie reasonably expected some quid for her quo. One day

she barged into my office. "It's time for a promotion. I can't take Enid and Leon anymore. They're ruining my sex life. How can I have a good time at night when I've spent all day working on their big new article, 'Rectal Orgasm: The Myth and the Reality'?"

"Just say to yourself, 'Get thee behind me, Satan honey.' "

"Come on."

"What can I tell you? You have to develop a professional attitude about this sort of thing."

"Oh, Mr. Wisdom, thank you so much. Do tell us, is it your professional attitude that helps you with the Fashionable Affair?"

"Who told you about that?"

"Never mind. I haven't pissed *every*body off around here, and believe me, *every*body's talking about it."

I explained I needed a project like the Fashionable Affair to impress the editorial staff or they were going to step all over me.

"I guess you couldn't trust that ball of fire Parker Burns to come up with good ideas."

"No."

"Well, buddy-boy, you're the one who should know from adultery. I don't know why you're bothering with all this research. You could write it from personal experience."

"I take it that you are alluding to a relatively brief stage in my recent past in which an unhappy man sought to slake his thirst for human warmth and affection with what admittedly were anonymous and exploitative relationships."

"What is this shit? You were screwing your gonads off. You're lucky you lived to tell the tale."

"Have it your way. But this article is different. Everything has to be tested. We're giving consumer advice. I'm going to be the Ralph Nader of fooling around. It also gets into fashion, decorating, and food. It's a LIFESTYLE concept. And the staff likes it."

"Yeah. One of them is really overjoyed."

"Ah-ha, it's Judy Gruber who has been telling you about my little scheme. She'll be happy to know she gets a break from me now. Gregory's going to check out intimate restaurants with her. You two are hitting it off, eh?"

Frankie looked at me defiantly. "So what? I like her."

"If she's as nice to you as she is to me, you're not going to have a laugh riot of a relationship. But even if you become best friends, I don't want her—or anyone else around here—to know that I could write this article from memory." I glared at Frankie so she would know I wasn't kidding.

"All right," she grumbled.

"Or my marital status either. You understand?"

"Okay okay. You still living at home?"

"We just haven't had time to resolve—"

"You're weird," she said. "Living at home while you're separated."

"I'm weird? The person who screwed a left wing for the Rangers in the penalty box at the Garden can't exactly refer to my sexual status as weird."

"Hey, you make it sound kinky. The Garden was empty at the time."

"Excuse me, Emily Dickinson of Seventh Avenue."

She grinned at me and I grinned back. We hadn't teased each other for quite a while. I promised I would do my best to get her away from the Malts. I tried to get Parker Burns to try her. But Parker was too afraid of me to take a chance on Frankie. I had urged him to exercise some editorial initiative; but when he paid $5,000 for a second-rate actress's ghostwritten account of how a particularly painful form of Oriental massage had brought her spiritual fulfillment and improved her backhand, I jumped all over poor Parker for not understanding the new LIFESTYLE.

Although hindsight offers us the unfortunate opportunity to berate ourselves for our mistakes, only once in a while does it offer an entirely different version of one's past. For instance, when Gregory Duplessix told me he would be unable to help me with the Fashionable Affair I was only slightly annoyed. But in hindsight I don't visualize a slightly annoyed publisher; I see instead a large clumsy fish—a carp, say—who has got himself tangled in a net.

"I hope you won't be too cross with me for backing out of your project," Gregory said. "You see, writing a cookbook is my dream. At last I'll be able to express my vision, my faith in food. But my publishers insist that it be published next spring. I must devote every spare minute I have to testing recipes and refining my theories."

Gregory, it turned out, was a kind of Kandinsky of food. He had evolved a theory of cooking based upon a complicated set of correspondences between emotions and ingredients. Each meat or fish, each sauce and vegetable, evoked particular feelings—feelings which could be modified by the style of preparation as well as by the accompanying foods. "Take something as simple as roast beef, George. Let us agree for the sake of argument that it is 'hearty.' Such a graceless emotion! But when heartiness is qualified by the poignancy of Brussels sprouts tossed with caraway seeds, and the ephemeral gaiety of puréed turnips, why then one has stated a certain vision of the human condition. In fact, lest the whole meal become too profound, I would follow this main course with the witty brio of a watercress salad."

"Doesn't the tongue play any role in this?"

"But of course. Once I thought it would be amusing to pour a very silly sauce such as fennel sauce Rocheloise over the saddest food I know, which is boiled cabbage. Believe me, George, pure *merde.* But you'd be amazed at the wonderful combinations you discover if you let emotions guide your cooking. In one of my most successful recent meals I started with an angry soup—my guests were nearly hitting each other—and then dish by dish I transformed that anger into a high-flying exuberance."

"It sounds like it's going to be a brilliant cookbook. You're excused."

"Don't worry, George. I've given a lot of thought to your Fashionable Affair, and I've assembled a list of places in which you will never be seen by friend or relative. I hope you understand, these places were selected not for the quality of the food but for their obscurity." He shuddered.

"I think the one thing that would make Judy Gruber happy would be to see me get caught."

"Poor George. I do feel guilty about leaving you to dine with her while I escape. I'm sure she'll be civil, but just barely."

Gregory's restaurant itinerary was cleverly planned. He figured there were two categories of restaurants or cafes in which lovers could meet without much risk of discovery. The first category was obvious: chic but out-of-the-way little bistros. The other category comprised those large, gaudy restaurants of which every city that attracts tourists seems to have an abundance. These places are generally known by such names as Papa Luigi's or La Bonne Duck or The Original Przcywski's (usually there are three places called The Original Przcywski's). They are all distinguished by a cuisine that is served without fear or flavor and they are ideal for discreet encounters, since no New Yorker would dream of setting foot in one. I wouldn't call them fashionable, exactly, but slumming is often stylish.

"No, you can't pick me up at my place," Judy said after I explained why Gregory had backed out. "That makes it a date. This is business. I'll meet you at the restaurant."

We met at the Aria Restaurant, a tourist trap near Lincoln Center which featured an opera motif. All the waiters were either aspiring opera singers or singers who could no longer aspirate. The walls were covered with old posters and programs from the Met as well as autographed photos of long-lost voices.

"I don't believe this place," Judy said with her usual charming lack of enthusiasm.

The full horror of the Aria dawned on her as the waiter began to sing his way through the specials. The only mouth that seemed to be watering was his—in a fine spray—as he concluded his recital by belting out "Striped Basso Profundo!"

"I'll kill you if you ask to hear the wine list," she whispered. "It seems to me we could leave right now."

"No, we're supposed to observe yet not be seen. It would be unfair not to stay long enough to give our readers a fair assessment of the odds of getting caught."

"And what happens if you run into your wife's best friend? Are you going to cancel the article?"

"That's a bridge I'm sure we won't have to cross. Anyway, we can't leave until Paul shows up at nine thirty to take a couple of photos. So relax and order some dinner. The Chicken Gudenov to Eat looks interesting."

Judy glared at me. "I can't stand people who tell me to relax."

"Why?"

"Because I can't relax." She picked up the menu. "Good God! Overtures instead of appetizers. And look at this: O Solo Meato. That does it. I'm not going to eat a bite. What makes you think an illicit relationship could survive a place like this?"

Luckily, Judy was soon drowned out by the waiters, who, with contrived spontaneity, kept bursting into duets. They would stand there singing, shoulder to shoulder against the music, while you waited in vain for a clean fork. As the evening wore on, the arias became softer and more romantic. Because Judy and I were the only couple at the Aria under the age of fifty-five who had not also dragged along several unwilling children, much of the romantic stuff was directed at us, to Judy's furious embarrassment. Paul the photographer finally showed up just as Judy, who had asked for the check, was yelling at the waiter for bringing it to me.

After the Aria experience we decided to try obscure places. In short order we tried a Chinese restaurant that served tripe prepared in eighteen different ways, a punk rock club on the Lower East Side that featured Velveeta cheese sandwiches, and a diner near the piers popular with transvestites. These experiences sent us back to another tourist trap, a restaurant in the Times Square area named Uncle Tonnato's. As we entered, the headwaiter told us how lucky we were to have come during their perpetual Saint Anthony's festival, and I suppose connoisseurs of the accordion might have considered themselves lucky. The restaurant was decorated with trellises through which were entwined garlands of plastic garlic heads and peppers.

"Who's Saint Anthony?" I asked Judy.

"The patron saint of lost appetites."

I made Judy stick around until Paul showed up though she was getting angrier and angrier as the strolling accordion players serenaded us. Paul arrived just as the restaurant's own photographer was insisting we have a picture taken for the folks back home. Paul was able to snap a shot of us shielding our faces from the photographer. It was perfect for the Affair, though Judy stubbornly refused to agree.

When we left Uncle Tonnato's I tried to console Judy. "We still have a pretty long list. Sooner or later we'll get a decent meal."

"Are you planning on publishing this article next Christmas? I'm beginning to think you're afraid to sit down and actually write the goddamned thing."

"I'm certainly not delaying it because of the pleasure of your company," I said. "Why don't you stop giving me all this grief?"

"What!" She began waving her arms in a curious windmill fashion and yelling at me. "Don't give *you* grief! That's like telling me to relax, you patronizing bastard. 'There there there, little Judy, don't give the clever publisher any grief.' I'll tell you this, pal: Watch out, because I give good grief."

She stormed off into the night.

My efforts to find a new job for Frankie were more successful with Robert Bickford, my Marketing Director. He had proved to be an unexpected asset to me. I couldn't have hoped for a more compulsively organized person to tend to marketing while I concentrated on editorial problems. Bob the Bachelor, as he was informally known, was a lanky, sandy-haired man of about forty-five, but his snub nose, jaunty stride, and incessant enthusiasm made him seem slightly boyish. He worked hard to keep himself in shape for the singles wars, running every morning and playing squash twice a week. There was something charmingly old-fashioned about Bob; instead of relationships he had dates, and he referred to his women friends as "gals." The gals mostly seemed to be successful, well-tailored women in their mid-thirties. Bob's year, he let me know in a firm way, was unvaryingly punctuated by a ski week in Vermont, a Caribbean week, and his summer house in one of the most established communities on Fire Island. Bob the Bachelor had everything under control.

I didn't know what impression Frankie had made on Bob, but he owed me a favor. My predecessor, Larry Roth, had slighted Bob's contributions to LIFESTYLE's success, but I had discovered that all I had to do was point him in the direction of a problem and he invariably found the most efficient solution. I had given him lots of authority.

When I popped the Frankie question to Bob the Bachelor he said he didn't know her, in a tone of voice which implied he knew *of* her and that was enough. But he was much smarter than Parker Burns. Bob didn't refuse outright; he left himself room to maneuver while appearing to be encouraging.

"You know her best, George, so I'm sure it's a great idea. And I could use somebody, especially with our sweepstakes promotion coming up. Of course, she may not like us boring types over in Marketing. Say, I've got an idea. You tell her to come see me. We talk. I tell her about Marketing; she tells me about Frankie. I take her with me on a meeting with a prospective advertiser. He tells us that Mongolian Creme Liqueur is looking for upscale media in which to tell its story. I give him the pitch for LIFESTYLE. He falls asleep. But if Frankie stays awake, she gets the job if she wants it."

Roughly translated, if Bob didn't like Frankie he would manipulate her into saying she didn't want to work for him.

"You mean you want me to work for Mr. Eastsider? Mr. Clean? Weekend Man?" Frankie said when I told her to talk to Bob the Bachelor.

"I think we're talking about the same person. But it's up to you. I'm merely suggesting that you speak to Bob and see how you feel about him and what he does. If you don't want to—"

"Okay, I'll talk to him. But I want to know if I'll have a chance to better myself."

"What do you mean?"

"I mean I want to do more than just be a secretary all my life."

"You've always said you like your life exactly the way it is."

"Well, now I want something different," she said stubbornly.

"What brought this on?"

"I went to a weekend self-actualization seminar."

"You mean one of those sessions where they get a bunch of people in a room and harangue them for thirty-six hours? I just killed an article by Leon Malt on self-actualization workshops."

"That's where I got the idea. It took place at this hotel in midtown. Only I didn't last thirty-six hours."

"What happened?"

"First they yelled at us for about ninety minutes and then they made us pair off and humiliate each other for a while. Then we were supposed to look our partners in the eye and tell them the worst thing we ever did to another person. So I looked at my partner, this schmucky *kid* who couldn't have been more than twenty-two. He still had a couple of pimples to go with his big blue eyes. And his mouth was hanging open like he's ready for some real hot stuff. So I asked myself, How am I going to tell this baby about the time I got my high school driver's ed teacher fired? And then I said to myself, 'Hey! You don't need this shit.'

"So I raised my hand and told the leader—this real fascist named Torbert—that I didn't think self-actualization was for me. And he told me I had paid for thirty-six hours and that was what I was going to get. Then I said, 'Keep the money. I'm leaving.' And he said the door was locked. So I pulled the fire alarm, and when the hotel security people came, I left."

"And this changed your life?"

"Yeah, kind of. See, I signed up for the seminar because I felt ready for some changes. But I really knew what I wanted to do. When I self-actualized myself into pulling the alarm, I figured I could self-actualize myself into getting a better job."

"I guess you got your money's worth. How much did they charge you?"

"Two hundred and fifty dollars."

"How many other people signed up for it?"

"About a hundred."

"Twenty-five thousand gross and almost no overhead for a weekend of work. What a business!"

"Yeah. Well, I've pulled the alarm, Georgie-boy. So help me."

My confidence in my ability to get my employees to be cooperative is probably exaggerated. But if I could get Judy to cooperate with me, I was sure the others would come around. Through an intermediary—Frankie—I got Judy to agree to go to one more restaurant with me. That would be all, I promised. On Gregory's list was a place called Quiet Encounters on the southwestern fringe of Greenwich Village. When I called for reservations they offered me a table in their very charming outdoor patio-garden. I accepted since we were having a balmy spring. I hoped it would please Judy, though I wasn't sure how I would tell.

As usual, Judy met me at the restaurant. She was doing her best to be tight-lipped and businesslike, but she acknowledged the pleasant garden with a little smile. Then I tried my next ploy.

"Here. This is a present for putting up with this difficult assignment." I handed her a little package.

She looked at me suspiciously. "Can't be money. I already got my raise." Inside the package she found a T-shirt on which I had had printed I GIVE GOOD GRIEF. She really smiled this time. "Okay, you win. But you're very sneaky."

After we ordered our meal we had a perfectly amicable conversation. At one point I told her that Bob the Bachelor had agreed to take Frankie on, and not as a secretary but as a kind of management trainee.

"That's terrific," Judy said. "She'll be so happy. She's been dying to get out of working for the Malts. And she's got all these new ambitions. She was afraid you'd say no."

"Afraid? That doesn't sound like Frankie."

"You're kidding. Don't you know she admires you like crazy? She thinks you're the smartest person she's ever met. She also likes you a lot. She would have been crushed if you had ignored her ambitions." Judy managed to say all this in a tone implying that, as far as *she* was concerned, the jury was still out on George Werble.

"You look embarrassed," she teased.

"I am. I'm not really so smart or likable but I am the most modest person I've ever met."

Judy winced, but in good humor.

"You and Frankie seem to have become pretty good friends," I said.

"We're the two shortest women at LIFESTYLE. That makes for a stronger bond than if we were the two most beautiful."

The waiter brought our dinners. The array of candles flickering in the night illuminated the patio so poorly we could barely see the food. Our recent experiences had made us suspicious.

"Coward," Judy said and plunged her fork into her plate as if she were pinning a tail on a donkey. She took a bite and wrinkled up her nose in disgust. "Ill meat by moonlight."

"We'll have to warn our readers that they're going to give up good food for the sake of the affair."

"I'm afraid of dessert."

"How about an imparfait?"

As I turned to summon the waiter, a rasp of nasal overtones cut through the night. "George Werble. It has been years. Where have you been?"

Standing before me in the gloom was Julia Simon, née Harrington of the Morrisburg Harringtons, a fellow emigré from the Best Families of Morrisburg, Ohio. We had come to New York at about the same time and, though we were not particularly close friends in Morrisburg, we contrived the sort of friendship that out-of-towners do during their New York novitiate. We exchanged news from back home and invited each other to our cocktail parties as we widened our circles of friends and obligations. After I met Helen we even double-dated once or twice. But Julia was determined to be as much a social presence in New York as her family had been in Morrisburg, and she couldn't understand why I didn't share the same goal. As far as I was concerned, her goal was to march to the beat of the humdrum, luxurious though it was, but I admired the determination with which she pursued it. She was a tall woman, neither attractive nor unattractive, neither charming nor unpleasant, and her family's wealth was only a little less moderate than mine. But she gritted her teeth and volunteered for thankless jobs with the right charity committees and cultural institutions. By the time she married Roger, who was not excessively older than she and possessed an identical world view, as well as a partnership in a major New York law firm, Julia had achieved such a stupendous state of self-satisfaction that I couldn't even bear to exchange Christmas cards with her anymore.

For a moment I was so busy trying to recall the last time I saw Julia that I forgot my "situation," of which I was reminded by a gentle kick under the table.

"It has been at least four years," I said.

We told each other how good we looked. Julia went to some lengths to let me know the only reason she was at this peculiar restaurant with her friend Pauline was that Pauline's husband was a client of Roger's and had bought Quiet Encounters as a tax-loss gift for Pauline.

Julia's eyes flickered over Judy, first assessingly, then knowingly, then judgmentally. "And how is Helen these days?"

I sighed. "Helen's fine. You probably haven't heard, but Helen and I are separated now."

"Oh, too sad, too sad," she said. "You two always seemed so . . . well-matched."

This *might* have been taken as a comment on Judy and, on the evidence of a less than gentle kick under the table, it was. At that moment we were all dazed by a blinding flash followed by two more flashes. As little stars danced before my eyes, I realized that Paul the photographer had arrived. It seemed an explanation was in order, but I didn't know where to begin. Luckily Judy was equal to the occasion. She snatched a roll from the basket on our table and threw it at Paul.

"Tell Helen to stuff her fucking photographs," Judy shouted.

She waved a clenched fist. "Blackmail won't do her any good now that I've left my husband. Georgie and I are for keeps."

Paul looked at me uncertainly. I gave him the thumb and he quickly left.

"Absolutely smashing to see you again, Julia," I said. "Give my best to your parents."

After Julia fled, I apologized to Judy for not introducing her. "You were brilliant. I hand it to you."

She laughed. "That was a pretty clever excuse you came up with. I figured I could pull any stunt I wanted after you told her you were separated. But aren't you afraid she'll call your wife and inform her you're separated?"

"No. Julia's really *my* friend, pardon the expression. And since her parents moved to Florida, they never see my parents. So I think it's a pretty foolproof excuse."

"In that case I won't insist you cancel the Fashionable Affair. But maybe it would be good to put in a little section—a sidebar, perhaps—of good excuses to use when you do run into someone you know."

"Great idea," I said.

On my late train back to Finchmont I wallowed happily in the recollection of the Julia incident. In a strange and marvelous way I had come up with a perfect excuse: I had told the truth and lied simultaneously. At last I understood relativity.

NINE

"*She*'s here. *She* wants to see you." As far as Teresa de la Iglesia was concerned, Frankie was unpronounceable.

"Got a sec?" Frankie said. She carefully closed my door behind her. I immediately grew tense. "Are you ready, George? It's showtime! *Ta-daa!*" she trumpeted and opened my door.

Enter Bob the Bachelor. It was late May but Bob was wearing a parka, a scarf, and earmuffs. He trudged into the office as if the weight of winter were upon him. "I can't stand January. It's so cold and dark and miserable. I sure feel terrible. Maybe there's something in the mail to cheer me up. Nope, nothing but bills and a letter from Aunt Sally, who thinks the town of Falmouth is persecuting her. What a drag! January is the lousiest month.

"But wait! What's this hot pink envelope that seems to glow invitingly here in my hand? Look what it says right here on the envelope: 'You may already have won an all-new lifestyle from LIFESTYLE. Enter the LIFESTYLE sweepstakes today. Special voucher enclosed. . . .'

"*Special voucher*, wow! Those direct-mail folks sure are clever. I'm just burning with curiosity. Why don't I open the envelope and read the letter inside? 'Dear Bob Bickford. . . .' Gad! My very own name. This letter must be from a real friend. And my friend is promising that my very own number, X37 8250 47AY, may have already been selected—oh, excitement is rising—selected to win a fifty-thousand-dollar remake of myself including two weeks at a health spa in Palm Springs, a designer wardrobe selected by Toni Marmoset, a wine cellar selected by

Gregory Duplessix, success counseling by Leon Malt, and ten thousand dollars' worth of plastic surgery. What a great prize! The way I feel about myself these days, I could use an all-new me.

"But what if I don't win? Why, it says here I'll still be a winner just by subscribing to LIFESTYLE at the special introductory rate. It says here LIFESTYLE is the talked-about magazine with lots of new editorial features and zip and zing. What a great letter! Let's see, who is my new friend? It's signed 'Sincerely yours, George Werble, Publisher.' Let me at that mailbox." He dashed out of my office.

"Come on, George," Frankie said. "Tell me what you think. Pretty great, huh?"

"It's a terrific idea."

Bob the Bachelor returned in seasonal dress. "Frankie has been a big help with this scheme. Lots of ideas. Lots of work."

"Me? Hey, thanks," Frankie said and blushed.

Modesty was not a common component of Frankie's emotional arsenal, and I was surprised to see her embarrassed by Bob's praise. I felt a momentary sense of loss: an old friend was slipping away. But if the new Frankie was a success I would console myself by taking most of the credit.

"How fast can you get the whole package ready?" I asked Bob.

"I've always assumed we were aiming for January."

"Don't assume. What if you crashed it beginning right now?"

Bob sighed, cast his eyes ceilingward, and began to count with his fingers and mumble to himself. Finally he said, "I mean, George, we're talking five million pieces in the mail, and all we have so far is the basic idea. If everything happened perfectly and we paid for lots of overtime, maybe we could finish by the end of September."

"Shit," I said.

"Do it in October," Frankie said.

"It has to be either September or January. Those are the best direct-mail months for us," Bob explained.

"Shit," I said again, a bit more loudly.

"I don't get it," Frankie said. "What's the big problem? Do it in January."

"What are you doing for lunch?" I asked Bob rhetorically.

"I'll cancel."

"We'll eat in my office."

"Great!" Frankie said. "I'll order us some sandwiches."

"No you won't," I said. "Teresa orders the sandwiches. And it's just Bob and I who are going to have lunch together."

"Oh." Frankie paused, then spun and hurried away in a state somewhere between huff and hurt.

I threw up my hands in exasperation.

"I'll explain to her later," Bob said.

I wondered if Frankie would take the point. It was ironic; managerial protocol dictated that Frankie should not order sandwiches because she was no longer a secretary; but as low person on the administrative totem pole now, she was not entitled to the same level of confidentiality she had enjoyed as my secretary.

When the sandwiches arrived I realized I would miss Frankie's way with delis. Teresa appeared to have requested "Two acrid tuna salad sandwiches on soggy whole wheat—hold the napkins." Nonetheless, the food was a perfect complement to the unappetizing problem I described to Bob Bickford.

It had taken me several weeks to figure out that LIFESTYLE's previous owner, the awe-inspiring Larry Roth, had made the deal look especially good to Schaefer/Gruppmann by spending almost nothing to build circulation during the previous eighteen months. Temporarily, the company looked cash-rich and profitable. But now the subscription list needed a real pop or we would run into cash-flow problems in a few months as the rates we could charge our advertisers dropped along with the number of subscribers.

The idea of going to Helmut Gernschaft and explaining that we were going to have cash-flow problems did not appeal to me. The bearer of ill tidings is traditionally the most important ingredient in scapegoat stew. I could see myself blithely telling Helmut the Panzers had paid too much for LIFESTYLE.

"So, George," Helmut would say, "we give you a free hand and you still blame us for your problems. The past is past, no? You must make the cash flow now."

On the other hand, the idea of *not* telling Helmut was equally unappealing. The only thing more upsetting than bad news is learning it the hard way.

"What it all boils down to," Bob said, "is if I don't get the mailing ready for September, you may have to borrow money from Schaefer to pay for it in January."

"That's what it comes down to. Now what are we going to do about it?"

For three hours Bob and I bounced strategies back and forth, but neither of us came up with any ideas that altered the basic problem. Finally we stitched together an approach best described as grasping at straws.

"Let me see if I understand what we're going to do," Bob said. "At the end of this meeting I go to my office and work like a madman. Make everybody around me crazy. After one week I come back to you, ravaged but triumphant. I tell you that there's a remote chance we can get the mailing done by September. You throw yourself at my feet, weeping in gratitude. You authorize all the overtime we need. We plunge ahead. More insanity. Screaming and yelling. Ego trips. Threats of bodily harm. Then we come to the fail-safe date: July fifteenth. If we're still on schedule to drop the mailing by September fifteenth, we go on with this madness. If not, we cancel. Either way, I become the marketing director most hated by his staff."

"That's our plan," I said. "It gives us the illusion of being in control. See you in a week."

Though I agreed to Bob's plan, I didn't like any of it. To be successful, sweepstakes offers cast a wide net to bring in large enough numbers of subscribers. But I was upgrading LIFESTYLE to appeal to a more select audience. My hope was to have my new editorial look in place by October—when Helmut and I were supposed to begin planning for the future. At that point I would propose the next logical move: that we drastically raise the subscription and cover price of LIFESTYLE and get rid of the subscribers who either couldn't pay the new price or lived in undesirable zip codes (median household income below $60,000—sorry, folks). And once we had our demographics in place we could actually *raise* our advertising rates and attract a whole new class of advertisers—high fashion! luxury cars! obscure aperitifs! whirlpool bathtubs! The new American dream.

Judy Gruber notwithstanding, the creative editorial idea had come first to me; but, as had always been my lucky experience, the numbers trotted right along in beautiful order. Unfortunately, if we ran out of cash before October, I might run out of luck.

Once I discovered LIFESTYLE's potential cash-flow problem, an image of Helmut hovered like a threatening cloud on my bountiful horizon. Then Helmut began to rain.

"George! How are you?" Helmut had an annoying habit of shouting into the telephone, as if any conversation with an American were transatlantic.

"I'm fine, Mr. Gernschaft. Say, this is a great connection."

"You know, I said to myself today, 'Gernschaft, you haven't seen George Werble in such a long time. Call him up and make a date with him.' "

It was nice to know that Helmut addressed himself in the imperative. "At your office?" I squeaked. Could a German recognize fear in English?

"We will meet for a drink, no?"

"No. I mean yes. I mean whatever you want." I was disintegrating quickly.

After we made the date I became quietly frantic. I don't believe in coincidences, yet as soon as my nasty little discovery ran to me, keening "Hide me, hide me," there was Helmut right on its tail. Could there be a spy at LIFESTYLE? Only Bob Bickford had been told about the problem, and as far as I knew he had no contact with anyone at Schaefer. I forced Frankie to poll all her Schaefer sources to see what was up, but according to the Panzers' secretaries I was still a fair-haired boy.

I realized I would have to wing it with Helmut. As the day for our drink drew closer I invented a scenario for the occasion which I rehearsed over and over again in my mind. I would listen very carefully to every word Helmut said. If he didn't say the right words I would try to draw him out. At the very first hint that he was on to my secret—but before he could really accuse me of anything—I would spill the beans. Though I didn't want to tell him, it would be better to confess than be accused. I even considered using the best-defense-is-a-good-offense ploy. Instead of merely confessing, I would explode indignantly at Helmut, accusing him of dumping this terrible problem in my lap. If I carried on unhappily enough, Helmut would be too taken aback to argue with me. Of course, this ploy requires that the ployer walk a fine line: you must sound more aggrieved than hostile; this allows the ployee enough room to reassure you that it's all a misunderstanding and that the ployee had delegated some negligent underling to tell you about the cash-flow problem.

As the elevator swooped up to the bar on the forty-third floor of the Gulf and Western Building, the other passengers edged away from the extremely tense magazine publisher who was mumbling to himself. Even though I was ten minutes early, Helmut was waiting.

"So, you are wondering why I am here already. I wanted to make sure we got to sit by the window. The view is very striking."

New York was at our feet; New Jersey lay beyond, glowing warmly in the lingering light of a serene spring evening.

"You are not afraid of heights?" Helmut asked.

"I'm afraid of something."

"It can't be me," Helmut said and laughed and laughed. I had forgotten how roly-poly Helmut was; fear made him loom larger in my imagination. His eyes were narrow and squinty; even while he laughed they darted about suspiciously.

"If you can rise to the occasion so can I," I said.

Helmut looked puzzled.

"You know, rise . . . heights . . . up high. . . ."

"Ach! I get it. I had forgotten you are a great kidder. I miss that at Schaefer now. Everybody is so serious these days. Give me that good old American humor." Helmut pounded the table humorously.

"But I can be serious too when it's necessary," I burted with stupefying earnestness. If I kept on behaving like an idiot I could easily learn to hate myself.

We ordered drinks. I ate all the peanuts. We ordered more peanuts. I ate them too. I pointed out the scenic wonders of New Jersey. We ordered more drinks. Helmut volunteered nothing but bland pleasantries. I finally decided to push him. "How do you like the reports I've been sending you? I hope they tell you everything you need to know."

"They are very good, George. Everything I could ask for. I like the way you present the numbers."

There is nothing like paranoia to turn a normal conversation into a kind of inverted image of itself. Whatever Helmut *didn't* say assumed ostentatious proportions. If he liked the "way" I presented the numbers, that meant to me that he disliked the numbers themselves. If I got him to say the numbers looked good, that meant numbers weren't enough and he wanted some interpretation. It made for a rather strange conversation.

"And I am no design expert, George, but I think the magazine looks very good. It has a livelier appearance."

"I'm trying to improve the writing. I've hired a new copy editor."

"I see. I am also impressed you have not lost any important staff members. Sometimes people quit when new owners and managers take over."

"I've replaced everybody that I fired or forced out. But if you think I should cut the staff . . ."

"No, George, I do not mean to suggest that. I leave it up to you."

We fell into an awkward silence. No matter how inviting I made it, Helmut refused to take any opportunity to bring up cash flow. I finally went so far as to say we were working on a sweepstakes promotion for new subscribers. He asked about its schedule. "January," I said and held my breath. But did he ask me how I intended to pay for the promotion? No, he surprised me.

"So, George, how is everything at home?"

"Home?"

"Your lovely wife. And Gretel the dog. You haven't mentioned my landsman Gretel. Or should I say with a chuckle, my lands*hund*?"

"Everybody's fine."

"That's good, George. You know, at Gruppmann we care about you and all our managers. A new project has great strain. You are anxious to make a good impression. You work so hard perhaps you forget what is important."

I was afraid he was going to give me an avuncular lecture on the importance of my imaginary dog and my imaginary marriage. Luckily he didn't know about my imaginary affair. I chided myself for my cynicism but then Helmut renewed my lack of faith.

"After all, George, an unhappy manager is a poor manager."

"That's important, all right, and you should know that I'm happy."

Helmut smiled benevolently, as if he believed he had bestowed this happiness upon me. "Let's have another drink."

I stared out the window while I collected my thoughts. The view was heartening but I was hoping for a more practical kind of inspiration. Lacking that, I decided to drop the issue of the financial problem. If Helmut wanted to have a meaningless conversation about my family he could have one. "My wife remains as charming as ever. And Gretel . . . Gretel has decided to go into show business."

"What? This is some sort of jest." Helmut was beaming too eagerly. Maybe he was relieved to be off the subject of LIFESTYLE.

"I'm serious. Every year Finchmont stages its famous Pet Pageant. It's a talent show for animals. We've entered Gretel this year."

"You have never told me Gretel is talented. Does she do many tricks?"

Damn that Sara! I thought. Why couldn't she have merely told me she got a haircut or a vaccination or something mundane? "Any dog can do tricks. We have Gretel the Comedy Dog. She does imitations, impressions."

"Of famous people?"

"Oh no. She's a dog, so naturally she does impressions of other animal personalities. For instance, she does a great Kermit the Frog. We've trained her to hop around on her hind legs and make a strange, croaking bark. And then we dress her in a pink undershirt and she dances to the Pink Panther music. And of course there's her famous Morris the Cat imitation in which she fastidiously refuses to eat any food that's offered to her."

"Such a dog!" Helmut exclaimed, which only encouraged me.

"But best of all is her fabulous Checkers imitation."

"Yes?"

"We put a cloth coat on her and she takes a wad of money in her mouth and goes off and buries it."

"Just a minute!" I heard Teresa cry. Frankie zipped into my office and Teresa trotted indignantly after her.

"It's okay, Teresa," I said. "I've got a few free minutes."

Teresa glowered at Frankie and retreated.

"You just love having women fight over you, don't you, George?" Frankie said. "You know, I'm still the same obnoxious person I've always been, but now Teresa blames it on the fact that I got promoted. I came to tell you that Bob the Bachelor explained what I did wrong the other day. I'm sorry I got so upset."

"It wasn't so terrible. You'll learn. Did Bob also explain that if I had let you stay it would have been insulting to him? It would have diminished his importance."

"Not in so many words. But I figured that was what he was getting at."

"Good for you. I take it he then dropped a few hints about our discussion."

"Yeah. How did you know? He told me not to tell you he told me."

"It is up to him to filter things down to you. But you better be able to keep his secret from the rest of the staff."

Frankie sighed. "It's all so complicated and tight-ass."

"Soon you'll learn to be a tight-ass like the rest of us," I consoled her. "So he told you about the mailing?"

"Yeah. He said if you don't get it out in time you would have to ask the Panzers to bail you out later."

I was actually relieved to find out that Bob had been a bit indiscreet with Frankie. If he had been a spy for the Panzers he never would have dreamed of telling Frankie about the problem. "The last thing I want to do is to ask the Panzers to bail me out."

"Well, that's where this really great idea I had comes in—which is the other reason I came to see you. It's great, really."

"Frankie, one of the things you need to learn is when you have a great idea you don't say so. You get other people to tell you it's great."

"Right. And that's what you're going to say when you hear it."

"I don't want to hear it."

"Hey! What are you pulling?"

"Think."

Frankie brooded for a few moments. "I get it. First I have to tell Bob 'cause he's my boss. Then he tells you."

I gave her the thumbs-up sign.

"See, George, I'm beginning to catch on."

"If Bob likes your idea, I'm sure I'll hear about it."

"He'll like it."

At least she didn't lack confidence. Before she left my office she told me I was supposed to go to the art department if I wanted to see the photographs Paul had taken for the Fashionable Affair. I didn't want to seem too eager to view my debut as a model so I waited until late in the day before sauntering over to the art department, the only other oasis of neatness besides my office. Cynthia Poly, the art director, pointed to a big table on which the photos were arranged. I was grateful to be able to admire myself in privacy, without risking embarrassment in front of my employees. Then Judy Gruber arrived.

"Some of these pictures are hysterical," she said as I was looking at one in which I was on the losing end of the world's longest strand of spaghetti.

Then Gregory showed up. "Your restaurant shots. How exciting!"

Then Frankie and Bob the Bachelor walked in. "See, Bob, I told you he'd be here. This'll really be funny."

"So these are your illicit rendezvous," said Annette of natural nutrition as she joined the party. "Tell us, Gregory, did you get this list from the Health Department?"

Cynthia Poly came over to see what all the fuss was about. Soon there were at least ten people sifting through the photographs and laughing at the boss. But I decided it was all in good fun; they seemed to be warming up to me at last.

I found the photographs less humorous than strange. There I was in stark reality; yet since I had contrived the situation I also felt I was looking at a figment of my own imagination.

"Yuck. What are you holding out to the camera in this one?" Frankie asked.

"That's where George tried to get Paul to eat some deep-fried pig's intestine," Judy said.

"He told me he was kosher," I said. We all laughed since Paul was a professional Irishman.

"Would you look at this one!" Frankie screeched. Everyone crowded around her and laughed even harder. Things were getting out of hand.

"Which one is that?" Judy said and took it from Frankie. "Oh, that's the time at Uncle Tonnato's when Paul got a picture of us just as the restaurant's own photographer was trying to shoot us too. Look how I'm covering my face. We really look guilty."

"Let me see that again," Frankie said and snatched it from Judy.

"Uncle Tonnato's!" someone exclaimed.

"Tourists!"

"Tackiness!"

"Boring!"

"Disgusting!"

During this volley of comments displaying the typical charitableness of New Yorkers, Frankie was staring transfixedly at the photograph. Suddenly she whirled. "Gotta go," she muttered. As she fled, she thrust the photograph at me.

While the crowd moved on to other delights, I studied the photograph again. In the foreground was the back of the head of Tonnato's photographer. Beyond him, Judy and I looked pitifully defensive as we tried to ward off his intrusion. Behind our table could be seen a few other tables, and at one of them were a couple of tourists who seemed to be quite fascinated with Judy and me. One of them was tall, one of them was amused; one of them was a stranger. The other one was Helmut Gernschaft.

"Gotta go," I muttered.

PART 3

TEN

For two days I did my best to avoid being cornered by Frankie. Nonetheless, when I passed her in the hall or encountered her in the elevator, she would glare at me fiercely and hiss, "What are you going to do about Helmut?" Sometimes she would hold her hands before her face as if she were focusing a camera and say, "Hold it. I think you're going to hate this picture." In response I would put one finger to my lips and shake my head, as if to say, Not here. But I really meant, Not anywhere.

Two days of doing nothing about the Helmut Problem extended easily into two weeks. As the waning of my marriage was teaching me, doing nothing about something important gathers a kind of negative momentum of its own. Each little procrastination, each "Tomorrow I'll call Helmut and set up a date," accreted to a growing corpus of little doing-nothings until the Helmut Problem became a huge ragged ball of excuses, evasions, equivocations that went hurtling through my life, crushing the occasional and feeble good intention I threw in its path.

This is not to say I pretended the Helmut Problem didn't exist. My days and nights were filled with speculations and scenarios. I wondered at times if the very richness and complexity of my anxious musings encouraged me to do nothing. I was like a spider who, carried away by the intricate detail of its pattern, heedlessly weaves itself into a trap, a Möbius web, perhaps, from which there is no escape.

Part of the difficulty lay in deciding what the Helmut Problem really was. There were two schools of thought in which I alternately enrolled. The first held that Helmut was mildly disturbed to think I was fooling around but would be quite angry to know that it was with my employee. The other school of thought said that Helmut didn't care who I screwed but would be furious to know that I was fooling around on my expense account and, worse yet, fooling around with an editorial project instead of marketing the magazine and sucking up to potential advertisers. Either way, the more Helmut knew about the truth the worse off I was—except, of course, for the fact that I wasn't fooling around with Judy. The very remote possibility that Helmut hadn't noticed us was enough to excuse me from broaching the subject with him directly.

One of my more unfortunate talents is the ability to carry on during difficult circumstances with my aplomb more or less intact. While my inner voice is whimpering, "Help me, help me, help me," I am outwardly benign and pleasant. And so I never get very much sympathy. (Don't you feel sorry for me?) Me and my aplomb buckled down to finish the Fashionable Affair. Although Judy and I were getting on so much better already, our mutual admiration really soared when I told her that I was turning the project over to her; though I would continue, for a short time, to participate, she was now the author. She no doubt attributed this to my generous spirit and not to my unwillingness to have my byline read by Helmut. I wouldn't say we became the best of friends, but we adopted an amused arm's-length relationship in which we took each other's insults and challenges in good humor and even enjoyed the sport.

One of Judy's favorite stratagems was to embarrass me at editorial meetings with difficult suggestions for our next tryst test. At one meeting she said, "It was all very easy to meet at my place for a roll in the hay, but what happens when *both* participants are married? Where do they go to make love?"

I certainly saw where she was heading, and I tried to convince the other editors that today's divorce rate had turned that particular form of double Dutch into a statistical rarity. "If you wait just a few months, virtually anyone you want will soon be divorced."

"What happens if the one you want is waiting for you to get

divorced?" Judy said. "I think we have to set up a hotel assignation."

"Oh, come on," I said thinking of the budget. But the other little bastards joined Judy in shouting me down.

"All right, all right," I said, trying to maintain a semblance of affability. "I'll choose a hotel and we'll all go over some evening for another *cinq-à-sept.*"

"Evening!" Judy exclaimed. "We also owe our readers a look at that great American institution, the nooner."

"Of course," Toni Marmoset said. "It would make an absolutely fabulous fashion spread. I've been looking for a way to do a feature on what the top designers are doing for business clothes—both men's and women's."

"Great," said Judy, "and since I'm writing this now, I get to choose the hotel."

If you go sucking after approval, as I was, you get victimized. Judy chose the most expensive and luxurious new hotel in New York, the Hotel Malmaison.

"What about the budget?" I objected.

"LIFESTYLE can't go second class," Judy said. As the other editors applauded, she winked at me triumphantly.

"Then I get to choose another hotel," I said. This time Judy objected; she knew enough not to trust me. But the other editors were on my side now. More fun!

"What's your choice?" Gregory asked.

I winked back at Judy. "We'll see."

Everywhere I turned there were little time bombs ticking away—the Fashionable Affair; Helmut's interest in my putative love life; LIFESTYLE's financial problems—and then one hot day another time bomb ticked its way into my life. It was the sort of day that makes dull people say, "Looks like a hot summer is on the way." I was preparing for summer by trying to compile a list of reasons why the LIFESTYLE staff should cease their selfish requests for expensive improvements to our very inadequate air conditioning. Given our strained finances, it was a short list:

"It's better than no air conditioning at all" was the only truthful reason. I had already tried telling them that the extra little air conditioner in my office made me uncomfortably cold, but that seemed to add fuel to their ire. I started suddenly; Teresa was standing before me, a look of hesitant anxiety on her face. I had asked her not to creep up on me; sooner or later her timidity would give me a heart attack.

"There's a man—" she began.

"Tell George I'll understand if he's busy," a voice boomed through the door.

"There's a man out there who says he's your brother-in-law."

"Is he large and kind of damp?"

She nodded disapprovingly and went out to get him.

"George!" Emerson cried. He pumped my hand enthusiastically while I mumbled appropriate sentiments.

"You look fine, George, just fine."

The Reverend Miller was a tall fleshy man who suffered from chronic dishevelment. His shirttails took only a passing interest in his pants and one side of his jacket had a tendency to slump from his shoulder.

"Oh it's hot out there, George. I carried my suitcase all the way from the bus station. And it's hot in here too. What's the matter, too cheap for air conditioning? Hey, just kidding." He poked me jocularly. Emerson was damper than usual; dark circles of sweat had soaked through his seersucker jacket and his round, boyish face was flushed and glistening.

"This is quite a surprise," I allowed.

"That's the idea, boy, a surprise. Just the sort of thing to buck up Irene and get that worried look out of her eyes. My plan was to race right up to your house and astonish the good woman. But as I was making my way over to Grand Central Station, I said to myself, 'Hey, let's check in with George first.' " He gave me an affectionate thump on the back. "I called your old office and they directed me here. This is . . . uh . . ."

"Quite a place," I suggested.

"You said it. Slick, real slick, George. LIFESTYLE has a good catchy sound to it." He rotated slowly, surveying my office while making clucking sounds of approval. "You've come a long way, George, and I want you to know that we're proud of you."

In Emerson's grammar, the first-person plural usually referred to him and Jesus; they had similar opinions about a lot of things. "By the way, George, what's the lay of the land up in . . . you know . . ." He jerked his head in the general direction of Finchmont Village.

"Are you asking me if Irene is going to welcome your sudden appearance?"

"That's it. Goodness knows, we've been through a bad patch together, but now I've got the old optimism back. And when the spirit is humming in me, things happen."

Emerson was one of those people who, with insistent intimacy, stand too close to you. His breath had a sweet, fruity odor, as if he had just eaten a cantaloupe.

"I think Irene will be glad to see you. But I'd take it easy at first. I wouldn't go charging in promising heaven on earth no matter how optimistic you are."

" 'Heaven on earth'—is that some sort of antireligious crack?"

"Just a figure of speech, Emerson."

"Huh. Well, I'll accept what you say about Irene. I know I looked stupid there in Fergus Falls. Speaking in tongues was the Lord's gift to me and I wanted to share it with everyone. But there were forces lined up against me, evil forces, and I couldn't overcome them. Yes, I disappointed Irene. I even disappointed Jesus. But I know in my heart that both of them are going to give me another chance. Why? Because I fought the good fight. The world is just too full of malice and gossip sometimes to accept the Word of God. Even though I failed, I'm proud I tried. And I'll tell you this, George: I'll be real disappointed in Irene if she doesn't welcome me back with yellow ribbons. I don't want any grudging acceptance. I'm a warrior. I want respect." He pounded his fist into his other hand. "You know, I never promised Irene a rose garden. And when the Lord called me He didn't promise milk and honey either."

"Did He make any promises? You should have gotten them in writing." I knew I was making a mistake the moment I opened my mouth.

Emerson walked across my office shaking his head in a mournfully appalled manner. He gazed out at the street for a few moments; then he spun around. "I *do* have it in writing, George. It's called the Bible. You know, we all have windows deep inside our souls through which we can catch a glimpse of divine promise. But with our greed and lust and impudence we smudge up our windows." He drew a finger across my office window and held it up as proof. It was coated with *something*. "The Lord called me to be His window washer. Yes, sometimes I fail. Sometimes my bucket of hope runs dry or my sponge of faith is dirty. Sometimes my strap breaks and I dangle over yawning chasms of evil. But I'm not going to give up. Why, every time I've been at a low ebb, I've been replenished, thank the Lord. And I can feel the sweet providence of inspiration coming on again."

"You wouldn't happen to have just a little hint about the form this inspiration is going to take?"

"No, but it's going to be good for me. A man with my potential can't be kept down for very long. You know, when I turn on the TV and see Jimmy Swaggart preaching away, I tell myself I could be just as big as Brother Jimmy. Or even that tight-ass Reverend Schuller. I *know* I've got the power. Why, when I'm hitting on all cylinders I can hold a bunch of sinners in my hand and squeeze 'em like they've never been squoze before. Oh, I've got the power. All I need to make it real big is a little luck."

"And maybe a job to tide you over."

"I've got something cooking in that area too. There's a congregation out in Dry Creek, California, that wants me to preach there in August for a trial run."

"Dry Creek sounds a lot more promising than Moscow, Idaho. I'm sure that Irene will be very encouraged."

"You think so? Say, that's great! That big beautiful lady needs me more than she knows. And I need her too. She's my mainstay, my rock. Besides, nobody trusts a preacher who isn't married."

I looked at my watch; I had a lunch date. "My wife and your rock are out this afternoon gathering signatures on a petition banning video game arcades within the Finchmont Village limits. It's a big election issue. Maybe you should find something to do in the city and come home with me tonight. You can leave your suitcase in my office."

"What's the matter? Too cheap to buy your brother-in-law lunch? Hey, just kidding. I know you're busy. That's a fine idea."

As I was showing Emerson out of the office, we ran into Leon and Enid Malt. I introduced them to Emerson, who regarded the couple suspiciously. "Are you the people who wrote that book *Good Self/Bad Self*?"

"That's us," Leon said. "What did you think of it?"

Emerson sniffed. "Just about the most pernicious thing I ever read. Don't think I don't know what you pop psychologists are up to. You want folks to feel good about sin."

"Emerson!" I said. The man was impossible. "Actually, Enid and Leon belong to a school known as Mom and Pop psychology."

"I'll bet you'd be surprised by how close our attitudes are about many things. I'm thinking of writing a piece on the Tao of John the Baptist," Leon said.

"Huh! All I know is if God didn't want us to feel guilty he wouldn't have invented sin."

Frankie's persistent attempts to make me face the consequences of Helmut's discovery seemed to have reached a peak of harassment. The next day, early in the morning, as I was on my way to a meeting, I saw her awaiting me down the hall. Her arms were folded and her face was fierce. Luckily I was able to duck into the men's room and wait her out. Later she tried to trap me as I left the meeting, calling out, "I need to talk to you, George."

I am never so deft as I am in evasion, and in one graceful slither I was past her and in the midst of a conversation with Bob the Bachelor, who happened to be walking by.

"I have a message for you," said Bob as we ambled along. "Frankie says she really wants to talk to you. It's important."

Oh was she a determined one! Back in my office I found a frieze of "while you were out" memos from Frankie stretched across my desk. And finally, on my way back from lunch, Frankie accosted me in the elevator.

"Maybe I put it wrong, George. I don't need to talk to you. You need to talk to me."

"Of course," I said condescendingly, "but this week is just too crowded. I'll tell Teresa to call you and set up a date for us next week."

Frankie's face darkened.

"Early next week," I offered over my shoulder as I pushed my way out of the elevator.

A few minutes later Frankie strode into my office unannounced.

"You're really going too far," I said angrily.

"You don't know what's good for you. And I don't know why I haven't given up."

My phone rang. "It's Mr. Gernschaft," Teresa said.

"Hello, Mr. Gernschaft. How are you?" I covered the mouthpiece. "It's Helmut. What do you suppose he wants?"

"That's what I've been trying to tell you all day, but it's too late now." As she reached my door she turned. "You're on your own, asshole."

Half an hour later I shuffled into Frankie's office carrying a bouquet of flowers.

"You treated me like homemade shit," Frankie said.

"I did. I'm sorry."

"I'm special to you. Treat me that way."

"You are. I will."

"You know, you get an idea in your head, George, and then nobody can talk to you. You just sail along like you're in a dream world."

"Helmut woke me up fast enough. He wants me to come over to his office tomorrow to meet someone."

"Who?"

"He wouldn't say. He was having his mean little joke with me. He said it was a secret, a surprise."

"Then I think I know who it is," Frankie said. "I really shouldn't tell you after the way you behaved, but I will. What I've been trying to tell you is that Larry Roth has been seen around Schaefer lately. He's had at least two meetings with Helmut that I know of."

"Larry Roth!"

I was upset. Larry Roth had avoided any contact with me after he sold the magazine to Schaefer Communications. As far as I knew, he had avoided everybody else at Schaefer as well.

"What does he want?" Frankie asked.

"Roth? I don't know. Helmut? I wish I knew. Maybe he just wants to keep me off-balance."

"You know what Helmut is like, a real mindfucker. There's probably nothing to it except he's doing a little number on your head. Too bad Roth is going to be there. You could have tried to explain what you and Judy were doing at that restaurant."

I spent the rest of the afternoon trying to get a line on Larry Roth. Judy Gruber gave me a suspicious frown when I approached her. "What do you want to know for?"

"Judy, can't I just ask a casual question and get a simple answer?"

"Not around here."

We stared at each other.

"Okay, okay," she finally said. "Larry was pretty crazy. Smart but crazy, and often very unpleasant to work for. LIFESTYLE was his child, and he took everything that happened personally."

"I thought that life here was smooth and easy when he was around."

"Just because we gave you a hard time? No, we disliked you on your own merits."

Disliked. It was hardly an endorsement but I chose to look at the use of the past tense as a positive step.

I made some more calls and prodded some other LIFESTYLERs. By the time I headed for Helmut's office the next morning, I had more of an idea of who Larry was.

He seemed like a lot of the media/marketing entrepreneurs one runs into around New York. He had launched a couple of one-shot magazines, sold design services, tied in some products to athletic events, produced special premiums for marketing promotions. He had had a few modest successes and a few modest failures. He had the usual ex-partner who thought he had been burned and the usual reputation for being creative but difficult. But there was really nothing out of the ordinary to his career until LIFESTYLE took off.

This was the first time I had been back to Schaefer's offices since my promotion. It was just as I had remembered: the neat buttoned-down look, the quiet determined hum, and the aroma of molded plastic that characterize the modern corporation. To my surprise, I felt uncomfortable; I had become accustomed to the noisy chaos of LIFESTYLE.

Helmut greeted me effusively. He proudly escorted me about his office, which had been redecorated since my last visit. All an executive has to do is mumble, "Nothing ostentatious," and the decorator immediately produces that apotheosis of corporate understatement, the beige and greige suite. In addition, Helmut had decided he could afford a special decorative perk, the "collection." Usually the decorator assembles a bunch of duck decoys or old photos of early airplanes or several antique clocks. But Helmut's decorator had impishly organized a group of plaques to comprise a wall of business bombast. There was "Think," "The buck stops here," "I don't get mad, I get even," "I don't get ulcers, I give them," and "When the going gets tough, the tough get going."

"So, George, I have not seen you since our nice drink."

"And now you have a surprise for me."

"Yes. You will let me tell you, however, that after we spoke on the phone I thought, Maybe I should not be so mysterious. There is no telling what somebody might think." He looked at me slyly. "You might have gotten worried, no?"

"I might. I thought you had been recalled to Germany and you wanted me to meet your successor."

"That is a good one! So, were you sad or happy that I was leaving?"

"That's *my* secret."

"Enough of secrets," Helmut said. "The reason I asked you—" The phone rang. "Very good. Send him in."

In walked Larry Roth. Since I was prepared to dislike him, I saw a narrow, mean face with a cruel mouth. No doubt his mother, children, and friends saw a visage of handsome, dark intensity. I think all of us would have agreed that he was tall and wiry.

"George Werble, meet Larry Roth." Helmut spread his arms with expansive bonhomie.

We declared we were glad to meet each other. We stated we had heard such good things about each other. We named several common acquaintances. We sat down on Helmut's beige ultrasuede couch and fell silent. Helmut offered us coffee.

"Is it true," I asked, "that you've decided it was all a mistake and you want to buy LIFESTYLE back?"

Larry laughed easily. "No, Helmut's been telling me what a great job you've been doing. I'm sure I couldn't afford it now."

"Now George," Helmut said, "I do not want us to think of this occasion as a business meeting. This is a social meeting, a casual gathering for the express purpose of introducing two interesting people to each other."

Helmut's remark was so patently untrue that it struck us all dumb. Neither Helmut nor Larry nor I would have dreamed of meeting each other for casual chitchat. When the sounds of sipping became unbearable I played first. "I'm glad to meet you at last. I tried to speak with you before I took over at LIFESTYLE. But I'm sure that was a very busy time for you."

"To tell the truth," Larry said, "it wasn't because I was so busy that I avoided you. Frankly, I hated you at the time—both of you."

Helmut and I looked puzzled but Larry smiled reassuringly.

"You must understand. I was selling my baby. I had nursed

LIFESTYLE from an ambitious idea into a successful magazine. I knew every department as if it were an extension of myself. Financially, selling LIFESTYLE was the right move at the right time. But emotionally—" He shook his head. "I was consumed by hatred and resentment. I hated Schaefer, who was paying me lots of money; I hated Helmut—and we know what a prince he is; and I hated you, George, for taking over my baby. I actually hoped that you'd all fail, that LIFESTYLE would fall apart without me. It was very irrational. I even went into therapy for a while."

"Feeling better these days?" I asked. Maybe it's my formal midwestern upbringing, but I'm always astonished at the way some people are on a first-name basis with their feelings, easily elaborating their passions, woes, and inadequacies. New York, especially, is full of people who, in the way that Eskimos have forty-nine different words to describe snow, have catalogued whole libraries of their resentments and anxieties.

"Much better. It took quite some time to work through my problem, but then my therapist and I agreed that the thing for me to do if I truly cared for LIFESTYLE would be to offer you any advice or help I could. You know, my friends told me to stay away. 'Take the money and run, Larry,' they said. But I couldn't."

Helmut was beaming. "You see, George, it's more than money that motivates us. We must care too for Larry's baby. It is easier to pass a needle through the eye of a camel than it is for a rich man to get into heaven."

"But I'll understand if you don't want my advice," Larry continued. "You guys probably have everything working so well that any advice I gave would be insulting."

He had an interesting way of leaving me no choice by offering me a choice. Helmut would surely not have set up this meeting unless he knew in advance what Larry was going to say, so I was being backed into a corner of some kind. But there's often opportunity in adversity. I saw an opening.

"You know, there is one area on which I'd like your thoughts. We've been breaking our backs to get a direct-mail campaign off the ground. Since there hasn't been much money spent on circulation for a couple of years, the files don't provide a lot of background. Maybe you could give me some idea of what worked and didn't work in the past."

There. I had almost said it. I wondered if Helmut were alert.

"Why, I'd love to help," Larry said without a flicker of guilt. "You're probably right to spend more on circulation. At a certain point a few years ago I decided to put more money into promotion and less into circulation—especially direct mail. Maybe it was a mistake, but I thought the magazine needed more image building and potential advertisers needed more stroking. But times change."

He spoke facilely but he was on delicate ground. Few magazines spend on promotion anything near what they spend to build circulation. I didn't expect Larry to admit outright that he used money that should have gone into circulation to make the bottom line look better, but we were getting close. I glanced at Helmut. He was beaming proudly, as if he were more interested in stimulating this wonderful exchange of ideas than in what was being said.

Larry and I agreed to meet soon so he could advise me on circulation. We nattered on for another half hour about miscellaneous matters. Abruptly, Helmut rose and brought the meeting to an end. On my way down in the elevator it occurred to me that this was the second recent meeting with Helmut in which he showed me he had some cards to play but didn't play them. I genuinely believed that Helmut couldn't fault my performance at LIFESTYLE (yet) so I assumed Frankie was right; he was one of those bosses who like to keep the pressure on their managers in sneaky, indirect ways—riding softshod over me. If he were dissatisfied with me I doubted he would hire Larry even if Larry and his therapist wanted the job. No, Gruppmann would bring in one of their own people if putsch came to shove.

ELEVEN

As Helmut's pressure squeezed me, I began to imagine that my plan and I were on a kind of pilgrimage. I was on a perilous road; danger attended every step of the way. If I survived the danger, there was still a crucial turning point.

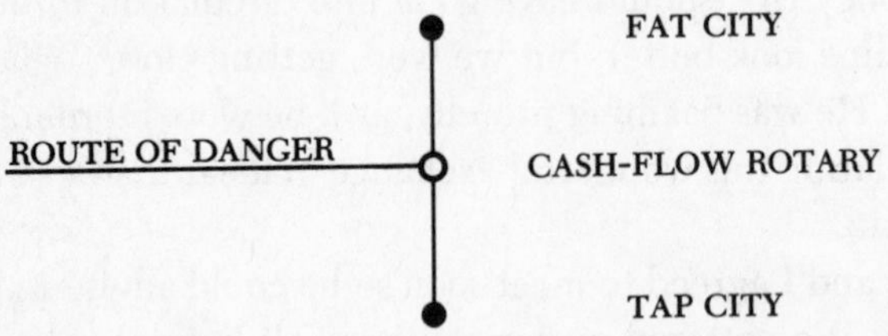

A few days after my meeting with Helmut and Roth, Teresa buzzed me.

"Telephone for you. It's Mr. Gernschaft."

Here comes the punch line, I thought as my adrenal gland prepared itself for a good workout. "Hello, Mr. Gernschaft. How did you like those figures I sent you?"

"Figures? Ah, of course. Very promising indeed. No problem there."

Then where? wondered my paranoia. "I enjoyed our meeting last week. Your new office is very handsome. Who was your decorator?" I was jumping about irrelevantly, trying to keep Helmut off-balance until I could get the conversation going on my terms.

"Who? I don't know. I must ask the office manager for the name."

"And I want to thank you for satisfying my curiosity."

"What were you curious about?"

"Larry Roth, of course. You know, he avoided meeting with me after we took over LIFESTYLE. It seemed strange to me, and I was eager to see if he were really as peculiar as he had acted."

"So tell me the truth, George; what did you think of him?"

"I was quite impressed. He's very smart," I said generously. "But I still think he's peculiar."

"Why?"

"That whole story of his about hating us—it was just off the wall."

"I see what you mean," Helmut said thoughtfully.

"There's something a little weird about Larry Roth." I was verging on overkill.

"So. You are absolutely correct, I believe. And you have helped me to make up my mind. I do not want somebody who comes off the wall to be on my staff."

Whew! My adrenal gland took a breather.

"But as you say, George, Roth is very smart. So I will employ him as a consultant instead."

The gland began to throb like a broken heart. "Consultant on what?"

"On new ventures, new acquisitions. We might even use him as a troubleshooter, somebody who would look into problems in our business."

I had been backed into the kind of corner from which only a direct and forthright appeal to Helmut's sense of propriety could rescue me.

"May I speak frankly?" I said.

"Of course, George. Don't we always?"

"I think it's all well and good to use Roth as a consultant for Schaefer. But as far as LIFESTYLE is concerned . . ." I waited for Helmut to say he got the point but he forced me to make it: "As far as LIFESTYLE is concerned, having the previous owner and publisher come in as a consultant would make things very difficult for me. I haven't made many charges at LIFESTYLE, but entrepreneurial types like Roth are often too personally involved to look at their own businesses objectively. He said himself that LIFESTYLE was his baby. And if he had any interaction with the staff—most of whom he hired—it would make it doubly difficult for me to manage them. I would find it an intolerable situation." I hadn't spoken so frankly in years.

"Thank you for saying what you have on your mind. I of course appreciate your situation and give you my utmost assurance that Larry Roth will stay far away from LIFESTYLE."

"I'm glad you understand," I said. "It's good that we can speak like this."

"And I must add, George, that I am sure that no troubleshooting will ever be needed at LIFESTYLE. I can tell by the figures that you are shooting all the trouble yourself." Helmut chuckled at his little linguistic leap and said good-bye.

I don't often lay things on the line, and for a few moments I basked in self-satisfaction. I rather liked the way I had defined the issue as *us* sensible managerial types against those emotional entrepreneurial types. Perhaps I had even achieved a new level of communication with Helmut. But gradually, as I rehashed the conversation, reality began to move in like a cold front. Finally I admitted it to myself: I had overplayed my hand.

I had resisted Roth because I was afraid he would call my editorial changes to Helmut's attention before I was ready to unveil my plan—which had been created in response to deficiencies I had inherited from Roth. But if LIFESTYLE's financial problems became apparent to Helmut before all my ducks were in a row, I might have Roth thrust upon me, Helmut's assurances notwithstanding. It would make it much easier to tag Roth with responsibility for his misdeeds if he were at the scene of the crime when Helmut found out about them. It was a sign that my confidence was wavering a little if I felt that I couldn't handle Roth. I had violated one of my basic business canons: Always accept in principle wrong, stupid, or malicious suggestions from one's superiors; they can usually be subverted or corrected in practice.

I needed a shoulder to lean on. I thought about calling Bob the Bachelor, but then I remembered I was lunching with a much more attractive pair of shoulders. Ever since our first meeting, Gloria Pastore's voice had resonated in my mind like a glass harmonica. Although we had had a few formal business meetings since then, there had been no opportunity for me to get personal. A lunch would give me another chance to overcome her better judgment, and I had wheedled and charmed her into agreeing to meet me.

Just before noon, as I was arousing myself with a kinky George and Gloria fantasy (based on what she said was a fondness for Caribbean holidays), Bob the Bachelor rang me.

"What if I have something to tell you that is so important it can't wait? What if I tell you something so incredible that you will sit up and say, 'Hey, Bob Bickford, we don't have a moment to lose. We must act this very minute'?"

"What do you mean, 'What if?' "

"Teresa tells me you're having lunch with Gloria today."

"And you want me to cancel? You're kidding."

"I'm talking about netting half a million dollars with almost no up-front investment."

Gloria was quite irritated when I canceled; I would not get another chance. Oh well, I would always have my fantasy to treasure: the moon . . . the fragrant Caribbean air . . . the murmuring palm trees on the beach . . . Gloria in and out of her black bikini . . . the perky waitress from the hotel . . . the gentle busboy from the hotel . . . the coke au vin. . . . Lovers come and go but our fantasies endure in perfection.

Bob appeared in my office in ten minutes. He carried no notes or props and he wore a pensive, uncertain look. He sat down. He got up. He sat down again.

"I've got a problem, George. First I was worried that I couldn't present this idea well and a great idea would die. Then again, it could be a lousy idea."

I sighed. "So you decided not to tell me. You're going to make me guess."

Bob ignored me. "But then I said to myself, 'If you don't present it like it's a good idea, George is going to wonder why you're wasting his time.' "

I cleared my throat in agreement.

"So then I thought, if it's a great idea, the first thing to do is whet George's appetite by mentioning the payoff: half a million net, not much investment, and the potential for lots more. That'll get him interested." He looked at me questioningly.

"That's already been established."

"The next step, I told myself, would be to tell George about one of LIFESTYLE's unrealized assets: it has never fully exploited its name or reputation. Look what other magazines do. You can go to Playboy clubs. You can buy Gourmet cookbooks. The Good Housekeeping Seal is everywhere. But then I thought, George will probably say, 'Hey, Bob, you idiot, do you want us to put our seal of approval on stylish things? Styles change too quickly. In the magazine we change our tune from month to month.' And I would say, 'George, that's a good point. But I'm afraid you're not thinking big enough.' As I said that, I would think, It's because George is such an open, tolerant kind of boss that I can speak so candidly.

"Now at this point, I figured you would be counting your assets before they're tapped, figuring that what's to come is some incredibly lucrative scheme for franchising the magazine's name and then, once I had you hooked, I would switch gears right in the middle of the conversation. While you were sitting there all eager and excited, I would say, 'George, you know you've got a real cash-flow problem staring you in the face. And I have to tell you, our sweepstakes plan isn't going to work.' It will take a moment to sink in, but suddenly you'll sit bolt upright."

"Just a sec," I said. "Are you telling me that our sweepstakes mailing can't be done on time after you said it could?"

"And I'll have to tell George that I have pretty good news and really bad news. The pretty good news is that more and more people are buying LIFESTYLE on the newsstand and some of them are even saying, 'I'm going to fill out this little card and get a subscription to the elegant new LIFESTYLE.' The bad news is that we're losing so many of our old subscribers so quickly that before we can even do any kind of mailing we're going to have to announce a lower guaranteed circulation to our advertisers. And there's no way we can hide that from Gernschaft.

"Then I thought, Oh dear. Poor George is going to be so depressed by this bad news that he'll forget about the great idea I was leading up to just a few moments earlier. I could just picture what would be going through your mind, George, as you worried if your career were going to derail and all those wonderful go-go years went-went. I decided to let you sweat a bit while you wondered if you should tell the Germans right away or wait. I knew that all of a sudden you would remember what I was saying, and you would turn to me and say something along the lines of—"

"Beats me," I said. I was getting a little stubborn about being a creature of Bob's imagination.

"I was pretty sure you'd say, 'Wait a minute, Bob. Didn't you just mention you had a scheme to net us a cool half million and maybe more? How quickly can this deal be pulled off?' And that's when I would answer, 'Very quickly,' and then I would point out that while half a million may not pay all the bills, if this idea works the Germans are going to be a lot more receptive when you come to them and say you need a bit of money to tide the magazine over until your brilliant new plan is in place. 'So, George,' the Panzers will say, 'anybody who can bring off a brilliant idea such as the Lifestyle Institute is going to go far at Gruppmann. Are you sure we can't give you more money?' "

"What is the Lifestyle Institute?" I said.

"That's it!" Bob cried. "Just what you're supposed to say. But I figured I wouldn't answer you directly. Instead, I would switch gears again, in my frustratingly oblique manner, and look you straight in the eye in a kind of serious, pompous way and ask if you knew how much money is spent every year on adult education and self-improvement instruction. I hoped you'd concede it was a pretty vast sum—middle ten figures, let's say."

"You mean you want us to start some sort of school?" I said, as I was destined to say.

"And then I'd know I nearly had you landed and I'd say, 'George, you know we bust our asses talking four hundred and eighty-five thousand people into forking over nineteen ninety-nine to subscribe to the magazine. Wouldn't it be easier to talk a few thousand into paying a few hundred dollars each?' "

"At long last," I said, entering into the spirit of things, "dear George begins to get a little tired of waiting for the punch line. He fears that Bob is going to ramble on and on, and he decides to tell Bob to put up or shut up."

"Aw, come on," said Bob, looking hurt. "I'm just about to get to the good part where I wonder how much you know about all those movie weekends and cooking weekends, all those hosteling trips and tennis camps and writers' workshops and increase-your-karma groups. And I also wonder if you know that half of the people who attend these things are only half interested in the subject and half interested in meeting other people who are half interested in the subject. And it is at this point that I feel you are finally ready for the big ah-ha."

"You mean the Lifestyle Institute."

"Ah-ha!" Bob said triumphantly. "Yes, at a lovely resort in the country, the Lifestyle Institute will offer seminars, lectures, and workshops to help you add a little style to your dull career, your dull home, your dull clothes, your dull body, and your dull opinions. Enid Malt will teach you how to be as polymorphously perverse as any jet-set sleazo. And if your food just lies there on the platter, Gregory Duplessix will show you how to prepare the kind of food that makes a statement." At last Bob was forced to address me directly: "What do you think?"

"It sounds very promising," I said carefully.

"I knew you'd be reluctant to just leap right in, so I thought I'd remind you that if we play our cards right the up-front investment is pretty small. We can test-advertise the Institute in the magazine. If it doesn't work, we can forget the whole thing."

"Considering that we're trying to upgrade the magazine, isn't your idea—"

"—rather tacky? I thought you might say that. But it's no worse than a sweepstakes promotion, and its real point is that only a class act like LIFESTYLE can help people escape from creeping tackiness. Only LIFESTYLE can teach you to acquire the objects and affectations that will give you an image."

I nodded slowly. I was getting interested.

"As I was thinking about how to tell you all this, I became worried. Some bosses refuse to back any idea that isn't their own. But then I told myself: Not George Werble. He's got too much integrity. He'll probably congratulate me on my brilliance. And that's when I'll show him how much integrity *I* have as I reveal that the idea for the Institute isn't mine at all."

"It's Frankie's idea," I said, finally figuring something out for myself. "Now I know what she was getting at."

"Can I call her? She's dying to know your reaction."

A few minutes later Frankie trooped into my office. "A great idea, right? And you like it, don't you?"

"I think so. Do I?" I asked Bob.

"You love it."

Frankie was delighted. She had of course gotten the idea from her self-actualization workshop. Diplomatically, she gave me some of the credit. "Of course I wouldn't have thought of it if you hadn't pointed out how much money they were making off us. Then I realized how many more people would shell out to be told how to have great lifestyles."

Frankie and Bob proudly outlined their plan. They had figured out which subjects would work and how much to pay our editors and other guest lecturers. They had made financial projections which showed we could break even with only 150 enrollees at $300 each per weekend and market projections which said we could get as many as 500 per weekend. They had even located a few hotels in the Catskill Mountains which could accommodate 500 lifestylers.

I was nervous about the idea. It had something of the "Hey kids, let's start an institute" spirit. It was the sort of project which should be massaged for a year before any action is taken. I turned to Bob and Frankie, who were hovering about me, eagerly waving their financial and demographic projections. I thought about asking Frankie to leave but decided she was as responsible for this as Bob.

"Aren't we lucky," I said, "to have this scheme to fall back on since we can't get our sweepstakes done on time."

They beamed.

"But something tells me that without this idea to distract you, we might have had our sweepstakes in good time."

They stopped beaming.

"So now that it is too late for our sweepstakes, what if this institute flops? What do we do next?"

They looked at each other nervously.

"We'll look for new jobs," I said.

To my knowledge, no American president's valediction has urged the citizenry to beware of the media/communications complex. But surely a warning is in order, for this complex has spawned a sizable corps of professionals whose entire careers consist of a series of projects punctuated by deadlines. There are major media projects and minor media projects, but every one has an air date, a publication deadline, a rollout date, or a premiere, and each of them is marked by generous complements of anxiety, misunderstanding, interpersonal hostility, and risk of imminent cancellation. In other words, even the most run-of-the-mill project bears a remarkable resemblance to a crisis, and so there are thousands of media people who don't know the difference between a true crisis and the normal state of affairs. Usually they just go right on scheming and screaming and spending lots of money without any sense that things have really gotten out of control until a public abomination is produced or they begin to sue each other or both. And that, my fellow Americans, is why television and movies are so terrible.

Had any of these thoughts struck me even a glancing blow as I approached the Hotel Malmaison, I would have instructed the cabdriver to turn around. But none did, and they appear here as a kind of post-dictive excuse for my heedless behavior. It was only four days after Helmut had danced a second threat before me, only three days after I had agreed in desperation to take a flyer on the Lifestyle Institute, and here I was in a taxi, my little heart pittering with delight at the fun good old George and his cohorts would have as the Fashionable Affair tried a nooner at New York's fanciest new hotel.

The plan was much like the *cinq-à-sept* at Judy's apartment. Judy and I would meet in midtown and proceed to the hotel to prove that the assignation could be managed between twelve fifteen and two. Once we registered the models would take over. Our plan had been slightly complicated by the Malmaison's emphatic suggestion, when we asked for their cooperation, that we select a different hotel for our tasteless project. In my rapture, I brushed aside the problem. "Judy and I will check in and then everybody will sneak up to the room."

According to plan, my cab pulled over to the curb at Park and 49th Street and Judy slipped in with her full complement of enthusiasm. "This is ridiculous. Why didn't *I* take a cab from the office and pick *you* up?"

"Me boss, you employee."

"There's a good reason."

"Just a minute," Paul the photographer yelled before our cab pulled away. "I want another shot of Judy getting into the cab." It took five more shots before a perfectly surreptitious length of Judy's calf vanishing into the cab was captured by Paul and we set off for the hotel.

"Now I know why I never got married," Judy said. "Adultery is too complicated. What's that?"

"That's our suitcase."

"What's that ugly strap around it for?"

"I thought that for the sake of tradition I should put telephone directories in it and for safety's sake I should put a strap around it."

New hotels flex their fanciness by dressing their employees in grotesque and humiliating uniforms. Until the Malmaison opened, the most abject depth of dress had been plumbed by a hotel that forced its employees to wear costumes based on a glitzed-up version of British military uniforms of the Victorian era; car parking, bellhopping, and room service resembled the Charge of the Heavily Decorated Brigade. In Crimean response, the Hotel Malmaison adopted its fashion vocabulary from the Imperial Russian Army during one of its French flirtations. As the doorman bent to help Judy out of the cab, his tall fur hat hit her on the head and knocked her back into the vehicle.

"*You* chose the hotel," I reminded her before her growl became a roar.

She got out on the second attempt and we were swept into the lobby by a troika of bellhops proudly bearing six copies of the Yellow Pages.

I joined a short line to check in. The gentle strumming of a zither echoed through the lobby. A group of perhaps fifteen couples milled about nearby, greeting and introducing each other as they checked in. They seemed to be in New York for a convention. "Oh look! Is it really her?" someone said.

It was. Fifi Hoffman, the well-known owner of the Malmaison, swept through the lobby, her ample flanks guarded by nervous assistants. She was on one of her famous fault-finding tours, pointing to lapses in hotel perfection which her troops quickly corrected. "What's this?" she said, indicating my check-in line. "No one should wait on a line at the Malmaison." She slipped behind the counter as the clerk blanched. "Why didn't you call for another clerk?"

"They all arrived at once. I was—"

"Never mind. I'll help you. There is no job at the Malmaison that I will not or cannot perform to ensure that my guests are treated royally from the moment they arrive." She raised her voice for our royal benefit.

The clerk was so terrified by her presence that the line moved more slowly. At 12:40 we finally registered. Judy was curious to know how I signed us in, but I leaned over the registration card so she couldn't see it.

"Let's see," said Fifi. "Mr. and Mrs. George Werble from Morrisburg, Ohio. Isn't that a coincidence! I'm sure we just registered someone from Morrisburg." The clerk shuffled through the cards and handed her one. "Oh, Dr. Tensor," she called. "It's these chance meetings that make innkeeping rewarding."

A slight dapper man detached himself from the crowd in the lobby. The ever-helpful Fifi introduced us, but Dr. Tensor looked puzzled. "I thought I knew every other dermatologist within a hundred miles of Morrisburg."

"Mr. Werble isn't with the convention," said Fifi.

Dr. Tensor was relieved. "Werble? You're not related to Arthur Werble, are you?"

"My father," I admitted.

"Why, your parents are patients of mine!"

Out of the corner of my eye I could see Judy shaking her head slowly. "I'd like you to meet the little lady," I said to the doctor. "Dear, this is my father's dermatologist."

"A pleasure," Judy said. "And a lovely coincidence. New York is like that. People you never expect to meet turn up. George, don't you think—"

She choked on her words as my finger jabbed her spine. Dr. Tensor was delighted by our encounter. He rubbed his hands together and smiled encouragingly. But I was determined that this relationship would go nowhere fast. After a few moments Dr. Tensor said, "I'm sure you were as happy as we were to learn that the little spot on your mother's cheek wasn't even precancerous."

I nodded.

"And your father's psoriasis is nicely under control now."

"I hope you have a great time in New York." I began to edge toward the elevators.

"We're planning on it. My wife Sally is going to do an article for the *Morrisburg Sentinel* on New York restaurants. Maybe you two would like to join us some evening."

"I'm so sorry," Judy said, "but we're only here for tonight. Tomorrow we take off for Paris."

"Kind of a second honeymoon," I said with a bashful grin as I squeezed Judy's hand affectionately.

When we were finally in the elevator, Judy said, "Caught again. Either you're very unlucky or Morrisburg is after you."

"It's not my parents I'm supposed to fool. It's my wife."

"Isn't she from Morrisburg too?"

"Only figuratively." A plaintive tone accidentally slipped into my voice.

"Ooh," Judy said in mock shock. "An almost personal remark from the Smooth One. Quite a day." She looked at me sternly. "Are you sure you've got your wife fooled?"

"She hasn't caught on yet."

"Maybe you should let her in on the gag. You don't have to prove anything to us."

"If you were my wife and I told you the truth about what we're doing, would you believe me?"

"Are you kidding? I'd kill you."

"You see? I'm stuck."

The bellhop awaited us at our door. He escorted us through our suiteful of histrionic luxury, pointing out the terry-cloth bathrobes, the complimentary perfumes and colognes, the authentic reproductions of eighteenth-century French furniture, the whirlpool bath, and the fresh flowers. Before he left he asked where we wanted our suitcase placed.

"Leave it there," Judy said. "I'll let my fingers do the lifting."

He was barely out the door when the phone rang. "Where have you been?" Gregory asked. "I've been frantic. The hotel wouldn't admit you checked in until a minute ago."

"Where are you?"

"I'm downstairs with Paul. He's got a lot of equipment."

"Well, divide up the equipment and come up one at a time. We're in Room 2327. I'll call the office and get everybody else here."

Gregory arrived in two minutes, carrying a case of Paul's lights, and Paul arrived soon after with another case. Gregory grabbed the room service menu. "Let me get my contribution over with as soon as possible. Look at this menu. How will I ever orchestrate a romantic interlude with food like this?"

"Romantic interlude!" Judy exclaimed. "Enid Malt says this is supposed to be a nice steamy tumble in the middle of the day."

"That's fine for steamy types like Enid," Gregory sniffed.

"But we've hired elegant models to model expensive clothes. I want the food to evoke a mood of erotic coldness, perverse detachment."

"That's romantic?"

"These days it's as close as one gets. Let's see what passes for nouvelle cuisine at this hotel."

"That's the spirit," Judy said. "There's nothing so coldly perverse as tiny piles of food on great big plates."

Soon there was a knock on the door and Cynthia Poly, our art director, came in. "Katrinka and Rusty are on their way up. I brought a few of their outfits with me. Toni is bringing the rest but she'll be a little late. The Armani clothes didn't arrive, so she's going to pick them up on her way here. But she said to get started."

"Okay," I said, "but we can't set up the lights until room service delivers." Gregory had been haranguing room service for the last five minutes.

There was a knock and Katrinka and Rusty arrived. Rusty looked wonderful; he nodded at us and smiled at his reflection in the mirror. Katrinka was another story. She was still basically beautiful, but on this day her face had a haggard, ravaged look that was hardly camera material.

"What happened to you?" Cynthia demanded.

"I went out dancing this morning."

"And you haven't slept? Very professional."

" 'Very professional, very professional,' " Katrinka echoed nastily. "Just give me a few minutes with my makeup and you'll get your lousy three hundred bucks per hour's worth. And somebody get me a drink."

"It's going to be a long afternoon for Toni and Cynthia," I whispered to Judy. "I'm glad I'm getting out of here at two o'clock. If you weren't the editor, you could leave too."

By the time the food arrived it already seemed like a long afternoon. I made everyone hide in the bathroom and dressing room. While the waiter set up the table, I could hear Katrinka hissing, "Don't push me, goddammit. I can't stand this pushing shit." When the waiter left we finally got to work. Paul and

Cynthia set up the lights; Rusty and Katrinka put on makeup; and Gregory sampled the food.

"What's the verdict, Gregory?" Judy asked.

"My theory was correct, but in practice . . . oh dear. I thought we should start with something sharp and pungent, to help our lovers forget their business problems. But the warm watercress salad is dressed far too sweetly. Then I went after a jaded, phlegmatic quality with nuggets of monkfish over slivers of jicama, but the sauce is insipid and the fish is overcooked. I'm going to send it all back and order again."

"We can't take down the lights and hide again," I said.

"You know, Gregory," Judy said, "it's almost one thirty. If our lovers actually ate their meal they'd have less than half an hour to make love. That's a little too phlegmatic. I think we should recommend that they bring their lunch with them."

"That's it!" Gregory said. "I know of the most exquisite little charcuterie that just opened. The owner used to be *sous-chef* at La Grande Tarte. I'll make up the perfect box lunch."

"*Déjeuner à l'hôtel* sounds a lot more romantic than 'nooner,' " Judy said. "The only thing our lovers will need from room service is a good bottle of wine."

"The wine! Where is the wine?" Gregory cried.

"There's the wine," Cynthia said.

The bottle was in Katrinka's hand. She had emerged from her dressing room transformed; the miracle of modern cosmetology had made her breathtaking again. "I look great, don't I? Absolutely fabulous. So I don't want to hear any more shit from any of you. Just keep off my case. And somebody get me a straw so I can drink the rest of this wine without smudging my lipstick."

"A straw!" Gregory shrieked. "That's a 1981 sparkling Vouvray sec. A wonderful wine. I must have a taste before it goes flat."

Katrinka glared at Gregory. "It tastes like sparkling dog piss to me." But she poured a small glass for Gregory, who pronounced it to be perfect.

"Let's get started," Cynthia said. "Toni wants Rusty in the Flusser and Katrinka in the Lagerfeld to start."

" 'Toni wants, Toni wants,' " sneered Katrinka. "Where is she, anyway? At least she knows what she's doing."

"I know what I'd like to do," Cynthia said, "but so far every model I've worked with has survived the experience."

Katrinka had us over a barrel. Since we had already shot the first feature using Rusty and Katrinka, it would be difficult to switch models in mid-affair. The jolly bunch finally got down to work, and we ran through several fashion changes. At one point Cynthia became so exasperated with Katrinka that rather than ask her to put on a funky little Kenzo jacket, Cynthia carefully draped it carelessly over a chair and told Paul to shoot it.

"Hey, I'm the goddamn model here. What is this shit?" Katrinka said.

"She made the choice between you and the chair on the basis of intelligence," Judy said.

"What's that, you stubby little twerp? Are you saying that I'm dumber than a chair?"

"But smarter than a newel post."

Things proceeded more or less on that level. Our efforts were accompanied by a background of Katrinka's mockery: "Pose, pose . . . stick your ass in . . . move your arm . . . stick your chin out . . . smile . . . don't smile . . . keep your hands off me . . . smile . . . raise your arm so you look like an idiot. . . ." Even Rusty's hermetic narcissism was pierced and he looked anxious every time Katrinka got near him.

"Just watch it, fatso," she said to Paul at one point. He had pulled a dresser up to the foot of the bed and was standing on it to shoot down at Katrinka, who was sprawled in a negligee next to Rusty, who wore only a discreetly draped sheet and a $2,500 watch.

There was a knock at the door.

"Toni, at last." Cynthia sighed in relief and ran to the door.

"Toni," screeched Katrinka, "it's about time we got a real pro here. These assholes are making me crazy with their stupid demands. Just get me off this bed before Fatso falls and crushes me. I swear this adultery idea is the stupidest—Who are *you?*"

Their shyness ever so slowly turned to suspicion, Dr. and Mrs.

Tensor stood in the doorway, searching for George Werble and his little lady.

"Join the party," Katrinka shouted. "Take off your clothes and make three hundred bucks per hour!"

The Tensors realized they were in the wrong room until they spotted me hiding behind an ashtray.

Mrs. Tensor nudged her husband, who said, "We . . . uh . . . brought this for you—champagne, you know . . ."

"Champagne!" Katrinka cried. As her negligee slipped off her shoulders, she leaped from the bed and grabbed the bottle.

". . . in honor of your second honeymoon."

I tried to thank them graciously. I started to introduce them to everyone in the room, but the sight of Paul's camera brought them to their senses: whatever our second honeymoon involved it wasn't going to involve them, and they hurriedly bowed out.

TWELVE

Although we had sheltered Irene during previous separations from Emerson, Helen and I had never before attended the reunion. Irene was on the porch that hot day when I brought Emerson home. As we emerged from the taxi, she bellowed and ran toward us. They threw themselves at each other with greedy enthusiasm. There were no apologies offered or requested, no charges or countercharges. Instead, a lot of fondling took place, successively, on the front lawn and the porch and in the living room, dining room, and kitchen. At each stage, Helen and I retreated to the next room, where we were soon joined by the ecstatic couple.

In the kitchen I whispered to Helen, "We better make our stand here. If we get too close to the bedroom they'll lose control completely."

But Irene and Emerson managed to find their own way to their bedroom while Helen and I improvised a celebratory dinner out of our haphazard larder: canned lobster bisque; three unfrozen little quiches; two guinea hens; a small steak with red wine sauce; two-bean-one-nut salad; and a choice of three pies that Irene had baked recently.

Emerson and Irene arrived at the table slightly dazed. Their eyes glistened and they appeared to be still out of breath. They were barely aware of the polyglut banquet set before them. Helen and I sat rigidly clutching our wineglasses. During the meal our guests acknowledged us mostly as mediums: "What do you think, George?" Emerson would say. "Has Irene put on a couple of pounds?" At that he affectionately stroked her neck.

"Tell us, Helen," Irene retorted happily, "do you think Emerson is in shape to speak to me that way?" She reached over and gently rubbed his belly.

"Maybe I should tell Irene about the job out in California," Emerson said to me.

"California! That could be great for us," Irene said. "We've spent so much time in cold midwestern places. Hey, have you guys ever been in one of those hot tubs?"

She said this to us as she winked at Emerson, who said, "Hot tubs; oh boy!" He squeezed Irene's arm and they both giggled. Helen and I stared at our plates.

"I've got a good idea for you, Emerson," I said. "You know all those drive-in churches out in California? Maybe you could get a whole bunch of hot tubs and people would come and sit in them while you preached."

For a second, Emerson looked thoughtful, but then he smiled. "You're kidding me. I can tell. But that's okay. I'm just too full of good feelings right now to get all riled up." He blew a kiss to Irene and they resumed pawing each other. After dessert, the happy couple disappeared upstairs again. I offered to help Helen with the dishes but she declared that they were her relatives and her dirty dishes. I retired to the West Wing.

Emerson and Irene's passion for each other remained at fever pitch for the next several weeks. Despite the embarrassments of living with a couple whose calmer moments could be reasonably described as foreplay, at least they had no time to think about the other couple, whose moments were all distant and restrained. Helen and I kept up a pretense of a relationship. The four of us frequently ate dinner together, and later we would assemble in the den to watch television. These postprandial gatherings rarely lasted more than half an hour before Emerson and Irene scrambled upstairs. Helen and I would sit tautly until the sounds of passion could be heard, and then we would quickly head for opposite ends of the house.

Helen and I acted as if nothing were going on because the lusty goings-on were too awkward to acknowledge. As moans and chortles wafted through the house, she couldn't very well turn to me and say, "Remember how you used to grunt like that?" Nor could I wonder if Emerson had elicited a distinctive peal of pleasure from Irene with the same little trick that I had once employed to elicit an almost identical cry from Helen.

Our feelings broke through one Sunday afternoon. Just as we were finishing brunch, Irene said to Emerson, "There's a little piece of smoked salmon by the corner of your mouth. Here, let me get it." She leaned over and flicked it up with her tongue. "And maybe there's another piece here, and here, and oh, here's another little piece." *Flick, flick, flick.* Emerson and Irene excused themselves, pausing on the stairs to rev their motors before racing on to their next pit stop.

Helen and I looked at each other furtively.

"Don't you think," I said, "that you could at least ask Irene to close the door to their bedroom?"

"I have. I've asked several times."

There was a certain urgent agitation in her voice, as there was in mine. We had been married long enough to know what that tone meant. It would not be the first time since our separation that we had acted on urgency; it would be the third. (But who's counting?)

"Succumb again?" I said.

I guess I seized the moment a little flippantly, for Helen shook her head emphatically. "No way." She hurried out of the room.

It was easy for her to decline, I thought resentfully, since she had her political campaign to absorb her excess excitement. My job was more nervous-making than consuming these days and I had nothing else to temper my energy. Well . . . I suppose masturbation *could* be considered a form of sublimation. It would not be the first time, either, since our separation. (But who's counting?) I at least had the good taste not to start things in the dining room. I went directly to my bedroom without even pausing on the stairs. *And* I shut my door.

Helen's fortunes as a political kingmaker had gotten off to a slow start. Al Brubaker's plan to reposition their candidate Bud

Horner as a tough hands-on manager of money didn't take hold. Their slogan, "He'll mind the store," was okay unless one had first-hand knowledge of the semi-chaotic organization of Bud's service station. I would guess at least 17 percent of all eligible voters in Finchmont had at one time or another stood at Bud's office to pay a bill while Bud shuffled through grease-stained stacks of invoices, purchase orders, and miscellaneous scraps. After a while Bud would usually look up and say, "Well, how does twenty-five bucks sound?" The first time I took my car to Bud someone warned me, "Just don't turn your back on him." I took this to be a euphemistic way of telling me that he was untrustworthy until I turned my back on Bud and he placed a friendly but very greasy hand on my cashmere sweater.

Out of boredom I attended some of Helen's election committee meetings. I would sit in the corner snickering and whispering with Sara, my ten-year-old friend from next door. Sara was allowed to come to the meetings because she was the only volunteer besides Helen who did much work; she stuffed envelopes and stapled posters to telephone poles with such earnest dedication that Helen was unable to mention to her that the posters had been affixed at a height which could only be read by other ten-year-olds. The strategizing at these meetings was dominated by Al Brubaker. Although he spoke at great length, he held himself apart—a slightly condescending consultant whose suggestions could not be faulted since they would never be followed efficiently.

Bud's deficiencies as a candidate were strikingly evident at the first Candidates' Night held by the League of Women Voters in the high school auditorium. All nine candidates for the five council posts were invited to speak. Four candidates were incumbents and considered shoo-ins. Three other candidates represented such fringes as antivivisection, pro casino gambling, and a libertarian who wanted to abolish the town council, property taxes, and the police department. That left Bud to face off against Andrew Hoyle for the fifth post. Hoyle was a stocky, prissy man with wet lips who taught biology at the high school. His slogan, "According to Hoyle," was obvious, but he actually had the officious quality of someone who makes a fetish out of playing by the rules. Hoyle addressed the voters in a vigorous, nasal tone about the needs of Finchmont. It was just the sort of speech that the old Bud Horner had given, except that Bud's presentation had always been duller, vaguer, and much more rambling.

The new Bud Horner scanned the audience nervously. He didn't begin speaking until Al Brubaker nodded, and then, in a herky-jerky manner, he started to punch the air, pound the podium, and declaim. Every time he got a little too carried away he would stop and look shocked, as if he had frightened himself. It seemed to me that Bud's speech said much the same things that Hoyle's did, but Bud's manner was so extraordinary that one lost track of his ideas. So did Bud, and he had to pause several times to locate his place in the speech. No one but Helen and her committee applauded when he was finished.

Bud's failure was followed by a number of uneasy committee meetings as his supporters wrestled with his "lack of viability," as Al Brubaker put it. Helen had certainly done her part; there were posters of Bud all over town and she had gotten plenty of endorsements from notable locals. But the repositioned Bud was taking hold no better than the old one. Al Brubaker persuaded the committee to switch to a "high-concept" campaign, which meant, he explained, that they needed to inflate a big issue which would soar off, bearing Bud Horner to victory despite his leaden personality.

"Now if Bud were a package-goods product," Al said with a tone of disappointment in his voice, "we would do some market research—opinion polls, focus groups—to find out what concept would work. But here in Finchmont our market is just too small to get statistically confident answers. As I see it, and of course I'm only hypothesizing here, we're going to have to fly by the seat of our pants. It's a risk, but I'm assuming there's no downside, because when you're losing you've got nothing to lose. Let's get some trial balloons in the air."

The first balloon was Helen's discovery that two cellos and a new piano had been quietly excised from the high school's budget. Bud was outraged at this insult to the arts, but Hoyle, who knew the proper place of the arts in a high school, announced that the only alternative was to cancel the order for two new goal posts and a blocking sled for the football team: "Is that what Bud Horner wants to do?" The Committee to Elect Bud Horner licked its wounds and looked to another issue.

"That Al Brubaker is pretty bright," I said to Helen one evening. "Is he married?"

"Yes, he's happily married."

"By answering my question instead of my very obvious implication, you've left me wondering."

"You're really impossible sometimes, George. But don't get your hopes up. There's nothing going on between me and Al. Nothing. And there's something else I want to tell you. Stop coming to my committee meetings. You're a bad influence on Sara. I really need her help now. Since Emerson arrived, Irene has been no help at all. I thought you might make some real contribution to the campaign, but all we get are supercilious comments that only you and Sara think are funny."

"I'm sorry. I thought politics was supposed to take place in joke-filled rooms."

One Sunday night Irene and Emerson scampered off to their revels unusually early, after which Helen immediately made her escape. Alone again, I retired to my room and drifted off into an unreveled sleep of care in which Helmut pursued me through a number of bad dreams. I awoke at one thirty and decided that a few offerings to my stomach might appease my fretful mind.

I crept down the back staircase to the kitchen. As I was constructing my crabmeat and avocado sandwich, I heard the sounds of someone else about. At moments like these one's sense of fear (the strangler! the burglar! call the police!) contends with one's sense of embarrassment (sorry, officer; it was only my stupid brother-in-law). So knife in hand I followed the sound through the dining room and into the living room.

From where I stood I could see into the den, and there I saw

Emerson. He was dressed in a billowing white nightshirt and, illuminated by the ghastly light of soundless television, he was engaged in a peculiar form of dance. He spun and writhed, froze for a moment, and whirled again, flinging an arm beseechingly to the heavens. He had appropriated a small figurine, an art nouveauish nude, from the coffee table and he clutched it in one hand and occasionally passed it from hand to hand, almost throwing it back and forth. Then he would lift the figurine to his lips and whisper to her passionately but unintelligibly. It dawned on me that none of Emerson's mental faculties had tenure.

Normally this is the sort of scene from which one discreetly retreats, but curiosity and my need for distraction prevailed. I put down the knife and cleared my throat. Emerson practically jumped out of his nightshirt.

"It's only me, Emerson," I reassured him.

He peered into the dark living room. "Hey, George, you almost sent me to my maker a few years ahead of schedule."

"Were you having trouble sleeping?" I was unable to bring myself to refer directly to his behavior, but Emerson got the point.

He smiled sheepishly. "I guess I must of looked pretty strange. Come on in the den here and I'll explain. I'm just practicing. I haven't been able to do much preaching lately, and I didn't want to lose my touch. See this guy here?" Emerson motioned to the television, where I saw a preacher plying his trade in a huge auditorium. "I taped him earlier tonight. If you turn the sound down you can concentrate on body language. He's got great moves. And watch his microphone work." As Emerson swung the figurine around in correspondence to the television image, I realized that she was a microphone substitute. "You know, George, the closer you get your mouth to the mike, the closer you seem to your audience. It's like your mouth is right up against them breathing the word of God into them. Spiritual resuscitation, I call it. But you also have to use the mike like a prop. Look at that guy! Behind the back smooth as silk. Where's the replay button? I want to see that again in slow motion."

With the critical detachment of football coaches, we watched the preacher run through his behind-the-back move three more times. Emerson then tried the move and, with a few hints from me, he finally got it right.

"Do you have much need for microphones?" I asked. "I thought that most of your churches have been pretty cozy."

"You're right, George, but maybe I'm too ambitious for these diddly little congregations. I still think I can make it real big. I've been doing some planning for a project I'm going to call the Emerson Miller Crusade. It'll be a great show! There'll be music and singing. I like a quartet myself—fresh innocent faces and blond hair, all harmonizing on some great hymn. I'll have lots of plants on the stage to give it a homey, natural look. Also, you need an assistant minister—somebody real sincere but not too exciting since I'm the main event. And then I'd get some old broken-down actress who used to be well known. And she'll come on and tell everyone how she threw away her career because she was promiscuous or drank or took drugs. But now she's found happiness through Emerson Miller. Check that: through *Jesus* through me. And we're going to travel around in our own bus. Maybe *two* buses. Maybe our own airplane when we get real big."

"Sounds good," I said. "If that's all it takes, why haven't you launched your crusade?"

Emerson shook his head. "There's a lot of competition these days. You need something special. I got into school prayer ahead of everybody and if it hadn't been for that janitor I would have really made it. And I almost got it rolling in Fergus Falls, but you know it's not such a big deal these days to get people to speak in tongues. No, I need a new signature, something that will distinguish Emerson Miller from every other preacher who has two buses and a reformed Hollywood slut."

"Something tells me that the new and improved model of Emerson Miller is ready to make its appearance."

Emerson smiled eagerly. "You've got to promise you won't tell anybody."

"You're the only preacher I know."

"Not even Irene."

"I promise."

"Okay, here it is: I'm getting into faith healing."

"Oh come on. Didn't that go out of style a long time ago? Nobody believes in that stuff anymore."

"You'd be surprised. But I've got a new twist. Something that's going to make me famous."

"I'm almost afraid to ask."

Emerson looked directly into my eyes. "I know what people like you think about faith healing. You think, one, that it's a fake. Or two, that people think they're cured when they're not. Or three, that people who do get cured really had psychosomatic illnesses to begin with. Am I right?"

"I haven't thought about it much, but those seem like three pretty good reasons for you to forget about this whole idea."

"Now George, I want you to take me seriously."

It was hard to take seriously somebody who was wearing a nightshirt and holding a nude figurine.

"Here's my idea, George. Aside from the outright fakes, the other two points make it clear that the mind is the most important element in faith healing. Right?"

"Right."

"So don't you see?"

"It's late and I'm tired."

"George, the Lord is telling me that he wants me to cure mental disease. That's where faith healing works. Why fight it? My job is to focus God's energy where it will do the most good. I'm not going to even try to cure anybody's body. But if they've got a problem in their head, that's where my faith healing will work."

"Can you be a little more specific? Are we talking neuroses or full-blown schizophrenia?"

"I'll show you how my idea works in good time, but I need to do some more research before I roll it out."

I wasn't sure what Emerson had in mind, but I was sure that

whatever it was I didn't want him doing it while he was living with me.

By her own account, it was Sara who finally got Bud Horner's campaign untracked. As she described it, her inspiration came one evening as she, along with the rest of the Committee to Elect Bud Horner Councilperson, sat in our living room comparing videotapes of Bud's and Hoyle's performances at the first Candidates' Night. According to Emerson, even if they couldn't get Bud to speak more forcefully, his body language could convey a stronger message. The Committee thought this was a great idea; surely any theory that combined psychology and electronics had to be good. They quickly discovered that Hoyle's body spoke in a clipped, staccato manner while Bud's body stuttered. But translating theory to practice proved difficult. Once Bud got a look at himself, his sense of inadequacy became a conviction and he was unable to rephrase his body.

The Committee had hit a mood of almost total resignation and Bud's self-image had assumed a fetal position, when Sara's ears pricked up. Someone had turned the television's sound back up and there was Hoyle declaring that he was uniquely equipped to guide Finchmont into the twenty-first century. At first Sara thought he was referring to his state of good health but no, he was making a pointed distinction between Hoyle the professional scientist and Bud the semiprofessional mechanic. Hoyle pointed to computers as an example of a technology that once seemed exotic but now was almost commonplace. "I've had a home computer for five years; I wonder if my worthy opponent even has an electric typewriter." Showing off, Hoyle went on to speak of genetic engineering as a strange technology to the layperson, but within a few years, he predicted, his students would be performing recombinant DNA experiments right there in Finchmont High School just as easily as they now dissected frogs.

Then Sara's brainstorm struck. "Oh, yuck. Those experiments are weird. If they do that in high school, we're in big trouble. I saw this movie once about this creepy scientist named Lothar who mixes his pig genes and rabbit genes which grow into these real disgusting animals. Anyway, Lothar hears about these explorers who find a dinosaur, a *Tyrannosaurus rex*, frozen in the arctic ice. So Lothar steals some of the genes from the dinosaur and he mixes them with the genes of a guy who's in prison for murdering prostitutes. And then Lothar grows this horrible dinosaurman with big teeth who escapes and starts to eat up most of the prostitutes in Los Angeles. Anyway, there's this real beautiful policewoman and she has to disguise herself as a prostitute in order to catch—"

"Just a sec," Helen said, her eyes narrowing. "Did Hoyle actually say that he's planning to do these experiments in the high school?"

"Well, uh," Bud said, "I think he was speaking figuratively."

"Maybe that's what *he* thought but it's not what anybody else is going to think. Al, at last we've got a big issue."

"What a fabulous idea," Al said.

"Hey, it was my idea," Sara said, who was beginning to learn how committees operate.

And so, at the second Candidates' Night, Bud challenged Hoyle on this point, summoning up a vision of legions of lethal viruses which would lay waste the high school football team, run amuck in the village, and then sweep south to devastate New York City.

Hoyle denied that he had any specific intention to teach genetic engineering in the high school. No one, he declared, would try anything like that unless it were perfectly safe.

"And how are we supposed to know when it's safe?" Bud asked, his voice dribbling with sarcasm. "Your . . . um . . . kind just expect us to accept your word that everything's okay. Well, that's not good enough. I want all . . . everyone to—uh—to know that my first act as—you know—councilperson will be . . . "—he looked over at Helen, who egged him on with a clenched fist—"to propose an ordinance which bans all these experiments in the high school. Oh yes, and in the rest of the Village too."

At this point Hoyle made his big mistake. Instead of caving in and agreeing with Bud—so the issue would go away—Hoyle declared that he was a professional scientist and educator and that any law censoring his ability to teach or perform such techniques would be the equivalent of book burning.

At that, Helen and her committee threw the meeting into an uproar by chanting, "Don't be a fool, don't pollute the genetic pool." When the din subsided, Bud went on to caricature Hoyle as Dr. Strangelove. The issue did wonders for Bud's rhetorical abilities; even his pauses seemed to be more authoritative.

Perhaps the right to produce designer genes in high school is worth a fight, but in the days that followed, Hoyle's integrity bordered on the perverse. Not only did he refuse to back down, he even incited his students to fight for their right to splice, which only enraged their parents. It was an issue made for Finchmont's pretensions. Every meaningful problem was forgotten as the town excitedly discussed the Big Issue. Even the *New York Times* had a little feature: WESTCHESTER TOWN DIVIDED OVER GENETIC EXPERIMENTS.

As the momentum swung in Bud's direction, Helen was transformed into a driving, possessed campaigner. She wore her exhaustion like a badge of honor. When she was at home her new politico's voice, hoarse and insistent, could be heard throughout the house. I had never known her to shout on the telephone at anyone besides her own family. But she wasn't home very much. I often encountered her when I arrived home as she was racing out, a jumble of papers clutched to her breast. On several occasions, however, she returned home in midevening with her taut, tired features relaxed and a glow in place of her pallor. I began to wonder. . . .

My vanity told me that the only way she could have turned down my proposition the other night was if she were having an affair. There were other clues. Finchmont is a small town; the election couldn't consume all the time Helen was putting in. And Helen glowed most visibly at eight fifteen on weekday evenings—just about the time a happily married man like Al Brubaker would get home after working late at the office.

I had almost no doubts. After all, the man who invented the Fashionable Affair should be able to recognize the signs. I even took a rather technical interest in Helen's affair. I wondered where they went and what excuses Al gave to his wife. Finchmont's size made subterfuge quite difficult.

My last doubts were dispelled one evening when I answered a phone call for Al Brubaker from a woman.

"He's not here, I'm afraid."

"Oh. What time did the meeting break up?"

"I think just a couple of minutes ago. I don't hear anyone speaking downstairs anymore."

"Then I guess he'll be home in a few minutes. Thanks."

But there had been no meeting at our house that evening. I had covered for my wife's lover.

One Saturday afternoon Helen came back from the shopping center with a car full of groceries. As soon as she pulled into the driveway there was a phone call for her. I unloaded the car while Helen was on the phone. Even allowing for the calories that Emerson and Irene were burning up in bed, there seemed to be a rather large number of groceries. An hour later I glanced out of my window above the driveway and saw Helen loading the groceries back into the car.

"What's the matter?" I called. "Are you returning everything?"

"Oh no. It's just that these aren't all for us. They're for a pot-luck supper we're having to raise money for Bud."

"I thought that pot luck meant that everybody had to contribute."

"Yes, but you know how people are. Some of them never bring what they promise. I have to make sure there's enough."

"I see."

What I didn't see was why Helen felt obliged to contribute toilet paper, laundry detergent, and toothpaste to the pot-luck supper. I surmised that Helen and Al had found a little nest somewhere and were stocking it.

I waited by my window until Helen finished reloading the car. About half an hour later she got into the car and drove away. It was two fifty so I figured she had a date to meet Al nearby at three. It was worth a try. I hurried downstairs and got on my bicycle. There were enough stoplights to give me a fighting chance to keep up with Helen if she didn't head for a highway.

After some furious pedaling I saw Helen turn onto Ronkers Road, a shopping area that had been eclipsed in the last two years by a new shopping center on the other side of town. One knows a shopping area has lost its cachet when its stores and shops become "outlets." I had to dodge a lot of traffic entering and leaving outlets for foam rubber, discount stereo, dinette sets, and factory rejects. Near the end of Ronkers Road Helen signaled for a right turn. To my surprise, she turned into the Moonglow Motel, whose proud motto, "Color TV in Every Room," towered high above Ronkers Road. There were only a couple of cars at the Moonglow, and Helen pulled up next to one parked at the rear of the motel.

I paused in the parking lot of the business next door to the Moonglow, a fast-food restaurant called Mr. & Mrs. Beef, while I figured things out. There was Helen, getting lots of pot luck in the motel; what did she need the groceries for? Mr. and Mrs. Werble were separately gripped by the two most basic biological urges; mine unfortunately was intense curiosity. I decided to eat a Bullburger. The restaurant was empty except for the proprietors, Mr. and Mrs. Beef themselves. I found a seat with a good view of the Moonglow and ate my Bullburger. After half an hour I ordered a Calfburger. Forty-five minutes later, as I was ordering some french fries, Mr. Beef said to Mrs. Beef, "Uh-oh, they're here. I better go change."

A birthday party of eleven eight-year-old boys arrived and proceeded to eat, throw, and spit a small herd of cattle. Unfortunately there was no other vantage point on the motel and I had to endure the shooting straws, breaking balloons, and Coca-Cola geysers. Soon Mr. Beef emerged dressed in a bull costume. The boys shrieked and pelted him with french fries and squirted him with ketchup. He seemed to take it in good humor until one of the boys got a rope around his horns and tied him to the door of the ladies' room.

All told it was nearly two hours before the door Helen had entered opened again. Al Brubaker must have torn himself away from his household chores; I was pleased to see that in overalls he hardly looked like a successful marketing man, much less someone who had just had a lubricious afternoon. (Okay, I admit it; I *was* a little jealous.)

He went to Helen's car and began to remove her groceries and load them into his car. It took a few seconds before I understood what a masterful stratagem I was witnessing: He had called Helen and given her his shopping list; Helen bought his groceries; he told his wife he was going out to do the shopping. Two hours later he would bring home the bacon. As long as no one got sick from spoiled or refrozen food, Al was home free. My jealousy gave way to professional admiration; I would have to think about persuading Judy to use this ploy in the Fashionable Affair. Well done, I thought, as he went back into the room. A few minutes later Helen drove off.

As I left Mr. & Mrs. Beef, several of the boys followed me out. They had tied several balloons to a Bullburger and were intending to launch their beefcraft over Finchmont. I was unlocking my bicycle when I saw Al get into his car. He sat in the car for several minutes and I grew worried. Had the boys attracted his attention so that he spotted me in his rearview mirror? He got out of the car again and slammed the door in anger. He went to the hood and opened it. I was relieved but, for some peculiar reason, I was also concerned for Al: his best-planned lay was going astray. He peered under the hood and then stepped back with his hands on his hips as if his engine were foreign territory to him. It was then that I was at last able to peer through my fog of preconceptions and see the truth. It wasn't Al standing there with his hands on his hips. It was Bud Horner.

PART 4

THIRTEEN

Bud Horner? Bud Horner! Bud Horner?

For days after the discovery of Helen's inamorato, my thought patterns resembled Bud's speech patterns—stunned and halting. It was the sort of implacable fact which refused to yield to any useful construction; it sat before me in mute repudiation, fraught with meaningfulness while I had not a clue to what it meant. After much brooding I did have one thought of a rather low order of insight: To have an affair with someone like Bud, Helen really had to love the guy. I mean he was hardly a likely candidate for an affair of the skin or a reckless fling. No, a relationship with a Bud either was deeply important or it wasn't a relationship. What was it, I wondered, that Helen saw in him? Could it be his . . . his very *Budness* that she loved? Oh, perversity beyond perversity! I imagined myself confronting Helen and saying, "What doesn't he have that I do?"

The mind is indeed a wonderful organ. Without even squeezing the considerable mental space set aside for Helmut, my Bud-and-Helen ruminations moved right in and claimed squatters' rights too. I was amazed at how difficult it was to evict Bud and Helen from my thoughts. It wasn't because I was jealous—at least I had no palpable sense of anger or privation—but it was surely more than idle curiosity that disturbed my concentration day after day. I finally had to admit I had a problem, but I still didn't know what it was. There weren't many people in my life to whom I could turn for advice. At last I asked Frankie to come by my office one afternoon.

"Would you believe this place!" Frankie said. "It looks like your one-piece-of-paper-on-the-desk style has been forgotten. Your office is almost messy."

"I hadn't realized," I said, "but you're right." My chrome and glass coffee table had vanished beneath an assortment of papers, magazines, and newspapers. There was a stack of file folders on one of my Barcelona chairs and, in the pot where my defoliated ficus stood shivering, a pen, the lid from a takeout coffee cup, several wadded memos, and a number of twisted paper clips had accumulated. Although my desk was hardly buried in paper, it was a far cry from the sterile obsessive look I had specialized in at Schaefer.

"Don't worry. It's okay," Frankie said. "The place looks almost human now."

"Thanks a lot."

"Hey, are you all right? You look a little ragged."

"There's something on my mind. But you have to promise—"

"You shouldn't have to ask. Your secret is safe. Sit down here and tell me."

I did. My account was punctuated by Frankie's astonishments: "Helen?" "A motel?" "Your mechanic?" "Holy shit!"

"So what's the big problem?" Frankie said when I finished. "Now you've got leverage. Maybe you can keep three quarters of your house."

"The thing is, I can't get the two of them out of my mind. But I swear it's not jealousy."

"Maybe you're embarrassed."

"Embarrassed?"

"You know, that your wife in name only, who you thought at least had enough good taste to live with you, is making it with a schmuck like this mechanic. Does that make you a schmuck too?"

"I don't think that's it."

"Okay, how about this? You've got a lot on your mind now and you're just a little depressed."

"No, I'm from the Midwest. We don't get a little depressed. Either everything's fine or we go to the roof of a building with a rifle and pick people off."

"Try to be practical, then. What are you going to do about Bud and Helen?"

"I don't know. I don't want to do anything. Should I want to do something?"

Frankie sighed. "I don't think we're getting anywhere. You know who's really great with these kind of problems? Judy Gruber. She's helped me a lot. She sees through all the bullshit and gets right to the nitty-gritty."

"The farther away she stays from my gritty, the better it will be for all of us. I'm the boss here. I've got to maintain a certain dignity and detachment."

"Dignity! Your little event at the Malmaison sure elevated you in the minds of your employees."

"You have a point. But I also think Judy would be pretty angry to find out that I'm separated from Helen after I told everybody that the Fashionable Affair was a *real* test for me. No, I don't want her to know about my problem."

"Problems."

"Problems. Besides, I'm going to get my revenge on her for the Malmaison. For the next installment of the Affair we're going to go to the Allegro Hotel."

"She'll kill you when she finds out what kind of a place it is."

I winked at Frankie. "Been there lately?"

"As a matter of fact, no. And you? You used to get a lot of use out of the place."

"Not lately. But I'll always be grateful to you for telling me about the best—"

"Yeah, but maybe you could do me a favor and forget I ever told you," Frankie said. "I wouldn't want everyone around here to know that I was once a regular customer at the Allegro."

"I thought you didn't care what people thought about you."

"Things are changing for me. My life as an impulse item has come to an end. Okay?"

"Your secret is safe with me."

"Speaking of hotels," Frankie said as she left, "don't forget that you, me, and Bob are going to inspect the Unity Hotel on Thursday. It's perfect for the Institute."

Despite Frankie's efforts, the happy couple were still honeymooning in my mind. Bud seemed like such a bizarre choice for Helen that I wasn't even disappointed in myself for not catching on. If Helen and I had been sleeping together, I'm sure I would have noticed some little clues—greasy handprints on her body or transmission fluid on her bra. But to *imagine* such a thing without a telltale hint? Impossible. In a whimsy, I tried to picture the couple in the throes of passion, their limbs flailing, Bud murmuring tenderly, "Let's see, if I put this there . . . uhh, no . . . that's not going to work . . . maybe I'll put my hand . . . no, maybe a little higher . . . um, let's try your leg this way . . . there, I guess we've got it, now start her up."

I suppose if I were able to resist such whimsies I might be better at figuring out what things like my nearly ex-wife having an affair with my mechanic did mean to me. And if I could get a leg up on that first *personal* rung of meaning, why then I might scramble right to the top rung and worry about What It All Means, which is why whimsy can be so useful in today's complicated world.

It appeared that the Institute for Lifestyle Arts, George Werble, Prop., had found a home. After exploring every hill, dale, and beach within an eighty-mile radius of New York, Frankie and Bob located a resort in the Catskills that had recently overexpanded and was accessible to the city (our major market) by train, bus, and car in seventy-five minutes. All that remained was for me to inspect the hotel, take a deep breath, and launch the Institute.

With that prospect in the offing, I had no choice but to take the initiative with Helmut. I couldn't keep the Institute a secret, but I would downplay it. I practiced getting a serious professional tone in my voice so I could say, "We're testing a new concept, Mr. Gernschaft," without making him too interested. There's nothing so earnestly professional in marketing as the Test, despite the fact that successful tests of exciting concepts usually precede the rollout of unpalatable products. It did me good to think about taking the initiative with Helmut. After weeks of dithering I was ready to move.

As I dialed Helmut, my spirits actually soared, for once one takes the first step, the next step is but a step away. After three minutes on hold, while I listened to Strauss's "Last Songs," my spirits deflated a little, though Helmut's secretary kept assuring me that he would pick up the phone momentarily. When he finally got on he said, "You know, I had just made up my mind that I was going to call you. We must be, as they say, on the same vibration."

Somehow my initiative had been appropriated. In my mind's eye I could see myself glancing over my shoulder, as if to assure myself that the foxhole from which I had just emerged was still there.

"What's up, Mr. Gernschaft?"

"Are you alone?"

"Yes." I began to edge back toward the foxhole.

"Are you sitting down?"

I ran back to the foxhole and dove in. "Yes," I quavered, "sitting right here and looking at a picture of Gretel."

Helmut chuckled. Then there was a long pause. He chuckled again. I cautiously peeked out of the foxhole. Maybe this was another little joke of Helmut's. "Tell me, George, have you ever eaten at a restaurant called Uncle Tonnato's?"

No joke.

I looked around the foxhole for a shovel. Maybe I could tunnel out.

"You are a naughty boy, I think." Helmut burst into a huge gale of giggles. "Yes, a naughty boy."

I'm glad I was too shell-shocked to do something stupid like deny ever having heard of Uncle Tonnato's. In fact there was something oddly encouraging about Helmut's laughter and his coy tone. I put my shovel down.

"I want to assure you, George, I understand such things. We are busy men. Our wives are busy women. Sometimes it is necessary to have a relief, an oasis, a special relationship."

This was all right. I began to climb out of the foxhole again.

"Perhaps I make you feel awkward, no?" Helmut said. "But in Europe such relationships are accepted as part of civilized behavior. I think it is the right of a busy executive. Do you agree?"

I hadn't exercised these rights lately but I was hardly going to argue. "I definitely agree." The smoke was lifting from the battlefield. As I walked happily across no-man's-land toward Helmut, I thought, We're going to be pals. Helmut and I have put our relationship on a new and frank basis. The hell with you, Larry Roth. And good-bye, Gretel. I don't need you anymore.

"In Europe," Helmut went on, "it is even considered proper to entertain for business with one's mistress. So, George, the two of us will go out together sometime with our mistresses. I know you agree that would be a jolly thing to do."

As soon as I was back in the foxhole, it began to fill up with water. But I couldn't climb out because Helmut was now lobbing grenades such as: "We will have a date next week. Thursday. Maybe we will all go to Uncle Tonnato's, where we first met." He giggled. He was having a fine time.

"Very busy next week," I called out and ducked.

"Then the week after. On Thursday. That is the night that Alicia and I always have together."

"That's the week I'll be at the convention."

"Of course. And Alicia and I have tickets for a play the following week. So it will have to be four weeks from this Thursday."

"We don't have a regular night. I'll have to check with my . . . my . . ." Words failed me.

"Oh you Americans. You have such love of surprises and improvisations. I am so stodgy with my regular schedule. When we are all together, you will teach Alicia and me to behave more freely. So we are agreed—four weeks from Thursday." He hung up.

I thumbed back through my calendar. There it was: Judy and I had visited Uncle Tonnato's on a Thursday. I started to call Cynthia Poly but thought better of it. I had to be careful. I called Frankie. "Remember that photo with Helmut looking at Judy and me?"

"*I* remember it. You're the one who's pretending to forget."

"Do me a favor and bring it to me. But don't let anyone see you."

"Here we go again. Just like when I smuggled the copy of LIFESTYLE to you back at Schaefer."

At the moment it wasn't a fond memory.

When Frankie arrived I said, "Have you been discreet?"

"I haven't told anyone that the head of Schaefer Communications saw you guys making a ridiculous scene at a restaurant. But I feel real guilty about hiding it from Judy. Don't forget, Helmut saw her too. And she's been so supportive of me."

I bared my teeth.

"I'll keep your secret. Why do you want to see this photo? Did the shit hit the fan?"

I described my conversation with Helmut.

Frankie failed to appreciate the seriousness of my position. "Hey, Helmut's got quite a spiffy number here. She's about three feet taller than he is."

"Let me see." Alicia was attractive.

"Why didn't you tell Helmut that you had broken up with your girlfriend?" Frankie asked.

"I was too amazed by his proposal to think that fast."

"I've got an idea," Frankie said. "You have to talk Judy into going on a date with you."

"Come on, Frankie. Can you really imagine Judy doing anything like that? Especially as a favor to me?"

"She doesn't hate you. Really."

"Maybe, but I've noticed that as the rest of the staff has warmed up to me lately, she seems to be cooling off."

"No way. She even said something nice about you the other day."

"What?"

"We were comparing the relative merits of the men on the staff. And after we got through your personal qualities, I told her that I thought you were very good-looking."

"I get it. After she said that I have no personal qualities, you said, 'At least he's good-looking.' Did she agree?"

"She said, 'If you like that type.' "

"Now there's a strong endorsement. Anyone who likes me that much is going to be a big help with Helmut."

"Wait a minute. I stuck up for your beauty so she finally said, 'I can't decide if he's a handsome average-looking man or an average-looking handsome man.' That's not bad."

"That's what I don't like about her. You can't win. She's always got some remark that keeps you off balance. I wouldn't trust her to help us."

"Then what are you going to do?"

"I'm probably going to wait until a few days before the date and tell him that we broke up."

"That doesn't sound very convincing."

"I know. Maybe I'll think of a better excuse in the meantime."

"See you in the morning," Frankie said.

Frankie and Bob were supposed to pick me up at 7:00 A.M. on our way to inspect the Unity Hotel. They had not arrived when I checked my watch at 7:07 and again at 7:27. I checked through the whole Boeing fleet until they showed up at 8:07 (7:67). They were barely apologetic for their tardiness.

"We didn't want to call so early and wake everybody up," Frankie said. "Bob was unavoidably detained."

"Unavoidably detained," Bob echoed happily.

The prospect of a jaunt in the country had put the two of them in a good mood. I was myself rather happy to escape the ringing of the phone and the clenching of the heart for several hours. Bob and I each politely insisted on driving until Frankie settled matters by parking herself behind the wheel and ordering me into the front and Bob into the back.

"What a beautiful day!" Bob said. "You know, Frankie, when George sees the place he's going to think, 'Gosh, that Bob and Frankie have done a job. They've found just the sort of place to put LIFESTYLE on the map."

"And wait till you hear about the deal we've cooked up," Frankie said.

"I hope George recognizes how hard it is to find a good place," Bob said. "You know, you hear about a place and you call them up and say, 'Sir, here is a list of our requirements for the Institute of Lifestyle Arts.' Then he says, 'I've got a place that fits the bill perfectly. And it's pretty as a picture.' So you go and look at it and then you say, 'I'm afraid the picture we had in mind wasn't taken by Walker Evans. And broken windows are not our idea of air conditioning. No, we don't think our guests should bring their own sheets, blankets, and towels. And a Pizza Palace on Route Twenty-five that will deliver is not our idea of room service.' "

Bob rattled on for a while, but gradually his voice grew heavy and when I looked back he was asleep.

"You know that problem you were telling me about," Frankie whispered. "I spoke to Judy about it."

"What! I thought I told you—"

"Don't worry. I didn't tell her it was you. I told her I had this friend who was separated from his wife for a long time and now she's going out with some guy and it bothers my friend even though he's not jealous. But he doesn't know why it bothers him."

"If she figures out that it's me—"

"No way. She asked me what else was going on in my friend's life and I said I didn't know and she said, 'Maybe there's nothing going on. Maybe he sees his wife getting on with her life and he's not going anywhere.' "

"That's just the kind of thing she would say to annoy me."

"She didn't know it was you."

"Besides, there's too much going on in my life. That's my problem."

"You'll cheer up when you see the hotel."

After an hour we were in farm country, and twenty minutes later we drove through the town of Moteville. I found its typicalness encouraging. Moteville boasted two antique shops (one shop and one shoppe); one store which sold postcards and tacky tourist stuff; the Genuine New York City Authentic Deli; and the appropriate complement of sullen natives.

"The bus stops here," Frankie said, pointing to the tacky tourist store, "and the Unity is only five miles away. There's a cab company in town that will give us a special rate to run a shuttle from here and from the train station to the hotel."

"See, we've got everything lined up," Bob said.

We took a small road from Moteville and soon we came to an arrow-shaped sign for the Unity that directed us down a quiet tree-lined lane. And there it was, a classic example of the Wood-frame Sprawling Heap, circa 1920. But with its new roof, a fresh coat of paint—white with green trim—and a wide and welcoming porch which meandered around its periphery, the Unity Hotel sparkled in the sunlight like a delicious promise. When we got out of the car, the country concerto of bird calls, cicada buzzes, and cricket chirps hit us.

"So far so good," I said.

"The guy who owns it inherited it from his parents," Frankie said. "It was pretty run-down. But he got some money together and renovated it. He added a new wing with meeting rooms so he can sell the hotel as a conference center for corporations or else to groups like us. In fact he had a deal for the summer with a chamber music festival, but it fell through because the renovations took too long."

"But it's all finished now," Bob said.

Several elderly men and women sat on the porch in rocking chairs. They rocked slowly and regarded us calmly. They too looked so typical that I must have smiled patronizingly because one man spoke up. "We're geezers and we're proud of it."

The others rocked a little faster.

"Is Mr. Martin Preston in his office?" Frankie asked.

"Who?" said a woman. She turned to her cohorts. "They're asking us if we got a Martin Preston here."

The others snorted.

The woman smiled slyly. "Maybe you mean Smarty Marty. A Smarty Marty we sure got."

"You got him in the office?" Frankie said.

"Don't get snippy, lady. He's in the office."

The lobby, which still smelled of fresh paint, had a carefully restored period look with knotty pine paneling, varnished counters, and, on the walls, faded photographs of white-flanneled tennis players, birdwatchers armed with binoculars, and a group of men in plus fours teeing off for what appeared to be the Unity Hotel Golf Championship of 1936.

"Howdy. I'm Martin Preston," said a middle-aged man in overalls and a plaid shirt. His puffy face, droopy eyes, and unkempt curly hair gave him a just-awakened look.

During introductions and small talk, I noticed that in addition to saying "howdy," Martin also "lived down the road a piece," and had a hog he was "fixin' to slaughter." And every time he was asked a question he rubbed the back of his neck in a doubtful manner before answering. But his accent was strictly New York City. Ironically, Martin seemed to be an essay from the previous incarnation of LIFESTYLE, which had run countless articles on getting "back" to the country.

I motioned to the photographs on the wall. "I didn't know you had a golf course here too."

"To tell you the God's honest truth, we don't. I just got my decorator lady to buy up a whole mess of old-time photos. Folks today want that old-fashioned feeling. Why don't I show you folks some rooms here in the hotel and then we'll take a look at the grounds and the conference rooms."

The rooms were simple but clean and attractive.

"We had the place inspected," Bob said. "All the sprinklers and wiring are up to code."

When we went outside to tour the grounds, the geezer chorus piped up again: "Hey, Smarty Marty, you got another deal cooking?" "You people, you better count your fingers after you shake Marty's hand." "Don't think you fool anybody with those overalls, Mr. Fast Operator." They all laughed derisively.

"I wish they wouldn't call me Marty," he muttered when we were out of earshot.

"They act like they're permanent guests," I said.

"They are," Marty said. "They're all that's left of the Central Committee of the Unity Cooperative."

He explained that his grandfather, a very successful doctor in the 1930s—an era in which success had not achieved the transcendental value it has in our own—bought the hotel as a haven for poor political radicals. Although Martin's grandparents were themselves members of an obscure Bakuninite heresy, they encouraged the full spectrum of left-wing factions to use the hotel. "The place was crawling with Commies, Trots, Socialists," Marty said. "All they did all day was argue." This made running the place difficult since the grandparents had allowed it to be organized as a cooperative. By the time Martin's parents inherited it, the political winds were shifting but they still maintained it as a cooperative with the Central Committee making all the decisions. Though the beautiful setting also attracted guests whose rejection of capitalist oppression went only as far as a weekend in the woods, the hotel ran downhill since the Central Committee could now, in addition to being unable to agree on what should be done, not afford to do anything. In the 1960s the Catskills' resort business in general entered a prolonged slump which made it impossible to even sell the place.

When Marty inherited the Unity, his parents' will required that he provide a place at the hotel for the last seven surviving members of the Central Committee. It didn't require, however, that he run the place cooperatively, and so battle lines were drawn. "They've all known me since I was born and they think they can say anything they want to me."

The new conference facilities were impressive. In one wing there was a small gym, a new pool, a weight-lifting room with Nautilus equipment, and a sauna. In another wing there were a number of meeting rooms and a kitchen big enough for Gregory to demonstrate cooking techniques.

"This must have cost a lot," I said.

"It ate up money like a pig eating slop," Marty said. "Just about cleaned me out. But my bank's still behind me. You see, it's just a matter of time before legalized gambling comes to the

Catskills and this area becomes bigger than Atlantic City. The day that happens, the gym becomes a casino, the dining room becomes a nightclub, and I sell out to one of them big gambling corporations. And then I get the hell out. Maybe live in Europe."

"You mean you can put the country in the boy but you can't keep the boy in the country."

"Sort of that way," he said, scratching himself under the bib of his overalls. "Let's go back to the office, pour ourselves a little white lightning, and make us a deal."

As Marty led the way back with Bob, Frankie said to me, "Isn't it perfect? There's a kitchen for Gregory, a gym for Judy, meeting rooms for Oswald and Toni and Annette. For the real popular lectures like Leon and Enid's we can use the dining room."

"How did you get them all to agree to work on weekends?"

"We promised them lots of extra money."

"You did what? Extra money? I thought we agreed on a budget."

"Shhh. Don't let Marty hear you. And don't worry. We've got new financial projections that are even better than the ones you saw three weeks ago. We're going to make oodles of money."

On the way into the office we had to run the gauntlet again: "Hey, look, it's Mr. Lucky back from the casino." "Can I buy some more chips, Mr. Lucky? I'll give you the title to my house."

When we were all seated in Martin's office he said, "I'm sure we can work out a fair deal without a lot of talk."

"Wait a sec," Frankie said, "we already discussed a basic deal. We give you twenty-five thousand dollars up front against fifteen percent of our net. That's for five weekends this summer with an option for four more in the fall. And we get the use of the whole hotel except for the rooms that the old people have. Right?"

"Yeah, but maybe you folks recollect I told you about the chamber music festival who wanted to use the place this summer. They came back to me after all and offered thirty thousand up front against fifteen percent of the *gross*.

"But we have to pay your out-of-pocket expenses. If you get a percent of the gross you're going to run up expenses on us."

"Okay, little lady, I'll settle for twenty percent of the net."

"I'm very sorry," Frankie said. "It looks like we wasted a trip. Let's get out of here."

Bob and I looked at each other in surprise but Frankie walked out with such decisiveness that we followed her.

"What are you doing?" I said. "The place is perfect. We can negotiate the difference. You said yourself there's oodles of money."

"Shh. I know what I'm doing."

As we reached the car, Marty caught up to us. "Hey, now don't get your bowels in an uproar. Listen to me for a mo—"

"No, you listen to me, Smarty Marty," Frankie said. "I don't want any more shit from you. My offer is now fifteen thousand up front against twelve and a half percent of the net."

"Okay, okay. I'll take the deal. I don't know why; I guess I like you folks."

"You'll get your contract next week."

We got into the car. I ended up driving, with Frankie and Bob in the back seat. "Congratulations," I said to Frankie. "It took guts to bluff like that. But I guess he was bluffing too."

"I wasn't bluffing," Frankie said. "I called that chamber music festival last week and told them I owned a hotel that would be perfect for their needs. I was trying to get a line on the deal they had discussed with Marty. But they told me they had already made a deal with a hotel in the Berkshires. So Smarty Marty, as down-home people like him would say, was left sucking hind tit."

"Well done," I said.

"I learned from you," she said generously, "that I should never negotiate from a weak position."

It had been a long time, I reflected as I drove, since I had felt in a position of strength. If we were happy on the way to the hotel, we were positively euphoric on the way home. Frankie and Bob sang songs in the back and I hummed along. Frankie and Bob laughed and giggled and snickered and . . . my God! I realized. They're having an affair. No wonder she asked me to be discreet about her past.

FOURTEEN

Frankie had a point. I really couldn't afford to offend Judy by taking her to a hot-sheet joint like the Allegro, even if it was the classiest such place in New York. But we needed at least one more event for the Fashionable Affair. The first installment, the *cinq-à-sept* at Judy's apartment, had just appeared to enthusiastic response; the nooner at the Malmaison was ready to go; and for another episode featuring resortwear, we had sent Katrinka and Rusty to the Caribbean. All Judy and I did for the resort event was to take suitcases and meet at the airport in New York. Then we went back to the office.

The focus of the articles were luscious, full-color photographs of our resplendently aloof models, Gregory's food, and Oswald's interiors. Sprinkled through the text were Paul's black-and-white shots of Judy and me as we scampered about; the photos of us had guilty-looking black bars over our eyes as if we were real adulterers. Everybody thought it was a witty idea of mine, but it saved me at least a little worry about Helmut (as did my mysterious insistence that the Uncle Tonnato photo be severely cropped). I finally challenged Judy at an editorial meeting to come up with a new idea for the last installment of the Affair.

"The only thing to do now is have them break up," she said. "The affair has run its course. Katrinka will shed a tear—I'm sure she has one—and Rusty will look poignantly pained and then they will go their separate ways."

"But where do they meet?" I said. "We've got the models all booked up for a week from Wednesday."

Any mention of an appointment reminded me of the Date, my

double date with Helmut. In my mind all time seemed to flow toward the point two and a half weeks away and then stop. I couldn't imagine that human life as we know it would continue beyond that day. My attention drifted back to the meeting, which had grown quite lively. Judy was gesturing excitedly in mid-idea. "*Cinq-à-sept* at my place was very traditional. Now we do something that's more up to date. The *six-à-huit* is a perfect idea."

"But eight is too late to leave for home," I said. "Besides, what difference does one hour make? It's still the same as five to seven."

Frankie, who was sitting next to me, kicked me too late. Judy looked at me coldly. "I guess you haven't been listening to me. I'm talking A.M. I think the last assignation should take place *before* work."

According to Judy, the crack of dawn was a gorge of passion. She claimed half the runners on the streets at that hour were on their way over to a lover's place. "How about all those women who tell their husbands they're going to have a swim at the health club before work—do you think there are enough pools in New York for them? And do you really believe that all those early-rising lawyers are trying to become members of their firms by getting to work before dawn?"

"You're right—what they want are firm members. But I'm a suburbanite. It's not fair to get me up so early."

"But you were so proud of how quickly you got home from my place." Judy smirked. "I'm sure you could do just as well in the opposite direction. What do the rest of you guys think?"

Naturally the rest of the editorial staff ganged up on the poor boss.

"Seeing each other at odd times—especially before the day begins—can help to deepen a relationship," Leon said. "One's defenses are much lower then. It is easier to communicate on a more profound level. You are children together, freshly born from the womb of sleep."

"And I'd love to add a piece about sex in the morning," Enid said eagerly. "You know, how bodies feel warm and soft in the morning . . . how, sullen with sleep, one moves against one's lover, gradually awakening together . . . then your hands gently—"

"Enid!" Frankie said. "The style of the Fashionable Affair is supposed to be tongue-in-cheek, not tongue-in-twat."

"As for breakfast," Gregory chimed in, "I can contribute a unique soufflé, a delicate mingling of eggs—crusty brown on top—and bits of smoked salmon. The combination of lightness and saltiness creates a sense of anticipation. And of course there's the fundamental bonding urge of orange juice and coffee."

"But Rusty and Katrinka will never show up so early," I objected.

"*They* can show up at nine," Judy said. "We'll start preparing my place as soon as you get there."

About the only concession I could wring from the sadistic bunch was that our episode would officially run from 6:30 to 8:30. And so . . .

I crawled out of my bed at 4:45 in the morning. In anticipation of my dopy condition, I had laid out my clothes, a shaving kit, and a squash racket. I don't play squash; the racket was a prop to fool my innocent wife. I crept down the back stairway and out the kitchen door. When I got outside, something told me to stop right there and assess the situation.

Seven thoughts stumbled through my mind in ungainly succession, rather like Keystone Kops, slipping and bumping into each other in hapless pursuit of intelligence: (1) It's raining; (2) I'll take my car to the station; (3) Helen's car is parked in back of my car; (4) I'll move Helen's car; (5) Uh-oh, I forgot my keys; (6) I'll go back in the house and get my keys; (7) I'm locked out of the house too. I was moist by my own petard.

At 5:15 A.M. a man wearing a billowing black plastic refuse bag and an "Elect Bud Horner" poster tied over his head was reported to have bicycled through the streets of Finchmont Village. The man arrived at the train station just as the 5:30 train did.

Although I removed my poster hat in the train, I left my bag on for Paul to photograph when he caught me scurrying over to Judy's place. By the time I got to Grand Central Station I was nearly awake and dying for some of Gregory's coffee. A man pushed ahead of me as I left the train. He ran along the platform and out toward the taxi stand. Because he was carrying a squash racket and because he was rushing, I decided that Judy was correct: this man had obviously given up squash for squish.

Paul was nowhere to be seen. For a moment I felt foolish in my plastic bag. But this was New York; my cabdriver didn't blink at my outfit. The streets were empty and it took only twelve minutes to get to Judy's place. Lazy Paul was probably waiting for me in her lobby. I figured I would give him a great photo opportunity by putting on my Bud Horner poster. As he counted out my change, the driver eyed me adjusting my bonnet. "Stay dry, pal," he said.

There was no one in the lobby. I'll give the whole gang a laugh, I thought. I'll wear the outfit as I enter. Judy's elevator was out of order—*still* out of order, judging by the nasty remarks scrawled on the out-of-order sign. I galloped up the stairs and knocked at Judy's door as I puffed and panted.

A very sleepy-looking Judy Gruber opened the door and looked me up and down. "A real laugh riot," she said sourly. Then she smiled in spite of herself. "Okay, you look pretty funny. But how can you try so hard so early in the morning? Come in. Let me take your hat and coat."

"Where is everybody?" I said, peering around the many corners of her apartment.

"I was wondering when you would ask. I know how bosses hate it if employees don't call when they're not coming to work, and I want you to know that everybody called. Toni called at ten last night to tell me that Katrinka had called her from a club to say she couldn't make it. Something about an overdose she either had had or was planning on having. Word spread quickly. In short order, Rusty, Cynthia, Oswald, Paul, and Gregory called to say if Katrinka's not coming they're not either."

"But why didn't you call me?"

"I did. At eleven. Your wife answered. She said you were

asleep. And when I realized that I could never explain to her what was happening I said there was no message. I'm sorry. Look at all these chairs and pictures and crap with which Oswald was going to transform my place again. And here are all of Toni's fashions. I can barely turn around. I'm so mad I'd keep this peignoir if it fit me." She held up something just this side of invisible.

"I really prefer your bathrobe," I said, trying to cheer her up.

"It's an heirloom." She was wearing a tattered green satin boxer's robe which said *Sunnyside Garden* on the back.

I looked at my watch. "Say, I made it door to door in only—" I stopped as a barrage of daggers flew from her eyes. "Okay, we'll forget about the Affair for this morning. Let's have some breakfast and feel sorry for ourselves."

"Coffee I can handle but I don't cook."

"I do. Did you get the stuff for Gregory's recipe?"

"Yes. Since I already had the food, he insisted on giving me the recipe last night on the phone. And here's the fancy cookware Gregory found to make it in."

"I'll take a whack at it."

It wasn't such a complicated recipe, and thirty-five minutes later we unfolded Judy's clever little dining table and sat down.

"Not bad," Judy said. "Do you do a lot of cooking?"

"Quite a bit."

"Your wife is lucky."

The rain picked up considerably and the wind whipped it against the windows. I felt quite cozy in Judy's little place.

"Tell me something," Judy said. "Why are you doing this?"

"Doing what?"

"Running around like a madman for the Fashionable Affair."

"It's been fun. I needed to break up my routine."

"Admit it. You wanted us to like you and respect you as a creative type."

"I already admitted that I was lonely. And you're the one who questioned my creative credentials."

"I think you've tried too hard to be likable. If they respected you more they would have shown up this morning."

"I guess I've really flopped. Now no one likes me or respects me."

Judy rolled her eyes.

"When I'm this tired," I said, "I'm entitled to a cheap bid for sympathy."

"And you're entitled to some cheap sympathy. You're not so unlikable."

" 'Not so unlikable.' Wow! My heart is swelling. What's not so unlikable about me?"

There was an extended pause.

"Take your time," I said. "I love the way my likable features are right on the tip of your tongue." I *was* feeling sorry for myself in a stubborn, perverse way.

Finally Judy said, "How's this? You were the first guy who ever came to my apartment who didn't make some stupid remark about how small it is. Maybe you thought something—"

"I did. I confess it."

"—but at least you kept your mouth shut."

"You're right. That's not so unlikable. Well, now that we've made it to double-negative status maybe we can try for a real positive."

"You *are* demanding."

"Come on."

"All right. I like you."

"I'm not convinced. You're under duress. Give me a reason."

"Give me a break." She thought for a moment. "Okay, you're a better-than-average example of what you are."

"Oh boy! Albert Schweitzer, move over, here comes George Werble, a better-than-average—"

"I was just teasing you. Actually I find you to be a charming mixture of narcissism and insecurity."

"That's likable? I suppose I asked for it. On the other hand, 'charming' isn't so bad. Now let's go on."

Judy pointed her finger at me. "Listen, pal, quit while you're ahead."

"You're right. Well, as long as you like me, will you do me a big favor?"

"I should have known. What is it?"

"Do you know who Helmut Gernschaft is?"

I hadn't planned on asking Judy to help me. I hadn't planned on anything except calling Helmut up pretty soon and telling him that my beloved was sick and couldn't make it. I told Judy the story of the photograph at the restaurant and how Helmut had proposed a double date with his friend.

"Two happy businessmen with their mistresses. Very nice," Judy said with a frown.

"It wasn't my idea. But could you possibly masquerade as my girlfriend? You've had lots of practice."

"This man is amazing," she said, appealing to the gods. "Can I give you some advice, George? I think you're really asking for trouble. Look, the magazine is in better shape editorially than it has been for years. And the Institute for Lifestyle Arts, appalling as it sounds, appears to be headed for a smashing success. Don't take a chance on screwing everything up with some crazy scheme for fooling your boss. Why not face the music and tell Gernschaft you can't do it? Tell him you broke up with your mistress."

"He'll be angry."

"So he'll be angry. But with all you've got going for you now, it won't be so bad. It'll be a lot worse if he meets me and then recognizes my by-line in "The Fashionable Affair" and imagines who knows what."

I nodded grudgingly. "You're right. It's better if I cancel the date."

Judy shook her head. "I can't believe that Frankie didn't tell me that Gernschaft had seen the two of us."

"Don't be angry with her. I threatened her." I looked at my watch. "It's eight thirty. Time for me to be leaving. I don't think we need to put ourselves through another morning like this. We'll send Rusty and Katrinka to Paul's studio to shoot them breaking up."

"I guess I better get ready for work. You won't mind if I'm a little late."

We walked to the door.

"It has been a great affair," I said.

"No tears now, I want to remember you just as you are. Seriously, I have enjoyed myself. And I don't think you should feel sorry for yourself. We're all beginning to like you."

At that moment I felt, to my surprise, a sudden rush of affection for Judy. I thought about kissing her—just a friendly peck on the cheek, please understand—to acknowledge that my gratitude was personal as well as professional.

I think she felt the same thing because she grinned at me in a friendly, sardonic way and said, "No matter how many others come after you, you're the one I'll never forget."

Then she shut the door.

Based on up-front receipts and reservations, the Institute for Lifestyle Arts was already a success. Each week Bob the Bachelor would report that another summer weekend was sold out. He would shake his head, as if he found the hectic action rather breathtaking, and say, "That Frankie—what a marketing animal! So much talent. Raw talent, to be sure, but she can do it all."

Words like "animal" and "raw" suggested that the fastidious Bob had allowed some primitive life force to sweep him up. What with various passionate pairings-off lately, I might have felt a little left out; but Judy's early morning counseling had helped to focus me on the positive side of my life. The magazine *was* clearly in better shape. After only two issues of the revamped LIFESTYLE had appeared, we won an award for creativity in design and editing. The mood changed. There were still the usual conflicts, but they seemed to take place within a new spirit of common purpose, constructive energy.

For a few days after the award was announced, my pride was tempered with fear. I thought it might alert Helmut to the changes I was making at LIFESTYLE, and Helmut was one area where Judy's advice had not produced positive results—not *yet*, that is. I hadn't quite managed to cancel our double date. Oh, I had called Helmut, fully intending to tell him about breaking up with my girlfriend, but my resolve turned to mush and I postponed the date instead for two more weeks. He accepted the postponement so benignly that two weeks later when I called him, again full of good intentions, it was all too easy to postpone the date again. And Helmut once more accepted the postponement without so much as a question.

Almost everyone at LIFESTYLE had taken up the new editorial point of view enthusiastically. Even Leon Malt was eager to give a lecture at the Institute. The only problem came to my attention when Frankie asked me for help.

"Gregory has gone off the deep end," she said. "I had him all lined up for a Saturday seminar on goat cheeses and a big Sunday morning session called "How to Give a Power Brunch for Power People." But he just told me he's only interested in teaching people how to think about food. I don't understand what he's talking about, but he said something about the destruction of food."

I found Gregory in his kitchen. "I gather there's some sort of problem about your lecture. Are you really going to talk about the destruction of food?"

"George, you just keep that little vixen away from me. She may be the hottest thing in marketing around here, but she's not intellectually equipped to understand my work."

"Why don't you try my intellectual equipment?"

"I was hoping to surprise you when my book came out, but since you ask I'll describe the intellectual journey I've made recently. For some time, I've been thinking about the application of structuralist theory to food criticism. 'Toward a Semiotics of Pureed Vegetables' was one of my important articles. And in a lecture given at the Museum of Ingestion, I pointed out that certain berry-based liqueurs are always served at the end of several unique meal structures."

"Cassis and desist?" I said.

"I even began to think that beneath all meals there lay perhaps five or six models—'deep meals,' I called them."

"So what's the trouble? Show everybody how to make a deep brunch."

"I'm afraid I've abandoned structuralism. My ideas have changed completely in the last month or two. George, I know how excited and proud of me you're going to be when I come forward as the world's first deconstructionist food *philosophe*."

"I'm not equipped for this."

"Bear with me, George. I ask you, what is it after all to be *sour*, to be *sweet*? These categories are different for every culture, not to mention for every person. We can know nothing in an absolute sense about food, and that is its tragedy and its glory. Each of us may consume an entirely different meal even as we eat the same food. You see, it's not what you eat but how you eat it. At my lecture at the Institute I shall reveal to my students the manifold meanings of food, the wonderful ambiguities of a meal, the way a meal may actually subvert its own intentions. I shall show how a pizza or a hamburger may be deconstructed to be as replete with meaning as a Beef Wellington. You know, George, I've reached a point of not needing to eat food to analyze it. Why, I can receive the same deconstructive pleasure from reading a recipe as I once did from tasting it."

I tried to think of some graceful way to persuade Gregory to abandon his principles for the sake of the Institute.

"And so I say to you, George, a chef knows nothing of what he does. It is the critic who performs the creative act of deconstruction. There are no cooks. There are only eaters."

"And I say to you, Gregory, that if you agree to show up at the Institute and tell no one about your theories, I won't fire you. As far as you and your students are concerned, the road to cachet is paved with goat cheese."

It wasn't graceful, but the next day Frankie told me that Gregory had capitulated.

For several days before my third call to Helmut, I thought a lot about being sensible and reasonable. Despite my conviction that with Judy's help I could have made the double date work, it wasn't really worth the risk. Maybe the challenge attracted me; or maybe it was the opportunity to forge a real friendship with

Helmut. But whatever the temptation, I couldn't afford to get Helmut annoyed by postponing a third time. Or could I? I'll never know because Helmut called me and postponed.

"I have to make an unexpected trip to Frankfurt next week. But the week after we will meet without fail. On Thursday, of course. You know, George, I have been so busy I have not realized we have had three postponements. We will not let that happen again."

"Indeed we will not," replied the reprieved.

Reprieved I was, but definitely for the last time. There was no choice now, which was something of a relief. The anxiety of indecision was over. I would enjoy the following weekend and then on Monday—not Tuesday, not Wednesday—I would call Helmut and tell him that my girlfriend had left me. I would confess, in my misery, that she had left me several weeks ago but I had hoped she would return, which was why I had postponed our date. Perhaps when I found a new girlfriend we could try again.

I didn't delay. First thing Monday morning I called.

"No, there's no message," I said to his secretary when she told me he had extended his trip. "I'll call him on Wednesday." I began to call him on Tuesday afternoon. On Wednesday afternoon his secretary told me he was definitely arriving on Thursday afternoon.

"Please have him call me as soon as he lands," I said. "Tell him it's an emergency."

I didn't leave the phone all day. At five it rang. "Mr. Gernschaft just called me from the airport," the secretary said. "I gave him your message. I told him you have interrupted me many times in the last few days. He asked me if you canceled tonight and I said no. So he said you can talk to him then. He is very tired. He is going to have a shave and a shower and he'll meet you at Uncle Tonnato's. I made the reservation for eight thirty."

"Would you happen to have the number of . . . of . . . of where's he having his shower?"

"Absolutely not," she said, which meant: I might know but I wouldn't tell *you.*

In my final, futile attempt, I had Helmut paged at the airport, but it was too late.

Judy wasn't in her office.

"I think I can, I think I can," I chanted in rhythm to the flat wheels of the F train. And I did believe I could persuade Judy to help me. We had not had much to do with each other since our morning together, but there was a residue of good feeling. When we passed each other in the halls we grinned as if we shared a secret. "I think she will, I think she will" was my second chorus.

I buzzed her apartment. When I tried to call her from the office there was no answer and I assumed, *hoped,* she was on her way home. A squall of static from the speaker answered the first of several prayers I had prepared for this evening.

"It's George."

"Who?"

"George Werble."

"Who?"

She finally gave in and buzzed open the door. My luck seemed to be improving: even the elevator was working. But it took half an hour for the super to free me after the elevator stuck between the second and third floors. At six thirty I knocked on Judy's door.

"You look awful," she said. She sat me down and fed me a drink. "That was you who buzzed before? Oh you poor man."

It had been a long time since anyone had really felt sorry for me. I was encouraged. As I told her the story, however, she got a tight look around her mouth and her brown eyes unsoftened themselves. When I was through she shook her head and then shuddered, as if she were trying hard to hold herself in check. She stood up and began to pace as she spoke.

"So you want me to help you make a fool out of Gernschaft. Has it occurred to you that he's my boss too? You know, I'd like to continue my career, preferably at LIFESTYLE. Maybe it's not the ultimate job for a journalist, but it's not bad. Maybe I'm not a star, but people recognize my work. I pay my rent, even though it's a small apartment. I'm reasonably happy. My life is progressing nicely. But of course from your point of view I should risk it all, throw it all away on some stupid scheme. You believe in nothing except yourself and your insane conviction that you can make anything work. I'll bet you never intended to call Helmut and cancel."

"It wasn't like that." In my mind's eye I saw a table for four at Tonnato's with one sad, unoccupied seat.

"And he thinks I'm stupid too. I know what you were up to that morning when you were so nice. You were coming on to me. You probably arranged for the others not to show up so you would have a chance to get into my pants. That way I'd have to go along with you on your date. You're just a sleazeball like the rest of your kind."

"Don't give me 'your kind,' you self-righteous bitch. That morning episode was *your* idea. Just who was trying to get into whose pants? It wouldn't be the first time someone decided to get to know the boss more intimately. You were ready to come on to me until my Helmut story scared you off."

"Oh you scumbag!" she shouted.

"Now don't get upset and cry," I sneered.

"Cry! Cry!" she screamed and kicked me in the knee.

I fell on the floor and writhed while she stood above me hurling threats and obscenities. The pain was immense. I finally struggled to my feet and thrust my twisted face up at her face and began to bellow in rage. Suddenly a terrible realization came over me and my eyes widened in amazement. Judy too was struck by the same mad thought and her mouth dropped open. For a moment all that could be heard was furious breathing, and then I said, "Oh no," and Judy said, "Oh shit."

We grabbed each other and as we pulled and grasped at our clothing we staggered to her bed and fell on it. The whole time we made love she kept murmuring, "Dammit, dammit, dammit." I didn't say a word. I wanted her so much I was afraid if I

said the wrong thing and broke the urgency of the moment I would cry.

Two couples, one alert and the other semiconscious, greeted each other at Uncle Tonnato's. I think Judy and I were both secretly relieved to have the date with Helmut as an excuse to evade responsibility for a little while; the need to figure out what had happened would be just as oppressive later on. We had dressed and made our way to the restaurant in a kind of dazed silence. When we spoke it was in a careful, perfunctory manner, and we avoided eye contact. There was something between us but neither of us was ready to find out if it was a barrier or a bond.

Helmut was in great form. He was full of little courtly familiarities, compliments, and jokes. He introduced us to Alicia, who obviously didn't want to be at Uncle Tonnato's. She was tall and dark and her basic expression was pouty-bored unless Helmut was paying attention to her. Alicia was Argentinian and she was working on an MBA in international banking at NYU. I was so drained that my anxiety about the date was reduced to an intellectual exercise. The conversation would veer toward a dangerous area—"Tell me, George, how long have you and Judy been together?"—and I would register the threat as if I were observing it from a great and safe distance.

Judy had more control. Though Helmut was not much interested in who Judy was or what she did, she sensibly got her professional credentials on record right away. "But our relationship is a secret at LIFESTYLE," she said. "Will you help us to keep it?"

"I love secrets," Helmut said.

Because I had fearfully anticipated this date for so long I found myself "pretending" that Judy and I were lovers even though it was now technically true. Helmut kept our glasses full of champagne; though Judy and I consumed a great deal, it didn't affect us. Helmut's good mood was excessive, given the occasion and the subdued spirits of his guests. He allowed himself to get tipsy and giggly. At one point he leaned forward and whispered, "And can you keep a secret also?" He could hardly wait to tell us. We promised to keep his secret.

"I think you must wonder, George, why you have so much been left alone at LIFESTYLE."

"I thought it was because I was doing a good job."

He chuckled. "Very good. But it is not my style to leave anybody alone. Even if you are good I must believe I can make you better. Otherwise what good am I for?"

"You're right."

"No. It has been very big trouble at Schaefer that has kept me occupied. You have heard of *CompuDiet?*"

"It's the first big success at Briggs and Schaefer in fifteen years," I said. Schaefer's publishing division had decided to see if they could fail less badly with software than with books. *CompuDiet* was a PC package in which, after you set long-range weight goals, you entered each day's consumption of food and expense of energy. Then the computer gave you food and energy instructions for the next day, even to the point of suggesting menus. The program remembered if you ignored its instructions; not only would it adjust for your failures, it would put up nagging messages on the screen, telling you to shape up, and even depict caricatures of your future obesity.

"How could that be trouble?" Judy asked.

"What happened is that eight people who used *CompuDiet* have died for unknown reasons."

"Why haven't we heard about it?"

"Nobody has put it all together. There were inquiries from their doctors asking about the program, but we have assured them that it has been examined by the experts. And it has. We cannot find anything wrong with it. Oh maybe there is a slight suspicion about electrolytes but nothing really conclusive. Those idiots at Briggs, they tried to hide it from me. I found out. That is the real reason Larry Roth is at Schaefer. We call him a consultant but he is running Briggs. The previous managers sit in their offices and as soon as this is over I will fire them all. But until then no one must get suspicious or we might be sued for millions. That is what I was doing in Frankfurt last week—protecting Schaefer as well as Gruppmann. We sold Briggs to a dummy corporation in Liechtenstein to make it difficult to sue us. Now we can safely phase *CompuDiet* off the market."

"Shouldn't you do it quickly?"

"These deaths, I am sure they are just coincidences. In two months our inventory will be gone and we'll have a new product called *CompuKid* to sell. It helps you raise your children."

"Have you thought about *CompuGod* for moral problems?" Judy said.

This date was turning into quite a boon. Not only had Helmut confided in me, I now knew that Larry Roth wasn't breathing down my neck. I was almost home free. By eleven Helmut was running out of gas. As he called for the check, Judy and I eyed each other apprehensively.

"I am tired from the jet lag or I would suggest a nightcap," Helmut said as we left the restaurant.

"Next time," I offered generously.

Alicia and Helmut got into a cab. Judy and I eyed each other on the street. I felt I was seeing her brown curly hair and dark eyes for the first time.

"So?"

"So?"

"Was this just a grudge fuck?" she said.

"What's that?"

"Sometimes when you have a lot of conflict or tension with someone, someone you don't even care for particularly, it can be kind of erotic to make . . . well, not love but something. You're free to *use* each other and the tension adds something."

"Was it a grudge fuck for you?"

"No," she said evenly. "For you?"

"No."

"Prove it."

FIFTEEN

I didn't go home for five days.

Among the many fantasies I had during my adolescence was an elaborate one in which I became the Perfect Sophisticate. Part of the fantasy involved my "place," a quiet, dark Manhattan bar and restaurant—usually called Augie's—into which I would saunter in the early evening just before going out on the town. (In my fantasy I was the kind of person who referred to New York as "a tough town but a great town.") "Nice evening, Mr. Werble," Augie would say. And Ciro, my favorite waiter, would say, "Hey, that's some nice suit." I would smile comfortably and join a small clutch of other Perfect Sophisticates at the bar. And then—and this was one of my favorite parts of the fantasy—I would nod to Benny the bartender and wink warmly. "The regular, Mr. Werble?" "The regular, Benny," I would reply with offhand grace. And Benny would make the regular *just so*!

Another part of the fantasy involved the sort of woman who complemented the Perfect Sophisticate. Of course in one's adolescent transport she was a P.S. herself, and life for us was an effortless duet. We were smooth, pliant, and strong; we intuited each other's needs and ensured that the only moods were good moods. We even looked alike. Often we walked through the city in the small hours of the morning and I imagined for us faint background music—*Rhapsody in Blue*, probably—and it was all we could do to keep from breaking into dance.

I didn't become a P.S., but some vestigial desire certainly prompted my attempts to veneer the hectic chaos of day-to-day life with good clothes, decent restaurants, and bad seats at the opera. The area in which I came closest to my fantasy was in my marriage. Not that Helen wasn't as imperfect a sophisticate as I, but until our actual breakup our relationship was genuinely effortless. Our backgrounds were in harmony and our foregrounds defined themselves over the years with hardly any conflict. There weren't many bad moods, since neither of us was particularly moody. I am sure some thimble-brained counselor would say, "Of course the marriage broke up. They didn't work at it." In an era in which marriages crumble more easily than cookies, this sort of hindsight is worth its weight in pigeon feathers. At any rate, even after our rupture I neither questioned nor regretted the effortlessness of the marriage. I think this means I still considered effortlessness to be some sort of ideal; which is why I was so surprised to find myself involved with someone who challenged me, mocked my values, derided my accomplishments. And astonished to find I enjoyed it.

I was also delighted to find I could go to bed with Judy without getting kicked in the knee first. She felt wonderful. Thanks to the exercise bike and the Nautilus machine she was fit and strong, and over her compact figure there was a thin layer of baby fat which felt almost velvety. I couldn't keep my hands off her.

"What makes me crazy," Judy said, about thirty-nine hours into the affair, "is how you get away with everything. You're not a bad person. I don't want to see you get punished. But think about it. You float into this magazine, behave like an asshole, and the magazine gets better. You float into some absolutely insane relationship with your boss, let him believe you have a mistress when you don't, and at the crucial moment you produce a mistress and he buys it. You float into my life, incite me into hostility and physical violence, and here you are having a terrific time in bed with me. Why should you get away with everything?"

"What is this 'floating" business?" I said. "What am I, a dirigible?"

"Yeah, and I'm Lakehurst, New Jersey."

"I didn't actually plan it all."

"I know. I envy people who are totally unaware of their own motives."

"You have to understand. I'm a representative of the New Service Class, capital NSC. We don't have a lot of motives or intentions except to make things work. We're kind of like lawyers who don't care if a client's guilty. We don't question whether something *needs* to be arranged or marketed or designed if it *can* be."

"Do you really believe that?"

"No, but I thought you might buy it."

"So you do believe it."

"Only if I can get you to believe it."

"You!" Her hand moved down my stomach. "Something seems to be working."

"That's a symbol."

"Of?"

"The rise of the New Service Class."

A day later: "You know, George, if you had actually failed to make something work, it might have humanized you."

"Made me a better person, eh? So that's what you want me to be—warm, caring, open, vulnerable, sensitive, and supportive."

"Are you kidding?" Judy said. "I'd destroy somebody that good. Not that you're cold, insensitive, and hostile. It's just that in your sneaky, affable way you're no pushover."

"Nor are you. I'm beginning to see that we have more in common than I thought."

"Maybe," Judy admitted. "I think you need someone who will give you a hard time, keep you off balance."

"It seems we're verging on one of those is-this-a-serious-relationship conversations—ouch!"

"We're not verging on anything except making each other feel good. We're two and a half days into this, and it's far too soon for serious conversations."

"You're right. We should get in a lot more fun before we—"

"Shut up and lick me until I whimper."

I knew I'd have to go home sometime, but I kept putting it

off. We were having an intensely sensational time; it seemed so unreal I was afraid I'd break the spell if I left. I was even developing an affection for Judy's apartment, small and hot as it was. Especially hot. Our first five days coincided with the first hot spell of the summer, and as we made love our bodies were always slick with sweat.

I bought extra underwear and a few new shirts but I knew I couldn't keep showing up at the office in the same suit without someone, particularly Frankie, noticing. We were careful about the office. I would get up quite early to take a taxi well before Judy left for work.

"I feel guilty for not telling Frankie about us," Judy said. "After all, she tried so hard to get me to like you. In fact it wasn't until you gave her a better job that I thought you might have some potential as a person."

"She made the most of it. The Institute is opening in less than a week and we've already picked up the option for four more weeks in September."

"At first I thought you put Frankie up to talking me into liking you. Kind of like Miles Standish, if you know what I mean."

"Not I. I'm definitely Miles Standoffish."

"It's funny, but now that we're really sleeping together Morrisburg hasn't caught us once."

"Not so fast." I reached for my jacket, which, as usual, was draped over a chair with the rest of my clothes. "Here, this letter came in the mail. It's from my mother."

"Oh no."

"Go ahead. Read it."

Dear George,

After you read this letter you'll understand why I sent it to your office. (I hope your secretary respects "Personal and Confidential" when it's written on an envelope. Miss Secretary: If you're reading this letter stop this instant! This is a personal letter from a mother to her son.)

George, my dear, several curious incidents have happened lately and I'm sure you'll have a good explanation.

Not that you owe me an explanation. It's simply the hope of a concerned parent. Firstly, a few weeks ago I bumped into that awful Edna Harrington at the mall. They live in Florida now, but she was in town to see her sister. She asked about you and I told her that you were fine and successful and happily married and then I prepared myself to listen to her run on about her precious Kent and her wonderful Julia. Instead she said, "I'm so happy to hear that George and Helen are together again after what Julia told me." Well, George, I just shut my mouth tight. I wasn't going to give her the pleasure of seeing me make a fool out of myself.

I was hurt to find out in such a manner. But then I thought, maybe it's a mistake. Maybe Julia misunderstood some remark or exaggerated a little spat. And just as I was beginning to feel better I read this article in the Morrisburg Sentinel *written by Sally Tensor (who happens to be the wife of our dermatologist).*

The clipping read:

> . . . and checked into our hotel, the famous and very expensive Malmaison (oh well, you only live once). Highly recommended! And wouldn't you know, we weren't the only Morrisburgers enjoying the Malmaison's luxury. There in the lobby was local man George Werble (son of Mr. and Mrs. Arthur Werble, 16 Apple Tree Lane). George and his lovely wife were spending the night at the Malmaison prior to setting off for Paris on a romantic second honeymoon. And very romantic they were indeed.

Well, George, that completely relieved me. Whatever had happened between you and Helen was now repaired (though I was surprised you hadn't told me you were going to Paris). And then this package arrived in the mail.

Please be assured that I would never have opened your mail but it was addressed to Mrs. Werble. I saw that it was from the Malmaison and assumed you had left something at the hotel which I could forward to you (though how it got to Morrisburg is beyond my comprehension).

Judy raised her head. "What was in the package?"
"Two things. One was this letter."

Malmaison

Mrs. George Werble
16 Apple Tree Lane
Morrisburg, Ohio 44654

June 20, 1985

Dear Mrs. Werble:

It's not easy to rule a château like the Malmaison. But my job is made so much easier by my dedicated subjects, my palace guard, my footmen, my ladies-in-waiting. My employees know that I demand a lot of them but no more than I demand of myself: diligence, care, honesty, and a desire to appear well-bred.

Perhaps you're surprised that we bothered to return this little item you left behind. But it doesn't matter to us if it is expensive or inexpensive.

My subjects and I want to ensure that when you're a guest in our kingdom, you are as happy and secure as if you were me.

Sincerely,

Fifi Hoffman

Fifi Hoffman
President

"And the other item?" Judy said.

I handed her a tiny silk camisole.

"Oh that. It sure looked great on Katrinka. Now what does Mom have to say about this?"

George, need I say that this is not Helen's size. It is not even her style. I cannot pretend to imagine what is going on. But I want you to know that your father and I hope that you and Helen can repair whatever breach has come between the two of you. You know we love and care for you and we love and care for Helen. We have always thought the two of you were the perfect couple. I hope you will tell Helen that no matter what trouble the two of you are going through, she is close to our hearts.

Love,
Mother

P.S. Of course if you and Helen have made an irrevocable break, please don't forget that your family loaned you the money for the down payment to buy your house (your father and I always intended to forgive the loan) and Helen has no right to drive you from that lovely home.

"Well, now you've met my mother. Tell me, if I can't escape from Morrisburg, Ohio, what can't you escape from?"

"A normally crazy, lower-middle-class neighborhood."

"What neighborhood?"

"Woodside, Queens."

"What does that mean?"

"If you have to ask, you wouldn't understand," Judy said. "Tell me something. Was there a point *before* we went to bed that you thought you might be interested in me?"

"Not exactly. I mean an awful lot of emotion came to the surface all at once. But looking back there was this occasion when you asked me if I had told my wife about the Fashionable Affair. And I asked you what you would say if you were my wife."

"I remember. I said I'd kill you. If that's when I began to interest you, no wonder a kick in the knee is what it took."

"You see, if Helen, my wife, found out that I was having an affair she wouldn't threaten to kill me. She'd be *very disappointed* in me. So when you said you'd kill me I thought it was interesting but no more than that. I mean I didn't think, Hey, that's what I need. Someone who will kick me, shower me with contempt, and, when I screw around, come after me with knives." At this point, the time seemed ripe for a happy confession. "I wonder, Judy, if you're curious about how I've been able to spend the last four days here."

"Not really. Given your amazing performance so far, I've assumed you have one of your fancy schemes working and your wife has swallowed it."

"You might enjoy hearing—"

"Stop right there. I don't think I would enjoy lying here with you and having a good giggle over how you're fooling your wife. And I think four days together is a little soon for us to discuss the state of your marriage."

She did see things with a certain forceful clarity—though in this case not as clearly as she thought. I had tried to tell her. Maybe it was just as well. I would save the news about Helen for the time when we had our is-this-a-serious-relationship conversation. It would be a nice surprise.

I had to go home. I needed some more clothes—especially casual clothes to wear to the Unity Hotel. Opening day of the Institute for Lifestyle Arts was three days away. The entire magazine was in a mild state of uproar as Frankie and Bob juggled schedules, assigned people to various duties, and negotiated with suppliers. Frankie had quite a time with Smarty Marty, who kept trying to screw her out of more money.

My fear that I would break the spell by leaving Judy was unfounded. As the train put distance between us I began to feel closer to her and to see more clearly how everything had fallen into place: LIFESTYLE was going to be a big success, the Institute was going to throw off hundreds of thousands of dollars *in cash*, Helmut had become my drinking buddy, and Larry Roth was off my back. And then there was Judy, the pièce de résistance; or, as she would be enraged to hear me put it, the resistant piece. I smiled to myself.

I arrived at Finchmont at nine. My bicycle was still chained to the rack but the front tire was flat. I made the taxi drop me off half a mile from home. I had the feeling I wasn't going to spend much more time in Finchmont. A farewell walking tour would be nice. It was warm and the air was heavy. Behind the lush trees and hedges, the houses of Finchmont seemed reserved, protective of their secrets, as if they suspected I was about to step from their orbit forever. As I approached my neighborhood I noticed that the street was filled with cars. Someone was having a party. If the hosts were people I knew, perhaps I would find a pretext to knock at the door. Surely they would invite me in and I could have a good-bye drink with my neighbors. I drew nearer and heard the music. I knew its source immediately: I was the only person in the neighborhood who owned a copy of "It Ain't the Meat, It's the Motion." In my figuratively split-level house a party was booming.

There's nothing like being uninvited to a party to make one feel superfluous, but the feeling was liberating. I had nothing to lose. I felt no obligations. I was going to crash a party in my own home.

By Finchmont standards it was a very raucous party. As I opened the door a wall of chatter and smoke hit me. A big handsome woman named Lenore, a member of Helen's election committee, registered my entrance with great surprise. Her eyes sparkled as she made her way over to me.

"Is this not a great party?" Lenore said.

"Where's the bar?" I replied.

I couldn't shake Lenore. She followed me to the bar and stood there while I drank two vodka martinis and started on my third.

"Everybody appears to be having a good time," I said.

"Especially Bud. I've never seen him so emotional. After twelve years he's finally made it."

It? And then I understood: This was Bud's victory party.

"And Helen," Lenore went on. "She deserves so much credit.

Bud got more votes than any other candidate. He's *head* of the town council now. You must be proud of Helen." Lenore was unwilling to get off the subject of Helen; she enumerated my wife's many virtues as a campaign director. "Did Helen tell you? Bud's going to make her the head of Finchmont's Task Force on the Arts."

"Which arts?" I said smirking to myself. But when Lenore's eyes widened slightly I caught on. She knew about Helen and Bud. I glanced around the room. At least three surreptitious stares at me were quickly averted. *Many* people knew. I was the party cuckold. If I felt liberated before, I now lost all restraint. I was really going to enjoy this party.

Now I understood why Lenore was being so persistent; she was trying to work me for some juicy reaction to gossip about. "Helen and I grew so close as we worked on the campaign."

"Campaigns will do that," I said, now deeply into my third martini and very obviously looking for another conversation to join.

As I edged away, Lenore said, "Helen told me you're from Ohio. I am too."

I refused to respond.

"Akron," Lenore offered.

"You know what they call an interesting person from Akron?" I said. "An anachronism."

I found Al Brubaker by the bar. I must have been swaying a little because Al looked slightly alarmed as I started my fourth martini. "Congratulations, Al. You guys have pulled off the upset of the century."

"Yes. It's very gratifying to know that the same campaign techniques which work on macrotargeted audiences can be effective with microtargets too."

"It must be a little sobering, however, to recall that the most important issue in the campaign was supplied by a ten-year-old child."

Al frowned. "She certainly didn't understand its implications."

"At least you've kept us safe from mutants. Say, Al, can I ask you a personal question? How come everybody named Al is called 'Big Al'? And has that been a problem for you in life?"

Al looked about for a rescuer.

"You know, Big Al, I owe you an apology. I'm usually not a suspicious kind of guy but you made me suspicious."

"Oh?" Al examined his pipe closely.

"You're not going to believe this, Big Al, but I actually thought you were humping my wife. But you're off the hook." I winked at him significantly. I spotted a familiar face. "Hey, Big Al. There's Buddy Boy—the power elite."

I'm sure Al wanted Bud to get as far away as possible, but I got a good grip on Bud's shoulder, which helped to support me.

"You know, Buddy," I said, "I was just telling Big Al here what a great job he did with you. I mean you can't pretend that you're leadership material."

"I think I've grown." Bud exchanged a nervous look with Al.

"Come on, Buddy. You've still got what Big Al here would call an image problem. I mean, did you ever watch the TV news when they've arrested some demented mass murderer? You're the pasty-faced guy they always find to interview who lives in the murderer's neighborhood. And when they ask you about the murderer, you inevitably say, 'Well, he always kept to himself.' "

There ensued a rather hazy period during which I am sure I behaved quite badly. I have the sense I spoke and laughed too loudly and that my abrupt motions knocked at least one drink down a dress. The next time things came into focus I looked across the room and saw Al speaking to Helen and pointing at me. Maybe he was telling her about the motto I had come up with for the Task Force on the Arts: *Ass gratia artis.* Helen started toward me. Here we go, I gleefully thought, but instead she found Emerson and enlisted him. He approached me with a look of patronizing concern.

"Hey, boy, looks like you're having a *very good time.*"

I knew Emerson well enough to know exactly where he was going. "No, Emerson, it only looks that way. On the surface I appear happy. But the delights of good food, good wine, and good flesh do not delight the soul. If your soul isn't having fun, you're not truly happy. Tell me, do you think your ability to cure mental problems can do anything for a hangover?"

"George, are you—?" He checked himself. "Let's talk this over." He put a consoling arm around my shoulders and led me to a quiet corner. "In our lives, George, we all search for something meaningful. You have great talent as a communicator, but I think you need a message. I know it can be a long search. Your maps may not be good, you may weather terrible storms. You know, I am reminded of the story of Jonah, who had a message but fled rather than communicate it. He sailed the seas—"

"Jonah?" I said. "I've always looked at that story from the point of view of the whale."

"The whale?"

"Yes, don't you see, it's about a whale who thought that if you want to give good head you have to learn how to swallow seamen."

After Emerson hit me, the next thing I remember is Helen herself standing before me and trembling with rage as we had one of those public confrontations which keep a suburb's gossip mills grinding for months. It was hard, in my state, to keep up with the stream of invective spewing from a woman I had thought capable only of disappointment. She didn't yell, but she spoke as loudly as it is possible to speak while one's teeth are gritting away. Many of her comments had to do with my five-day absence and my lack of faithfulness. I suspected this hypocrisy was for public consumption and so I felt free to suggest that if I were absent it only made it easier for her to cavort in my house with her lover—whom I unfortunately referred to as "your little grease monkey." Then, thanks to my mother, I reminded Helen that the house had been supplied by my parents.

I remember lying in my bed as the West Wing spun around me and wondering if I had really cut all my ties. Was it possible that Helen's last words to me would, uncharacteristically, be: "You can take your house and shove it"? And that my last words would be: "If you don't get out of my way I'm going to throw up on you"?

SIXTEEN

"What have we here?" Judy said the next morning as she opened her door. "A man and his suitcase. You look awful."

I felt worse. I had awakened at four thirty in the morning because a vulture inside my head was pecking at my skull. I packed my suitcase and, in a supreme testament to the indomitability of the hung-over human spirit, I repeated my early morning trip to New York. This time, however, I took a cab to the station.

I was grateful to discover that Judy could occasionally refrain from giving me a hard time. She helped me into a comfortable chair, made me coffee, and left me alone. Her movements about the apartment were already familiar. The sense of intimacy was reassuring, soothing. When I awoke, she was gone.

I managed to get in to the office by noon. I considered taking the day off but it was two days before the Institute opened, and there were a lot of payments to approve. At the end of the day, Frankie and Bob took off for Moteville. I knocked on wood.

I was feeling somewhat better by the time I returned to Judy's. With the concession to my hangover that could I stay on my back, we were able to pick up right where we had left off. I expected Judy to ask me how or why I had ravaged myself so completely in only eleven hours; but since most of our conversations took place before, during, or after one of us was doing something moist and delicious to the other, the subject never arose.

A day later, on Friday afternoon, we took the train to Moteville. Judy was one of those New Yorkers who always seek an advantage in any situation. In this case she disappeared ten minutes before the train was ready for boarding. When I found her on the train she was hoarding the four seats at the end of the car. She sat on the aisle with her feet on the opposite seat and a look on her face that would have kept Marvin Hagler from stepping over her legs.

"Here, sit down," she said as she lowered her legs for me. "People are so pushy. The car ahead of us isn't full. I don't see why they had to give me a hard time over these seats."

"Maybe they didn't want to carry their heavy bags all the way to the next car."

"And maybe they might be on their way to the Institute for Lifestyle Arts. People who come by lifestyles naturally are bad enough; I couldn't take the guilt of sitting with someone whom we've convinced to pay to have one."

Judy was also the kind of person who provoked a certain hostility in others. The red-faced conductor, whose tight uniform made him look like a badly stuffed knockwurst, took his time with our tickets while he stared at Judy. Finally he said, "You mind taking your feet off the seat?"

"I took off my shoes." Judy sighed at the tediousness of it all.

"That's not the point, little girl."

Judy made no move.

"Is that how they raised you to sit at home?" the conductor said.

She turned to him with wide-eyed innocence. "They didn't much care how we sat at the orphanage."

I was pretty sure I was in love.

At Moteville a line of vans and taxis met the train and transported an impressive number of lifestyle acolytes to the Unity Hotel. Frankie and Bob met us in the lobby. They both looked exhausted.

Frankie raised her arm in triumph. "It's going to work. It's going to work."

The hubbub in the lobby was encouraging. The arrivals looked happy and eager as they arranged for matriculation.

"How's Marty behaving?" I asked.

"Around my little finger," Frankie said. "When he actually saw how many people were showing up he tried to talk me into running the Institute through the winter."

"You think so?" I said.

"Let's see how it goes. But I'll string Marty along."

About half of the student body was due in Friday night. The rest would arrive the next morning. Judy and I had agreed we could risk traveling together—after all, we were coming from and going to the same places—but at the Unity Motel she would room with Frankie. The boss got his own room. We made plans for her to sneak into my room after dinner. "We've been practicing this for months. Let's do it when it counts," I said.

But dinner wouldn't end, and Judy and I didn't even get to sit together. We spent the evening childishly making faces at each other. Following the meal, we were treated to the first lifestyle lecture. It was an address by Tamara Nevergelt, one of the magazine's favorite new free-lancers. She specialized in personality profiles of money masticators from the Street, political power brokers, media moguls, fashion designers, important hostesses—people who draped themselves in success as if it were a richly embroidered cloak. Although their financial success seemed to require a minimum of eighteen hours of work each day (a staple of each profile was the photograph of the subject hunched obsessively over desk or drawing table as darkness descended or the sun rose) they also managed to embellish their profiles with important friends, charming country estates, important dinners, charming spouses, important cultural events, and service on the boards of two or three important foundations.

Tamara's lecture was on choosing a private school for one's children, and it was immediately obvious why a journalist with her credentials should tackle education: Since private schools make an essential contribution to the lifestyles of the parents, they should be chosen on the basis of the parents whose children attend. Tamara described the various permutations of fame, fortune, and ethnicity which defined the Parents' Associations of a number of private schools. "Show business people may be fun to meet but too many of them make a school trendy; and too many social-register types may prove to be boring as well as unfriendly.

"But we must never forget," Tamara went on, "the considerations that are even more important than the social ambience of a school. After all, private schools do not exist solely to provide a social life for the parents. No, the school you choose for your children can also have a decisive effect on your career. Lawyers, for instance, will be exposed to a large number of potential clients. Money managers will find many fortunes in need of managing at the right school. And real estate developers and politicians go hand in hand. In this light, the cost of private education is greatly exaggerated by its critics. The expense will be returned many times over by the contacts your children make for you."

There was enthusiastic applause as the lecture ended. As they left the dining room, the student body was debating the finer points of Tamara's lecture. I made my way over to Judy but Frankie was already beside her.

"Come on," Frankie was saying, "I'm about to collapse. Please don't come in late and wake me up."

Judy looked at me forlornly. I shrugged. There was nothing we could do. That night I lay in my lonely bed listening to a mosquito circling for a landing. I comforted myself by taking the long view. After all, did a single night of pleasure mean that much when I was on the threshold of a great affair? Yes.

The next day saw the Institute in full swing. There wasn't much for me to do. I wandered from classroom to classroom, sampling the varied fare of lifestyle arts. I paused in Oswald Propper's colloquium on interior design. He had persuaded Jacques and Kimberly Sue de Musset (the perfume heir and the fast-food heiress) to speak about the many notable interiors they had commissioned for their many notable homes and apartments. Jacques and Kimberly Sue were at the forefront of something called the New Eclecticism which permitted people of style to push unlikely objects into exquisite proximity to each other. We were treated to slides of Chinese bronze candelabras reflected in art deco mirrors; English marine paintings above

Corbusier chairs; a pink fluorescent light on a Regency table; and a collection of kitschy Victoriana on a high-tech étagère. The secret seemed to be something Kimberly Sue referred to as a "free zone" between the contrasting objects; without it eclecticism didn't work. The students dutifully scribbled the term in their notebooks and one raised her hand to ask, "How do you tell how big the free zone should be?" Jacques sniffed, "One cannot measure it. One feels a *frisson.*"

I moved on to an enlightening seminar on the Terrace Reconsidered. At lunch, Gregory, fresh from his goat cheese triumph, gave an amusing account of the six worst wine stewards in New York. After lunch, Enid and Leon addressed the group on Personality and Style.

I had been wrong about the Malts. Enid was the one having trouble adjusting to the new LIFESTYLE. Sex was just too biological. But Leon had blithely abandoned the homiletic milkshake of humanistic psychology for a new therapeutic version of behavior modification. According to Leon, the therapist was now a kind of feedback mechanism who helped the patient redesign the way he or she is perceived by the world. Say you owned a highly lucrative sweatshop that you had just sold for a pile. Rather than remain a shirt-sleeved slob with a vicious temper, Leon would help you to acquire the accent, gestures, reactions, and perceptions which make up the sleek demeanor of the Successful Entrepreneur Who Dabbles in Film Finance.

In midafternoon I caught up to Judy in her gym kingdom. She was dressed in shorts and a T-shirt and she had a whistle around her neck.

"I feel like a camp counselor," she said. "Except at camp we would have a chance to make out."

"Maybe this would be a good time for us to slip into the sauna for a nice sweat."

"Would you listen to Mr. Free and Easy! I've got to give an aerobics class in half an hour." She threw up her hands. "Look what's happened to me. I started out to be a journalist and I've become a phys-ed instructor. You know, I hadn't stretched a hamstring in five years when I heard about the job at LIFESTYLE and talked my way into it. Now I've ended up with a whistle around my neck." She regarded me contentiously. "Don't look at me that way."

"I like it when you vent your spleen."

"Yeah, but it means you don't take me seriously."

"Where would we be if I took everything you did seriously?"

"Not here with you trying to talk me into the sauna. Forget it. We'll try later."

And later and later. Either Frankie or Bob was hovering nearby or I wasn't or Judy was busy. I would have been willing to skip dinner, but after the meal I was scheduled to introduce Bob for a commencement address.

I managed to sit with Judy, but Frankie was at our table too. Was it the glint in my eye or the giddiness of our banter that made Frankie stare at the two of us with thoughtful suspicion? I was glad to leave the table to introduce Bob, who gave a competent reading of the auspicious-occasion speech. He concluded by putting the idea of lifestyle into historical perspective.

"I wonder how many of you know this, but in the 1930s the Unity Hotel was the favorite summer resort of radicals and Marxists. We've come a long way, baby! [Cheers from the audience.] As a matter of fact, I got to thinking today: What if Karl Marx himself came to the Institute for Lifestyle Arts? I could just picture him lumbering around this weekend, visiting our seminars and workshops, stroking his beard, and muttering to himself. Thanks to our *good weather* [more cheers from the audience] and Karl's big-guy build, he'd probably sweat a lot and get pretty tired. So I'd come up to him and say, 'Hey, Karl, either get out of those heavy clothes or get out of the sun. How about a drink?' And I'd lead him right into the Unity Bar, sit him down on a stool, and say, 'I'm buying. How about a frozen daiquiri?' After we sipped a bit, I'd pop the question that had been on my mind all day. 'Come on, Karl, tell me what you think of the Institute.' He'd shake his head ponderously—as if he didn't understand the Institute but was pretty sure he didn't approve of it anyway. And then I'd say, 'You know, Karl, I'm not surprised you don't understand. When you were writing, people made things and sold things. But you've seen something today that is bigger and better than socialism. You've seen marketing democracy in action. Everybody here is being given the tools to market themselves in today's exciting, marketing-oriented society. Why, there is no habit, interest, or practice of the rich and elite that cannot be acquired by anyone. Thanks to LIFESTYLE magazine and its Institute, we can all position ourselves as sophisticated, civilized, fascinatingly tasteful products of our society.' "

The student body applauded vigorously and went off to drink and carouse. Frankie and Bob organized a private party for the Institute's staff. It was a happy occasion, though I could see that the party was going to preclude yet another get-together for Judy and me. We managed to find a quiet corner to talk but I saw Frankie giving us the eye again. I bided my time until I saw Frankie with Bob, and then I made sure she saw me giving the two of them an equally fishy stare. Our eyes locked. We gazed at each other stubbornly. Back in my own room, I surrendered my chasteness to the mosquito.

I was up early on Sunday morning. Frankie was up too. She found me in the lobby. She faced me with the kind of nervous-ashamed look which says: I don't want to tell you but you better ask.

"What's wrong?"

"I know about you and Judy."

"And I know about you and Bob. No big deal. Just a couple more secrets to add to our burgeoning storehouse."

"No, you've got to listen. Last night I told Judy about me and Bob, so she would be morally obliged to tell me about you and her. And she did."

"I'm not mad at her."

"But when she told me, I said, 'That's great since I like you both so much. But what makes it even better is that you probably started off kind of depressed because he's married and then you found out he's not really married.' "

"You didn't."

"How was I to know you hadn't told her? She's real mad."

"I tried to tell her. But it's basically good news so I'm sure she'll calm down."

"I wouldn't bet on it. She went crazy. She didn't sleep all night. I'm not sure even you can dance around her enough to patch it up."

"Where is she?"

"She may have gone already. She said she was leaving because she was afraid of what she'd do if she saw you. I'm sorry, George. I didn't know. Give her a couple of days. Maybe . . ."

I didn't want to see anybody, especially Judy, until the sick feeling went away. I started to head for my room when I heard Frankie exclaim, "Shit! I didn't think *he'd* come."

Helmut Gernschaft walked into the lobby as if he owned the place. In his red Bermuda shorts and his red-and-white striped shirt he looked rather like a beach ball.

"Who invited him?" I asked.

"I don't know. He must have been on one of the mailing lists."

He caught sight of me. "George, I did not think you were the sort who would surprise me."

"Don't you remember, in my June report, the thing I called 'Test: Untitled Education Project'?"

"Yes. But there was no money involved. I didn't think much of it until I got a brochure in the mail."

"We got enough money up front to cover the expenses for our little test," Frankie said.

"Little? This is what you call little?" Helmut waved his arm at the lifestylers who were streaming past on their way to breakfast.

"It exceeded our expectations," I said.

"By how much?" Helmut's eyes glittered carnivorously.

"Even with all the start-up costs, we're going to net forty thousand dollars this weekend," Frankie said. "And we're going to net at least seventy-five thousand in each of the next eight weekends."

"It just mushroomed, Mr. Gernschaft," I said.

"First someone will get my suitcase from the taxi. Then we will talk."

"Let me." I ran out. Parked before the porch was a taxi with an open trunk. The driver was saying, "Hold on, lady. Let me get this suitcase out before you put yours in."

By the time I found out that was no lady, Judy had seen me.

"Am I sorry to see you," she said. "And are you going to be sorry you saw me. How could you lie to me! And to everybody!"

"I didn't lie exactly."

"You lied exactly. *You lied!*"

"I even tried to tell you."

"Tried! You should have told me. You deceived everybody on the magazine. I can still hear you: 'I'm good at fooling my wife but not that good.' You disgusting man. And you deceived me. You pretended to be married when you're not."

"Isn't that good? And I am married."

"He calls that a marriage! I heard the story. That's no marriage as far as I'm concerned. If you don't know what a marriage is, you sure can't know what an affair is."

I tried an offensive. "If you're this upset, maybe you really *wanted* a married man. That makes it simpler to avoid a commitment."

"What a pathetic cheap shot. It's *your* behavior that's shitty. And I've had it with you. I should have known. Your type can't be honest. You don't know what honest is." She gave a great yank and Helmut's suitcase flew from the trunk. It landed on the ground with a thump.

"Careful, please," the wrong voice called.

I turned around. Helmut had joined the small audience assembled on the porch.

"You!" Judy shrieked at him. "You're as bad as he is. You're both sleazeballs." She glared up at me. "Look at me closely. I'm not crying. And I'm not going to kick you either. I'm never going to touch you again." She got into the taxi and slammed the door shut. "Move it," she said to the driver. "Take me to the station."

He threw her suitcase into the trunk. I watched the cab disappear. When I turned around, Helmut was approaching me. "I don't understand, George. Did she think you are married or not married?"

"I guess she didn't approve of the relationship I have with my wife."

"How is that relationship?"

"You could call it formal and distant."

Helmut brightened. "Why, so is mine. That's marriage. What did she expect? And who is she to think it is her business? These women are so hysterical."

On top of everything, I had to feel guilty for not defending Judy's emotional stability. I didn't know what to do with Helmut. I stood there nodding mournfully. He didn't know what to do with me so he nodded in response. We bobbed back and forth until Frankie rescued me. "Let's find someplace to leave your suitcase, Mr. Gernschaft. And then I can show you around. It's too bad you only came for this last day."

"I'll see you later, George," Helmut said.

I needed to be alone. I would have to compose myself to deal with Helmut. I wandered over to the gym. I was trying to get closer to Judy in a symbolic way. As soon as I saw the sauna, I knew I had found the perfect place to hide and unwind. It was hot and empty. I took off my clothes and stretched out on my back on the lowest level. I closed my eyes and tried to wish away the last half hour. Judy's departure was talismanic; I now believed I was going to lose everything. I did feel that Judy had acted too quickly. I deserved some benefit of the doubt, though I suppose she had nothing but doubts about me now.

There was a violent sizzle as a pail of water hit the hot sauna rocks. Through the billowing steam I made out a lean body as naked as mine. With her white hair and deep tan, Enid looked like an apparition.

"This is a pleasant surprise. It's not often one's boss is so . . . so informal."

She lay down on the level above me and surveyed my body. I just lay there. It seemed a bit late in the day to hide my dignity behind a towel. Enid reached down and gently rubbed one of my nipples.

"I don't think . . ." I said, which was about as truthful a statement as I had managed in quite a while.

"You don't think a boss and his employee should make love." Enid continued to stroke me.

"That's it," I said halfheartedly. "I don't approve."

"Oh dear. But you don't want me to stop."

We know morality exists by how quickly we attempt to rationalize our lapses. By the time Enid started on my other nipple, I was trying to get angry at Judy for being so self-righteous.

"Maybe we could compromise somehow," Enid said.

"What do you mean?"

"We don't have to go all the way. I'll settle for a hand job if you will."

I'm a slut. I could have said no. In my defense—and it's not a very good one—my recently departed sense of well-being, of getting it all right, had a strong sexual component. It seemed, in my desperation, that sex could at least restore the good feeling if not Judy herself. And so I gave myself over to Enid's vice-like grip.

Helmut and Frankie saved my life. After Enid left, I fell asleep. If Helmut hadn't asked Frankie to find me, no one else would have thought to look in the gym. And if she had checked the sauna only half an hour later, sound medical opinion says my blood would have parboiled my brain.

The first thing I remember is a circle of anxious faces above me. They were pouring water over me and fanning me with towels. Frankie's most successful mailing list had pulled in thirty-three doctors to the Institute, and while five of them discussed whether the little scar on my chin from a childhood accident could be removed, eleven others decided that I was going to live and probably didn't need to go to a hospital.

Helmut took charge and commandeered Bob's car. I was too

woozy to question where I was going. They piled me into the back seat and we took off. I fell asleep again. When I awoke we were on the Thruway.

"Are you all right?" Helmut was looking at me through the rearview mirror. He handed a bottle back to me. "Here is some water which you must drink. You have had a bad day. You should lie down and rest. And don't worry about the Institute. It is in good hands."

We drove on for a while. I had occasional moments of dizziness, and bright purple cobwebs flashed across my eyes. I groaned.

"Do you want me to stop?" Helmut asked. "We should be at your house in less than an hour."

"Don't bother to stop." My house. Helen. Since I was pretty sick, I doubted if she would make a scene no matter how badly our last encounter had gone.

"At least there is something good come of this day," Helmut said. "I finally get to meet that wonder dog Gretel."

"Maybe you should stop somewhere, Mr. Gernschaft."

At the gas station I borrowed some change from Helmut. "In case there's a pay toilet," I said. "No, don't bother to come. I'm feeling much better."

As I got out of the car, I realized that I was dressed in a white terry-cloth bathrobe from the gym and my shoes had been left behind. We were one hundred miles inland but I told myself to act as if I had come from the beach. My toes squirmed on the hot oily asphalt. At the phone in the men's room I could barely remember my own number. It rang and rang. Finally Sara answered.

"What are you doing there?" I said.

"Helen asked me—"

"Is she there?"

"No, and Mr. Miller's out back in the tent. I had to stay here while they delivered the chairs and call Helen when the other trucks got here."

"Oh." I decided to focus on essentials. If Helen wasn't there,

Sara was the next best person. "Look, Helmut is coming home with me. He wants to see Gretel."

Sara giggled.

"Please listen. This is important. Helmut will go crazy if he finds out there's no Gretel. Helen doesn't know anything about Gretel. You've got to find her and explain the whole thing to her. Tell Helen not to mention Gretel, but if Helmut asks she should say Gretel is sick and at the vet's."

"I got it. This is neat."

"No it's not. Also tell Helen that if I lose my job, there won't be any alimony."

"Okay. I know where she is. I can leave now."

"Wait a minute. I've got a better idea. Just stay there. If Helen's not there when Helmut drops me off, there won't be a problem. If she shows up, tell her the story."

"Okay. Good-bye."

When I got back to the car Helmut said, "You are feeling better. I can tell by looking at you."

And I was. I wasn't any happier but my adrenaline was pumping as I tried to get control of the situation.

"I hope someone is home to care for you," Helmut said. "The doctors insist we must be careful."

Tent? Chairs? "Don't worry. I think my wife is having a political meeting of some sort at our house. She's very civic-minded. There will be lots of people."

"But you must rest."

And then I thought: What if Helen arrives home *while* Helmut is dropping me off? To be on the safe side I said, "I have some bad news for you. Gretel died last week."

"What! You didn't tell me."

"She's been very sick."

"This is a bad dream you had while you were in the sauna."

"Oh no. But my wife doesn't know yet. She was away. She'll be very upset. If you see her, don't mention Gretel, please."

"I understand."

I had all the bases covered. I sighed pitiably and collapsed in the back seat again. I pretended to be asleep until the car slowed down and left the highway.

Helmut cleared his throat. "From here I need directions, George."

We wound our way through the streets of the town I thought I'd never see again. "And one left and there it is." I saw two Red Dot moving vans in the driveway. As we pulled up, the truck from Fenton's Party Rentals ("Have Your Affair with Fenton—Chairs, Tables, Bars, and Tents for All Occasions") was leaving.

"Do you need some help?" Helmut asked.

"I'll be all right. Thanks for the ride."

"I must not leave you alone. It looks very quiet."

It was quiet. As we spoke, two men emerged from the front door, which was propped open. They were carrying the living-room couch. They set it down in the front yard and paused to catch their breaths. I opened the car door and headed for the moving men.

"What are you doing with that couch?"

"Sitting on it." They were both perspiring heavily.

"And then?"

"Into the truck with the rest of the furniture," one of the burly men said. "Hey, would you mind closing your robe? You're hanging out all over the place. No wonder she's moving, with neighbors like you."

Oh God. "I'm not a neighbor. I live here."

"No wonder she's moving."

"What's going on here?" It was Helmut.

"We're sending the furniture to be recovered," I said. The purple cobwebs flashed before my eyes again and I staggered.

"Maybe you should lie down," the moving man said.

I sat on the couch. There was a humming sound in my head that sounded like faraway organ music.

"He's quite ill," said Helmut.

"What are you, his keeper?"

When I felt steady enough to stand, Helmut helped me into the house. The place was stripped: no pictures on the walls, no drapes, no chairs, no cute little objects on handsome coffee tables. But somewhere in the house, if tradition held true, there would be a bitter note from Helen to me.

Two more moving men came down the stairs carrying a mattress.

"You're having a *bed* recovered?" Helmut said.

I changed the subject by groaning.

"Here, gentlemen. I want this mattress on the floor for my companion." Helmut's Teutonic authority worked. I fell on the mattress. The organ music in my head grew louder. "You lie there, George. I'll get some water." He came back with a paper cup. "I don't understand. There are almost no dishes left in the kitchen."

It was time for delirium. "Is this the hospital? Call my doctor. I'm a prisoner here. A prisoner." I grabbed the phone. "Hello, Central, give me Doctor Jive."

"George. Perhaps I should take you to a hospital."

"No, just let me rest."

I lay down again. Helmut found a small stool. He placed it near my head and perched on it while he stared at me. The moving men kept up a steady pace. The organ music was even louder now, and I could swear I heard angels singing. Maybe I *was* delirious.

"George, when I was in the kitchen, I saw a big tent in the backyard. There at least fifty chairs under it and seven or eight people sitting there."

"So what?" I said.

"I mean—" Helmut shook his head slowly. He had a stubborn angry look. He didn't like what he was seeing but it didn't make enough sense for him to say anything.

I was only half a step ahead of Helmut. I had the moving-men part of the equation worked out, but the rest eluded me until the organ sound reached a crescendo that definitely did not come from my head. There was silence for a moment and then an amplified electronic squeal made us wince.

"And now, my friends," boomed Emerson's voice, "we come to the healing part of the service." The microphone squealed again and I imagined Emerson passing it behind his back. "There are a lot of preachers who say they can heal the body. But Brother Emerson Miller stands before you with the power to heal your minds."

Helmut raised his eyebrows.

"My brother-in-law," I offered weakly.

"Belief is all it takes. You believe with your minds, do you not?"

"Yes, oh yes!" I heard Irene shout.

"And so belief will soothe your mental afflictions. Now I want you all to close your eyes and let the spirit enter you." Emerson started humming; with loudspeakers the spirit sounded like a large vacuum cleaner. "Now is there someone sitting before me who's got perverted lusts? *Hmmm-hmmm.* Somebody who loves his mother too much? *Hmmm-hmmm.* Then stand up and come before me. Maybe there's a man out there, *hmmm-hmmm,* who, when his wife goes to the PTA meeting, *hmmm-hmmm,* he puts on her clothes. Stand up and be relieved! Don't be ashamed to come before me. Yes, there's a woman with pain on her face. Let me hold your hands, my child. Tell me, please, what is your affliction? Oh, my Lord, she says ever since she's been a little girl, she's had to take four showers a day . . . oh, my dear . . . and she can't use any other bathroom but her own. Heal her, O spirit! Let her use any bath—"

There was a loud yell from the front yard. "Stop it! Stop it!" a shrill voice yelled.

"Get the fuck off me," a moving man yelled.

"I can't hold on!"

There was a clatter on the porch and then into the living room bounded an enormous, hairy dog, which ran over to me and begin to lick my face. Right behind the dog came Sara.

"Look, George, it's Gretel. She's all better."

SEVENTEEN

The house echoes because there's still no furniture to absorb the sound. During the first month, every step I took reminded me half a second later that I had taken it. In that unhappy, self-critical period, I made rather a lot of the echo; nature was telling me that every step one takes has its resonance. Luckily, by the second month I had grown used to the echo and didn't hear it or think about it as a metaphor. After all, one has to go on living.

And it is not a bad life. During the second post-LIFESTYLE month I announced that I was a magazine consultant, and this month I actually began to earn enough to put food on the little table I bought at a yard sale and enough to put meat in Gretel's bowl. I bought Gretel from Sara for the $15 she had paid the dog pound. I like the responsibility of caring for Gretel, and she adds a kind of arbitrary order to my life.

I speak to Frankie every so often and am assured that things are fine at LIFESTYLE. She's tacitly second-in-command though Bob is still too afraid of Helmut to give her a better title than Associate Marketing Director. A few weeks ago, when Frankie told me that Judy had found a new job, she confided that Judy had made her promise not to tell me where.

"So what," I said.

But of course I think about her all the time. Last month everybody was talking about her free-lance article in *The Atlantic Monthly* which exposed the *CompuDiet* scandal. These days I picture her walking to work. She's still a little distant with her new co-workers, but I imagine they are beginning to discover they can rely on her for all kinds of suggestions, advice, and support. I'm pretty sure she thinks about me, even after three months. She probably thinks I'm a real coward for not even trying to patch it up. But even if I try I know what she'll say: "Please stay out of my life, George. If you want to do something constructive for yourself, learn how to face reality and give up on your schemes for redesigning it. Apologize to me like a normal human being and go away."

Just what I need: a conscience that speaks to me in Judy's voice. Now I have all the disadvantages of the relationship and none of the benefits. Worse yet, she's right as usual. But what good would it do for me to abase myself? No, I'm not going to apologize. Besides, I've already found out which magazine she's working for and I had lunch with its publisher last week. He didn't realize it until he met me, but now he's quite convinced the magazine could profit from the advice of a good consultant. He wants me to get to know the staff. . . .